this book belongs to...

Curious Cat Books

RACHAEL HARDCASTLE
TO HOLD AN INFINITY

Harvest Fields
Mousique
Manaia Forest
Pouki's Cabin
Casper's Cabin
Orc Pit
Drakonta
Highman's Point
Wolf Territory
Recruit Lair
Haeylo City

Demonic Territory
Volcanic Ruins
Marshland
Petrified Forest
The Land Bridge
The Depths
Queen's Port
Entit Sehde Palace
Rulecast Tower
The Edge
Abandoned Dwarf Mine
The Valley
Recruit HQ
Temple
Enzo
Enzo Beach
Drakontan Mountains
Barren Fishtail
Tribal Settlement
Mirror Of The Soul

ONE

9281 AD – *1 year after the battle for Pandora's box*

Blood-curdling was the scream, the one imprinted in Arriette's exhausted mind—lodged as a dramatic memory, a brutal scar on her existence. Both she and this mysterious screeching woman were bound for trouble; somehow, she knew, as she sat bolt upright in bed.

Last year, the war over possessing Pandora's box produced a variety of similar sounds, all of which Arriette associated with the deaths of her innocent supernatural friends; the war to find and protect the ancient Greek relic had worn her organisation thin—their ranks had depleted, as had their supplies. At least the box was in safe hands, stored where Arriette and her dependable supes could access it.

"Arriette, are you alright?"

Unexpectedly, a concerned face nudged her shoulder and as she forced a smile, Tobias's unshaven stubble grated her skin. He squeezed her clammy palm. His mousy hair, strewn across his forehead, had grown out, hiding hazel eyes and a furrowed brow. The past months of chaos left little opportunity to visit a barber, and Arriette didn't trust herself to cut it for him, lest he look twice as dishevelled (but still rugged and handsome) by her hand.

"Go back to sleep. I'm fine."

"Liar."

Following the groove of her first scar, sweat trickled down Arriette's spine and pooled on the bedsheets, causing her to wriggle in discomfort. Originally the agonising outlet for her wings, Arriette remembered how far the Recruit had come since their feathery materialisation in the streets of Haeylo's city. These days, when she liberated them, she didn't notice. She was accustomed to their weight and how to manoeuvre them.

Tobias brushed away her soggy brunette locks and took her temperature with the back of his hand. After blowing a sharp breath, she kicked the sheets off.

"You're burning up. Still hearing voices?"

"*A* voice, in a recurring nightmare—a stranger."

Arriette clenched her fists and swung her bare feet off the bed. She stormed to the window, frustrated by the past three insomnia-tormented weeks, and threw open the latch for fresh air, hanging her head out in the darkness.

"You can't stand there; someone could fire an arrow," Tobias argued. "You're the leader of the Recruit now, Arriette, *and* the keeper of Pandora's box. You're a princess too technically, remember? Need I say more?"

"You're going to," she muttered, ignoring a further plea to close the latch, and fingered the box's key which hung on a chain beside her Everlast pendant. "Am I a princess if I don't pursue the title *or* investigate my heritage?"

"Yes."

"Guess free will is out the window."

"If somebody grabs a hold of you, *you* will be." He groaned and strode to the foot of the bed. "The voices you hear at night aren't real, but Tabitha said that although there are no physical symptoms of your pregnancy, magic will make up for it through your emotions, your spirit, your—"

"Sanity and patience?"

"Thankfully, *not* on your sense of humour, I see," he uttered.

"You know I'm the strongest supe on this planet, right?" she reminded him. "I can deflect an arrow with telekinesis, or shift my head's shape so it flies right through me, or turn the arrow into a flower with my dreaming. Or..."

"Or not see it coming... and die."

Arriette folded her arms and puffed a loose strand of tangled hair from her face. Upon catching her reflection in the glass, she cringed at how tired—depressed—her khaki eyes were. Dark circles and crow's feet consumed them. She'd been avoiding mirrors for that reason—she did not need reminding how bedraggled she was.

She ran a gentle hand across her stomach, wondering what carrying a human child would be like. As their friend Pouki Hallidae, their trainer and a skilled telepath promised, Arriette's supernatural pregnancy had perks. Thanks to her unaffected lean physique and excitable energy, her position as leader of their organisation and the guardian of Pandora's box could remain top priority. However, during her sacred alone time in their library, she'd seen pictures of baby bumps, read about morning sickness, light-headedness, and other undesirable side effects. The human in her longed to experience it nevertheless.

"Magical pregnancies pose fewer risks in our circumstances. You're not regretting the decision, are you?" Tobias asked; he knew her too well.

"Course not. I agree with Pouki that it's practical. I was born a human, Tobias, so this isn't standard for me.

It'll take some... *adjusting*."

"Nightmares are nothing but a brain's way of figuring out what troubles us. Like a natural filing system," he soothed, then grinned. "Thanks to me you're a dreamer—it's not uncommon to have an animated imagination."

"I should know! I've been a dreamer long enough."

Longingly through the open window, Arriette gazed. A light mist was descending on the local village from the ocean it peered over, and she imagined it swallowing her whole. Though Enzo was alluring and peaceful, she felt that pang of loneliness, as if Rosewood Cottage in Mousique was calling her name.

"I've been stuck here for my *safety*. Our daughter won't have a normal life."

Tobias shook his head, shocked by the realisation. Neither of their little girl's parents was 'normal', as Tobias was a scale two dreamer and Arriette a magical mix of her friends' blood.

"Expect to hear voices as you're part angel, and they get messages from the creator so it's all connected to your gifts."

He paced around their chilly bedroom to meet her, then ran soft fingers through her matted hair with one hand and closed the window with the other.

"Every other supe has *one* set of side-effects to worry about—two max if you're Baby A, juggling time travel and her angelic responsibilities. Not fair! *I* have..." Arriette didn't have the spirit to count her powers on her fingers, "... *too many!*"

The tension in his shoulders released, and he initiated a warm hug, but said nothing.

Against his chest, she murmured, "I don't look pregnant."

"Better to be comfortable and pain-free, as we made a *lot* of enemies, Arriette, and if they found out you were the mother of a future saviour *and* a royal, they'd rally. To guard you both is the priority."

"A *royal?*" she said with a raised brow. "Until last year, none of us knew royalty existed on this planet, and by 'they', you're referring to Christine Kaines, and whatever minions are living in that kingdom. Christine dubbed herself Queen; someone can strip the title with ease. And you mean enemies like Falkon Lou."

"True," he agreed. "*Ze Entit Sehde Eyeh* has *no right* to call herself your grandmother, not after the way she treated your mother and aunt. She's Queen for now, but we'll nose around when we're able. Our research has proven fruitful; we know where she is. Falkon isn't going anywhere but he had acquaintances in the city and the Underworld who may be bitter about his fate."

"Hmm, I miss the peace and the serenity of Mousique, in Rosewood Cottage surrounded by stacks of books and teacups."

"Something greater chose you," Tobias whispered. "Pandora gave half her soul because she believed in Casper's choice."

Arriette recalled the vivid sensation of Pandora's soul splitting in two; half of the goddess's lifeform seeping through her skin and infecting her bloodstream. The creaking of her bones and stretching of her muscles to accommodate that responsibility had been beyond painful because she hadn't envisioned or wanted it.

"Since we found and called the gateway evils back," Arriette countered, "Pandora's soul hasn't surfaced from my body. She lives within me... *somewhere*. Or perhaps in my pendant. If it's a symbol of everlasting life—she's ancient! How can I be sure she and I bonded? What was the point if not to cheat her punishment and prolong her survival?"

She scolded herself. Ma always taught her to be a good hostess.

"If you *had* bonded, you'd be able to interact?"

Arriette perked up at the idea. She periodically thought she sensed the goddess, but hadn't considered Pandora's involvement in the perturbed voice or attempted to communicate with her in-depth. Was the screaming woman Pandora, trapped?

"Presently, I'm about as sure as I am that Christine is my grandmother. Knowing Casper was my ancestor is comforting, but *her*?"

A sigh. "Why would Ma lie?"

"Right. I'm sorry," she said and pulled a disgusted face. "I don't reckon the voices are a side-effect of my pregnancy, or the piece of Pandora's soul she gifted me. I think our creator is trying to tell me something. It's... *symbolic*."

"Until you figure it out—"

Arriette hugged him tighter, interrupting what she predicted to be another suggestion that she stay protected inside their new headquarters.

"I know I haven't been a ray of sunshine, but I'm—"

"*Scared?*" Now it was his turn to interrupt.

"Do you blame me?"

"About giving birth or marrying me?" Tobias's gaze widened. "Is *that* what this is about? Are you getting cold feet? Are you the screaming woman?"

Hands trembling, Arriette whacked him across the stomach. "I *love* you and I *want* to marry you! When we find time. That's not what I'm afraid of. It's these weird nightmares and that female with a high-pitched voice. She's in *so much pain*. How? Why?"

"Should we discuss with the others the possibility of Zïnnyi warning us? It's worth running past Tabitha and Pouki, because it may not be good for the baby. They're your doctors, after all. Uhm, sort of."

"I wish Zïnnyi would give me some time off if I'm pregnant and put a different angel in charge. Baby A is better than I am. More experienced. There are plenty of supes here. It's the Recruit's brand new HQ, for goodness' sake! Since you guys built this place, supes from all over the land have swarmed for guidance. Not short of help, are we?"

Tobias offered a comforting smile and kissed her sweltering cheek.

"Baby A wouldn't have made you an angel if she didn't expect you could handle the liability, no matter your circumstances. Let us believe in you."

"Casper bullied her into it. Anyway, Zïnnyi needs to come out with it. *'Arriette, you're in danger'* or *'Hey, go save this woman'*." She snorted.

"Loves a good puzzle, he's subtle."

They both giggled as Tobias retrieved their gowns and led Arriette to the corridor.

"Every voice in the past has been disturbing," she admitted, following his navigation through the shadowy bedroom, digging her toes into the long pile of the carpet, "but this woman sounds worse. Her misery is mine. Zïnnyi might want me to save her," she said, halting him. "No, Tobias, we can't go. Pouki will be sleeping."

Tobias nudged her forward with a playful bump of his fist. "Trust me, Pouki knows we're coming. In his sleep, he hears our thoughts. You're projecting enough emotion to penetrate his consciousness. Even *I* can sense your aura, and I'm just a dreamer."

Arriette smirked at the word 'just' as she closed the door behind them.

"A *measly* scale two. That's *all* you are," she joked. "On the HPS, the second deadliest supe species to exist on the planet, but you're *just* a dreamer. What a ghastly curse!"

"Yeah, well, being a telepath is Pouki's," he said, ushering Arriette along as she mocked him.

"Oh, I'd hate to think what nightmares *he's* been having."

TWO

In their pyjamas, Arriette and Tobias shuffled down the corridor to Pouki's room, keeping their footsteps light so as not to wake an audience. It was a chance to enjoy the unusual calm of HQ's labyrinth of passages.

Out of habit, Arriette gave the office doors a quick rattle as they passed, checking they were secure, even if they did not directly lead to the external grounds or anything of value, like the basement where the box's vault had been installed. This mundane act distracted her momentarily from how uneasy the silence made her; the lack of scurrying Recruit members and followers going about their noisy business seemed... unnatural. Unsettling.

Dangerous.

But in this wing, the rooms were residential or unused, anyway.

Since moving into the building in Enzo a few months ago, Arriette had grown used to the bustle and chaos of a larger organisation. She missed the natural surroundings at Rosewood Cottage, and even the crammed comfort of Casper's secluded wooden cabin. Reiko and Tobias promised her when they met that they'd build her a new cabin. Oh, the enormity of their creation! It was technically their home now, though, and she'd just have to perfect her grateful smile.

Wherever Tobias is, I will be safe, and warm, and

loved. I will be home.

Before Tobias rapped on his door, Pouki opened it inward. The old man had not long since been out of bed and wore his usual white robes and sandals, but hadn't had time to comb his white hair or knee-length beard.

"Tobias Shallow. Took you long enough," he said.

"She's hearing voices," he replied, ushering Arriette in. "Again."

Pouki scratched his head. "Not the only one."

"Yeah, mine, and *you're* used to it," Arriette growled.

"You're always hearing voices, it's part of your angelic—"

"Part of my gift, Pouki, *yeah yeah.*" She huffed and pinched the bridge of her nose. "People *really* need to stop using that as a damned excuse. This is different."

He yawned through saying, "Fine, fine."

When Arriette walked to the base of Pouki's bed, she was suddenly exhausted and guilty for involving anyone else in her pregnancy blues. There was a good chance this was, indeed, nothing. At only three feet tall, Pouki stood to examine Arriette anyway as she slid against his sheets and sat cross-legged on the floor.

In unison, they yawned again.

After a few minutes, Pouki asked, "Insomnia?"

"Isn't that apparent?"

"If it was, would I have asked?"

He raised an eyebrow at Tobias, who shrugged. Arriette's mood swings were increasing the closer she got to her due date. Whether because of her birthing fear, royalty worries, this mysterious voice, or harbouring half of a powerful goddess's soul, they couldn't tell.

"I know why you're here, Arriette. It isn't because you're stressed about a random dying woman's voice."

Arriette accepted some water and grimaced as he poured in a lilac powder, then mixed it with a spoon. A gentle tinkling filled the room as it bounced off the glass.

"A little sleeping concoction courtesy of our potions master," Pouki interrupted. "I wouldn't give you anything that might harm the baby, so don't ask."

"Was I going to?" She scowled. "And Reiko's making potions for you now? You're a telepath, not a sorcerer."

"A few basics, you understand. Lavender is nature's goodness. I'd have made it myself but he insisted on getting the practice. Drink it all, then rest. We'll talk about this more tomorrow."

Arriette took a swig and gagged. The water smelled soothing, but it was bitter.

"We didn't wake you for potions," Tobias said.

Pouki ignored him and turned to Arriette again. "This female voice is not your unborn baby. You'll be a wonderful mother."

Tobias glared at her. "Is *that* what's worrying you?"

Arriette narrowed her eyes. "No!"

"These voices are, perhaps, nightmares because of your magical pregnancy and the swirl of hormones, or even the beginning of your daughter's powers. The female body should naturally bind them until birth, but with *you two* as parents, she's no doubt an extraordinarily powerful child, capable of de-tangling the masking spell we applied with ease. It is similar to the binding potion Casper once made for Baby A. Speaking of angels, our creator calls on you with visions; it may be your daughter is similar?"

"My daughter might be an angel?"

"If that's what's happening. Not all visions require action, though. Your daughter may be *amplifying* a perfectly harmless one."

"The baby can't do any damage from the womb, or harm Arriette accidentally?"

Pouki placed a gentle palm on Tobias's forearm. "I shouldn't think so. If she's anything like her mother, she'll be strong-willed and in control of any powers she *inherits* soon enough. But most supernatural mothers will naturally bind the baby's powers until their birth."

The telepath released Tobias from his momentary gesture of understanding, then winked as the dreamer rubbed the spot in thought.

He kissed Arriette's forehead. "Stop fretting. If I'm wrong and Zinnyi *is* trying to tell you something, the dilemma will reveal itself. Drama always does."

Forcing a smile, Arriette struggled to her feet and groaned as she towered above him.

"So you agree it *could* be a premonition?"

"Time will tell."

"Hmm, I'm confused. Somebody told us our daughter would be born human," Tobias interjected.

Pouki balked. "Somebody?"

Arriette and Tobias stared at one another, ashamed to admit they'd taken medical advice from a wiccan. She shook her head and cringed, gesturing Tobias should say no more, but the secret was already out, and they'd face the full force of Pouki's wrath.

"Oh dear, oh dear! Still, you surprise me, after all we've been through." He cleared his throat. "I'll need to hear more about this when we're all rested."

But Tobias stood firm. "We're foolish for visiting a palm-reader?"

"Not at all, but you should understand by now how readings can change because free will bends. As the baby develops, so will her powers and her future. If the wiccan's reading was accurate, it was based on Arriette's mindset and the child's development *at that time*."

Pouki yawned once more and gestured for Arriette to drink up.

"That makes sense," she hummed.

"Of course it does, because *I* said it. Now, both of you, please, try not to worry."

On their way out, Arriette grabbed Pouki's hand and squeezed it.

"I really *do* appreciate your help."

Pouki tapped his forehead. "I know you do, Princess."

THREE

The little sleep Arriette managed helped to refresh her mind and body for the day ahead, but she worried about the screaming female.

After showering and changing, she slid into a burnt orange knee-length dress and brown boots, then set off down the hall alone to study in the library, sorting through endless piles of notes and paperwork as a distraction.

Shelves packed with hardback books surrounded her. Floor-to-ceiling, their dusty jackets and colourful spines beckoned Arriette to lose herself in their romantic adventures. Here, she felt a great deal of comfort. In this space, books were harmless friends with nothing to offer but pleasure, entertainment, knowledge, and answers to endless troubles. Within the pages, she'd discovered the queen lived across the Barren Fishtail, an empty, dying land bridge between their glorious green landscape and the Edge—a city balanced atop a cliff.

It wasn't long before Tobias was trespassing in her Eden. He stood beside her with a breakfast offering—a bowl of fruit and orange juice on a tray in one hand and a folder filled with applicants in the other. But Arriette didn't want to hire anyone else... ever. The building was plenty busy, and she loved their dynamic the way it was.

In truth, they needed some extra administrative help. The Recruit were tired; emotionally scarred from the battle, but strong and trusting of each other. With the influx of flocking supes to their HQ, there were too few of her friends to help them all right now.

"Decided on a receptionist yet?" Tobias asked, stealing a strawberry.

She batted his hand away. "I don't want to."

"Let me help you."

He rummaged through a pile Arriette had marked for the bin and thrust one across the desk.

"Here. Done."

"I'll look through them later, Tobias. I'm busy."

She pushed it out of his reach using her telekinesis, narrowing her eyes, and avoided meeting his gaze.

"I like this one. If you ask me, I'd say she's capable. Got a pleasant smile, ideal for the front desk."

"I didn't ask you." Arriette reached out and took the folder for a second glance anyway, then groaned. "Annie Barker. 24 years-old. A young, single retainer with *no* office experience? I think you're a little too obsessed with her *pleasant smile*."

She blinked and dumped it in the bin to her right, then re-focused on her paperwork. Now she and Tobias were engaged *nothing* was going to stand in their way. Not some young, pretty genius.

"Just give her an interview. She can learn. It's what retainers do, and she'll want to bank the knowledge. We can't put this off any longer. At least a retainer has more enthusiasm for study, and she might even know about supe pregnancies. We need someone who won't quit at the first sign of danger and who can keep this place organised while we're away."

Arriette scoffed. "Tobias, we've talked about this. We're *not* going away on some crazy 'find-my-unstable-family' mission until the baby is old enough to travel because I won't drag an innocent little girl into my twisted affairs. Christine Kaines could be dangerous. You want to introduce her to an unstable magical toddler and her *deranged* mother? Besides, I don't need a stranger prodding and poking my stomach, or anywhere *else* for that matter, when Pouki's diagnosis and examinations are dignified and honest. I trust him. And Tabitha does, too. She's the only retainer I want... uhm... down there."

"It's already been a year since your mother came clean about who you are, Arriette. We can't leave it much longer. Christine might decide to attack us instead."

"She can *try*."

"Just think about hiring Annie," he said, fluttering his long, tantalising lashes, "for me?"

"Maybe."

Tobias sighed. "That means no."

"No, that means maybe."

"Fine." Tobias held up both hands and turned for the door. "Eat your breakfast, sign your paperwork, and I'll see you at the meeting in an hour. *Don't* be late." Before he slammed the door, he stuck his head back in and added, "And you're not deranged!" then disappeared.

Arriette flicked through a couple more applications when he'd gone, but through her frustration, decided instead to set off for the meeting early and think about Annie's qualifications on the way. She ran her delicate fingers along a row of spines on her way out, whispering a gentle goodbye to her confidants, then dropped her dirty dishes in the canteen. She scurried down the corridor, saying hello to some carpenters on the way to build a second stable, then bounded through the doors at the end to be greeted by a group of friendly faces.

"How are you this morning, Arriette?" asked Tabitha Hope, the Recruit's head retainer, acting physician, and one of Arriette's closest friends. She often worked with Pouki Hallidae, who no doubt had told her everything about their discussion.

Privacy was a thing of the past now.

"Better. Got a bit more sleep."

Lies.

As one of the youngest members of their organisation, Tabitha was always cheerful and excited to take part in any Recruit business, including their boring weekly meetings, research, or scouting missions. Her bright blue eyes were wide and eager today and her shoulder-length brown hair was in a flawless bun. Arriette envied Tabitha's beauty, wishing she could turn back the clock to when she was Tabitha's age, ignorant of Haeylo's truths.

Lots of familiar faces welcomed her, and she smiled at each of them. *I'm happy. I'm present. Let's do this.*

Lies.

"Everyone's here already?"

A young, plump boy named Sebastian Sky hid beneath a pointed sorcerer's hat and traditional purple robes. His auburn hair poked in various directions, and as the light caught his emerald saucers, Arriette remembered their first encounter in the caves beneath the lair. He'd given her his robe to use as a towel and introduced her to the concept of *Indalo*. If not for Sebastian's kindness that day, she might never have dared enter through to witness the lair's beauty.

Dion Delavious sat beside him, chatting with the sorcerer about potion bottles and unrealistic love spells. Despite being a 'vegetarian' vampyr with the ability to change her red hair and eye colour to camouflage for prey within seconds (plus a bunch of other terrifying abilities Arriette refused to acknowledge), Arriette was most excited to see her. In Manaia Forest, Casper introduced Dion to Arriette, promising she ate only animals, and that human blood made her nauseated. Arriette noticed she'd adopted the same blazing red locks as she did that night, which (being her preferred appearance) suited her attitude and showed Dion felt calm.

Tabitha stepped aside to allow Paulei Leigh, a telepath like their trainer, Pouki to kiss her cheek and shake her hand. Paulei was older than most of her other friends and he was getting fatter and greyer every day, but never failed to shave or dress in a smart, tailored suit. She wondered if in his spare time he'd give Tobias the trim he needed and if his fashion sense might rub off on the rest of the group. Paulei respected Arriette's authority, just as he had respected Casper's before the war. Between dealing with Dion and now Susan's quirky undead personalities and running a chaotic HQ, Arriette was more than grateful for his patience and understanding when she made a mistake.

When she needed grounding, she turned to Paulei.

"Progress in the stables, I see," Paulei said.

When she shared his relief they were expanding to allow more and more supe visitors from across Haeylo, he gave her the thumbs up and, with a spring in his step, returned to his seat.

The Recruit's dazzling everlast, Joy Johnas hopped down from sitting on a desk at the far side of the room when she saw Arriette was free. She ran to wrap her arms around her, knocking Paulei aside and stealing the room's attention. Paulei and Arriette both laughed, and she puffed the everlast's midnight hair out of her open mouth, pleased that this one excitable friend would never age, never change.

"Good... to... see... you... too," she managed through squashed lungs. "How do you always lift my spirit?"

"It's a gift." She winked. "Oh, Jet sends his apologies; he's having *power problems*. Tabitha is going to examine him later today in the infirmary, so don't worry."

"Same symptoms?"

Joy grimaced. "If *I* could turn invisible, even without warning sometimes, *I'd* be taking advantage."

Meaning you'd be loitering where you shouldn't be, Arriette thought and rolled her eyes. She pushed a few chairs aside and started towards the front.

"It's a shame we don't have others with invisibility or we'd be able to ask. Jet can't be alone," Joy voiced behind her. "Will you find somebody else like him when you go on your trip?"

"Uh, I'm looking forward to it."

Lies. Lies. LIES!

Joy danced back to her seat.

Arriette leaned against a bare cream wall and waited for everyone to find a perch. Most of the rooms in HQ were similarly decorated except for private sleeping quarters and the foyer, which was open-plan with marble flooring and two ornamental grey and white pillars beside the main desk. The Recruit were still working their way through the corridors and offices painting, polishing wooden floors, and adding welcoming furnishings such as rugs, lamps and artwork. The process was slow and expensive, but thankfully, Arriette now had friends in high places and the city was not short of creatives.

Tobias was already at the back next to Reiko Port, his

bald-headed human hunting buddy, and the Recruit's potions master. She glared at them both to behave. Reiko was busy scribbling on a sheet of parchment. His tongue poked through the gap in his front teeth and Tobias watched, mesmerised.

Arriette hoped he wasn't still angry at her.

"We're missing people," she realised. "Susan and—"

"Me, me, me!" Baby A rushed through the door, leaving it wide open. She backtracked and clunked it closed with her foot. "Sorry! You lend a guy your keys and POOF! he's conjured a puff of weird fog and poisoned half of Enzo. What on *Haeylo* we're going to do about that kid is beyond me, and whose idea was it to invite students to practice in our laboratories again?"

Reiko's pen halted, and he sank a few inches. As potions master, those students were his responsibility, even if their presence was as a favour to Charles Melovich, now the city's most influential everlast leader. The man who had paid for Arriette's medical bills and Susan's 'funeral', before discovering she'd turned into a vampyr. The city's highest-ranking everlasts had selected Reiko Port to offer some work experience for the university's marvels. How could they turn *that* down?

Arriette hushed Baby A and scowled at Reiko for forgetting his priorities.

Sebastian interrupted, "We need to train our young to use magic. Under supervision, of course," said the sorcerer, tipping his hat to her.

"Wait, you gave a stranger your keys?" Arriette asked Baby A before she could agree with Sebastian. It niggled at whatever caused her to check the doors on an evening, and whatever made Tobias *insist* on their bedroom window remaining latched.

Baby A moaned. "I had to! I was late for a meeting and nobody else was available to let them in. Our reception desk is understaffed... *still*."

Arriette shot Tobias a warning stare and folded her arms. Her body language said, *don't you dare*.

He said nothing.

Good.

"They were only unsupervised for ten minutes. I told them not to touch anything until I could find a wiccan to oversee the lesson. The poor boy claimed it was accidental and I'm sure it was, but he's gone now and we can't find him anywhere. I've been up all night trying to investigate what he mixed because he couldn't remember, and all the vials are empty. Now, he's gone."

"You're not the only one who has been awake all night," Pouki mumbled.

Arriette shot him a scowl, too, but the telepath didn't back down.

Tobias said, "I thought the carpenters were supposed to be fixing the lab's window today. Would the potion have escaped had they done *their* job?"

"They were, but Arriette asked them to finish the stable first. Everyone travels here on horseback. They'll get to it. I don't think it would have made any difference, honestly," she assured and slumped in her seat, exhausted.

Lies, but not Arriette's this time. Ones she appreciated, though.

"Isn't a security issue more important than shelter for animals?" asked Paulei, cringing as he awaited their leader's reaction.

She declared, "*All* life on Haeylo matters. Not just those on the HPS."

"You're missing Ira Wilda, but I mean, this *is* the

Recruit's new HQ after all and it's not finished, so if anywhere will be a target for magical mayhem, it'll be this building. And the potions lab? That's just *asking* for trouble," he added.

"Let's not talk about Ira," Arriette grunted.

"It's fine," Baby A assured them, tucking her short blonde bob behind both ears. "The window closes. It just rattles a bit. Paulei, read my mind and see for yourself the day I'm having. By the end, though, I will solve *all* our carpentry issues. Anyway, I'm late because I assigned someone to scout the damage before the fog reaches Enzo's village. It's drifted and settled by the cliff at the minute, so when we're done here, I'll need Reiko to mix an antidote."

"If it's urgent, you can go now," Arriette said.

"I had a few vials under quarantine—no antidotes yet. It will not make much of a difference if the kid released one of those. If he's mixed something new, it's a day's work at best," Reiko said, shaking his head. "I lock the room for this reason! Was there anything missing, Baby A?"

"No. Only used. He tried to clear up after himself—a spell went wrong, that's all."

"*That's all?* Spells are deadly, right? So I'm the only one in here who knows when you chant, mix chemicals, and waft smoke around stuff happens. Why wasn't I made aware of a quarantine, Reiko?" Arriette snapped, taking them both by surprise. "If I'd have known there was something *so* dangerous in the lab, I wouldn't have re-assigned the carpenters and I'd have postponed lessons. Charles would have understood. Can the effects of this spell or whatever the hell went wrong be reversed?"

"*I* don't know. We were testing a power-stripping

substance to run alongside Susan's binding experiments, but it didn't work," Reiko replied. "I wanted to run some more before we tried anything further. If it's *that* spell, it's unpredictable. The fog will disperse, but I can't do anything about the damage already done."

Arriette's fingers, now resting on her hips, tapped. "Are we sure it's not just ocean mist? This morning I saw fog and... wait a second, *why* is Susan working on a binding spell when we have the one Casper developed years ago?"

"She made me promise not to say anything. She knows you've got a lot on right now with the baby and hiring people. No idea why, before you ask. She's unhappy and wanted help to learn a bit more about her condition," Reiko said. "Casper's potion is temporary and not at all strong enough for a vampire. Dion's helping us."

Tobias asked him, "In exchange for what?" and the hunter glared.

"I don't judge them like you lot do."

"Being a vampyr is *not* a condition, Reiko!" Tabitha scolded. "If that's judgemental, then I'm judgemental."

Dion growled at them both to stop being stubborn, causing Tabitha to jump from her seat, though she cryptically directed her anger towards Reiko.

"All due respect, but isn't that up to Susan? Plus, I remember until Dion met Arriette, getting bitten and turned into a vampyr didn't exactly thrill her either."

"Don't involve me in this, Reiko!" She hissed and flipped her red hair.

The secret was out. The new vampyr was still struggling with her identity and had now turned to wiccan potions and spells to reverse her 'condition'. Arriette was furious with Susan, Dion and Reiko for entertaining the idea, but it was the least of her worries.

"Let's not argue," she managed, though she did fancy a kick and a long scream into her pillow given the chance. "Nobody else is to brew potions or cast spells without me knowing. That goes for you too, Reiko."

"What did *I* do?"

"Supplying Pouki with 'the basics', as he put it?"

"I'm the potions master! Isn't that my job?"

She massaged her temple, wishing everyone would shut up and leave before she said something she'd regret.

"How do you know a power-stripping potion won't kill Susan?" Baby A continued, switching back to the vampyr conversation. "I mean, she's *dead,* but not *'dead dead'.*"

Dion hissed, this time with visible fangs. "What the hell is *'dead dead'* supposed to mean?"

"Sorry Dion, I mean *undead.* Stripping away Susan's immortality might leave a corpse, though I guess she can astro-project too, *so...*" She swallowed hard.

Reiko groaned and stood up; the force of his frustration tipped his chair, and he swiped his notebook and pen off the table.

"I don't know, Baby A! How 'bout *you* drink some first and we'll see if that pretty blonde hair of yours turns green?"

"Alright, alright." Arriette hushed them.

She gestured for Reiko to sit before Baby A's pride exploded and blinded them all in a freak electric light show. Arriette remembered all too well how terrifying and effective *that* display was.

Tobias gripped his friend's forearm and tugged him down. He straightened the chair and sat back, sulking.

"None of this was malicious. I'll speak to Susan later.

Until then, let's get the lab closed off and authorised experimentations only to be carried out in there from now on. I mean approved by me," Arriette said, pointing at herself with both index fingers. "Keep spells in books, not lying on tables. I'm not mad, OK, just... tired."

LIES!

Reiko folded his arms. "Fine."

"Fine," said Baby A.

Then he and the angel shot daggers at one another as Arriette handed out a wad of papers—something she'd thrown together in the library over the past few days. Despite the work gathering research involved, she knew the information in those pages would help her team in an emergency, especially once she and Tobias set off to study her family history. If it wasn't for her accidental pregnancy, they'd be there already, discovering her real bloodline and the possibility she was, indeed, a princess.

Ugh, a princess.

The delay pleased Arriette. She wasn't ready to face the truth.

"This is a draft I've been putting together. I think it's important we record our history and the magical beings we cross; those we defeat and how, those we save and why, for future generations. It contains all my primary concerns and potential dangers we're yet to face, plus how we can use our powers more efficiently. I've included some personal diary entries; they could help to document our experiences, and I'm calling it *The Chronicles of Pandora* given that our entire mission so far has been to reverse what she originally caused."

Sebastian glanced at the notes, tipped back his hat, and frowned. "So you're starting a grimoire?"

"Suppose so."

"Didn't Pandora suck the evils back into the box? What else do we have to fear, Arriette? Why all the extra measures? I'd suggest *The Chronicles of the Recruit*."

How about The Chronicles of My Last Nerve.

"At the moment we're safe, Sebastian, but Pandora only called back the *gateway* evils—sickness, death, turmoil, strife, jealousy, hatred, famine, and passion—not the damage they did or the practices they created. Those seeds have grown and spread. We've put a cork in the source, but it's important to mop up what manifested because of those things, and dams can break or leak. It's peaceful now, but it won't be forever," Arriette replied. "We can never eradicate evil, even though the box is secure in our vault. I just want us to learn as much as we can and be prepared, especially since Pandora herself hasn't resurfaced since I encountered her."

"Are you worried about Pandora being inside you?" Sebastian asked.

"She's dormant, but when our baby is born, things will change for the better. When she's old enough, Tobias and I won't be here to guide you because we'll have a crying infant, then a sarcastic magical teenager. If Pandora comes back, things will get complicated, but I'll be my own person again at least."

"Can't we come with you to find your family?" he said. "We're strongest together. We can help with childcare and supernatural tantrums. There are lots of supe followers to hold down the fort here and guard the box. Right, guys?"

The room nodded, humming in unison.

"The box goes where I go," Arriette said.

With the friendliest smile she could muster, she placed a hand on Sebastian's shoulder. None of them had experience taking care of a child. HQ needed them.

"I'm going to be a mother and Tobias a father. We'll have newer responsibilities and challenges only *we* can face for the first few years. We've got to learn this stuff and can't rely on you guys or retainers all the time, nor you on us. When we're gone, we'll need you to keep things running. What if something delays our return? That's why we'll be hiring some extra help before we go."

Tobias snorted. "Reluctantly."

Arriette glowered. He faked zipping his lips.

"Why are you worrying about this *now*?" Tabitha asked. "We have a few weeks until your due date. A grimoire is taking things too far."

"Think of *The Chronicles of Pandora* as a history... a story. So supes can carry on our mission."

Tabitha was right, but Arriette couldn't shake the sense they were heading for yet another catastrophe.

"I want to get a head start. If we all get distracted by the next trauma—and there *will* be a trauma because there always is—it'll be too late. I trust you all with my life and I'd trust you with our child's. I just fear for our future. We lost so many friends in the battle last year and I can't lose anyone else. Casper's death was eye-opening; I realised what this organisation is protecting and how we're sacrificing. I need to be sure having a baby doesn't disrupt *your* lives further. If something happens to Tobias and I, you should be able to fix it fast. *Please* read what I have so far, even if it never goes further... for me?"

Baby A nodded. "Of course. We can add to it, too. We all keep diaries of our own; let's sift through and include anything suitable for you to read when you get back. You're afraid—we understand, but you should remember we did OK before you became the leader, so we'll be OK when you take your break now we have Pandora's box locked away. We're stronger than we were a year ago."

Arriette exhaled with relief. "I've written a summary of how I came to be here, so perhaps you can add your perspectives on that as well. Get us to the current year."

She finished the meeting within the hour, discussing the Recruit's expenses, the new stable, stock levels for food and supplies, clothing for the Enzoian monks, maintenance of the temple, security of the crumbled tunnel, and of course, removal of the dragon's rotting carcass piece by scaly piece and storing what they could use for potions and trade. Even a year on, they hadn't scratched the surface.

She'd considered discussing the voices in her head, then thought better of it, not wanting to worry them or start a lengthy debate.

Pouki was probably right. *Nothing to worry about.*

And... more lies.

When they had finished, Arriette dismissed her friends and headed to the foyer where a stack of fresh applications waited. But as she approached, she felt sick and faint as bile filled her mouth and her eyes streamed, burning as if spiked with spicy peppers. Tobias, too, lost all colour and was covering his mouth and nose with the sleeve of his shirt. Several followers were hunched and leaning against the desk, the pillars, and each other.

"What's that *smell*?" He sniffed Arriette.

Arriette slapped his arm. "Don't be rude."

"What?" he said, grinning.

"Tobias, I'm pregnant; you'd *know* if it was me."

Then a follower screamed.

It was an all too familiar sound. Arriette turned to find the source and, through the largest of the foyer's gleaming windows, she saw thick grey fog rolling in from the already consumed Enzoian village, heading for HQ.

She pushed open the main doors and went outside to get a closer look. The stench increased.

"Get back here!"

"Tobias, I'm fine, but look."

The flowers at her feet wilted. The grass withered and turned brown. Flocks of birds and swarms of bugs flew in the opposite direction, blanketing the sky. Arriette ducked to avoid a face full.

Then her skin itched.

"Do we have any gas masks we can hand out?" she asked him, waving people inside. "This is... malevolent."

He nodded but said nothing, transfixed by the incoming threat. Baby A yelled for them to come back and they complied, locking the glass doors behind them with Arriette's skeleton key and a metal bar.

After a few minutes, the stench subsided and Arriette felt better. Her skin, though, was flushed and dry, itching and fiery as if covered in tiny stings or nasty sunburn. She had some ointment in her quarters she could smear on later —a gift from Baby A to care for her delicate pregnant skin.

"Did you open a new wormhole in the basement yet?" Arriette asked Baby A absent-mindedly.

"A few days ago, like you asked. The vault's down there, though, and I didn't want to activate anything unless you said so, as it would draw too much attention."

"Is it one-way?"

"For now."

"Pandora's box is in the basement vault. Nobody can access it but me. Let's evacuate everyone."

"Is that necessary? The lair is a war zone, Arriette.

The clean-up is going much slower than we expected. Lots of dead demons still to find out in the fields. The smell isn't much better. Perhaps we should move the vulnerable first and send any remaining students back to the city?"

"Something isn't right here, Baby A. Please, just do it. It's not wise for anyone to travel."

Tobias snapped his fingers. "Find me that clumsy student who did this first—perhaps *he* can help us reverse it?"

"I've been investigating with no luck all night, Tobias!" Baby A said, setting off to find Reiko. "I'm telling you, he's gone. He panicked."

Tobias shouted after her, "Then tell Reiko to write what *he'd* been experimenting with around that time!"

Baby A waved an acknowledging hand at him as she disappeared. When he turned to ask Arriette for a decision on the vulnerable, she was already halfway down the opposite corridor.

"Don't let anyone else go outside, Tobias," she called. "Keep those doors barricaded!"

"Wait, where are *you* going?"

FOUR

rriette's stomach warned her to beware of Reiko's dangerous concoctions with a nervous squeeze as she entered the lab. The Recruit's only potions master had a tremendous responsibility; if Arriette kicked something over, he'd be working overtime (if they survived the no-doubt *catastrophic* consequences). But Arriette knew exactly what she was looking for. She could side-step the deadly stuff, meander past Reiko's quarantine-worthy mixes, and head for the planet's most nourishing vitamin, Brollirium, which, despite being told in the meeting they had plenty of, now appeared to be in short supply.

Damn students using up all our essentials!

She slammed the cupboard, groaned, and added it to her mental shopping list. When the fog disappeared, they'd have to dispatch a scavenger party.

After a few more minutes of rummaging, the only Brollirium she'd found, using her ability to shape-shift to her preferred cat-like senses, was smoking gently over a burner at the back of the room. She simply followed her nose.

Casper's power came in handy often for similar jobs, like locating certain herbs for medicinal purposes; forming tools in place of her hands when they were short of a hammer or a key (or locked in a werewolf prison cell!);

stretching her legs to reach a top shelf, or mimicking an enemy to confuse them on the battlefield. It wasn't one of Arriette's favourite powers, but by far the most useful.

The first substance was naturally light green, salty, and harsh. The second was maroon and sweet, so something else was mixed in. Its fragrance was inviting, and it took all her strength not to stick her fingers in the vile and lick them, as if the potion was... *calling her.*

"What ya doing?"

Arriette jumped and drew her hand away. "Dion! Get *out* of here."

"This stuff is more dangerous to you than me."

"Reiko's students have been working with silver, and there's power-stripping stuff in here. I don't want a vampyr exposed."

"I'm not as fragile as I look, an' silver is painful, but it won't end me."

"Touch nothing." She paused, startled by Dion's brighter eyes and warmer complexion. "Something's *weird* with you."

"Reiko synthesised some blood. Been testin' it an' workin' on my speech."

"Under whose authority?"

"Uhm, yours?" she said, scowling. "No?"

Arriette ground her teeth and clenched her fists, smashing them against her cheeks in frustration.

"Nobody *bloody* LISTENS to me!"

Dion swallowed hard. "Oh, well, it's only for emergencies; it's doin' me some good an' those I encounter are takin' me more seriously. Ideal for long journeys, that sorta thing."

"There's nothing wrong with your accent. You're planning on taking a trip, are you?"

Dion cringed. "Well, not exactly. But it means there's no need to hunt or kill anythin'. Works almost as well as the real thing, but doesn't taste as nice. I mean, I eat animals anyway, so it's not really for *me*, but I'm an ideal candidate to test..."

Arriette zoned out, angered that Dion was planning on crashing their trip to confront her grandmother.

Wait, she said synthetic *blood? He's finally done it!*

She'd suspected something was up. Late nights in the boring lab, extra strong coffee, and dark circles around Reiko's human eyes; all a sure sign of a harrowing project. Unnatural as it was, Arriette thought the remaining rogue vampyrs in the vicinity might agree to the Recruit's terms if promised tasty alternatives to their usual menu. She'd heard Reiko suggest it in the past, but Arriette couldn't understand why it was tempting her too.

"What ya about to stick ya hand in is lunch," Dion said, lifting the second vial of Brollirium from the flickering flame. "It's devised mostly of animal blood an' vampyr venom. Reiko didn't want this body rejectin' it. Only downside is the silver."

"It smells... inviting," Arriette admitted.

"It's supposed to."

Brollirium could be easily drawn from the sap of an aged venom tree and there were plenty in Manaia Forest. Arriette noticed after several minutes of cooling, this mixture thickened and looked more like blood than a potion, showing there was indeed animal blood and vampyr venom in there. The green substance must have been the 'before' version.

"Does it hurt when he takes the venom?"

"Nah," she said, "we don't feel the same way you do. I heal fast. The Brollirium gives ma body vitamins."

"And the silver is what, a *dare*?" She sniggered.

"No, it burns ma throat so the potion can be taken into the bloodstream quickly. Helps circulate it too given ma, well, *dead* heart. For Susan, I imagine *quenching one's thirst* is a matter of life an' death, so we're both pleased."

"That's disgusting."

"Nah, tickles. Reiko said I can stop an' hunt anytime I like. Susan's on a... *tighter* leash."

"I guess we should thank him. *Now* I understand why Susan wants to be human again."

"We can make money from this, too. Feedin' all these people can't be cheap. Help fund HQ?"

"Personal gain," Arriette said, shaking her head. "We should use it to help the remaining vampyrs integrate into our new society. And Charles is happy paying for this research facility; he and other agreeable everlasts in the city owe us. We want the human population to thrive again. We, uhm, I mean *they*, are a dying species."

"Still not used to bein' a supe, huh?"

"Less so since my pregnancy," she replied blandly.

Arriette gestured for Dion to eat her dinner, then inspected the lab for other leftover vitamins. It was white and bland like every other room in HQ until further funding arrived, but Reiko kept it well-organised, with cabinets, cupboards, draws and shelves neatly labelled and clean. The tiny jar of Brollirium in storage had not yet been prepared for use and there wouldn't be enough to achieve her plan.

"Where did the supplies go?"

Dion shrugged. "Odd. Here, take the rest of this. I can help ya look for whatever it is ya need. Vampyr senses." She winked.

"Got my own. Something I *enjoy* about being a supe

thanks to Casper."

Arriette really *did* miss her mentor—her grandfather.

"Remind me what am lookin' for."

"I wanted pure Brollirium to burn on some firewood in the garden. It's the only thing I can think of to counteract the effects on the plant life."

"What if Brollirium was in the potion that caused this?"

"Brollirium wouldn't cause damage. It's not a long-term solution, but it's a start."

Dion brushed back a loose strand of scarlet hair. "What 'bout Irami, the acid? Under the right conditions, doesn't it form a gas? Reiko said it's nourishing."

"*I* don't know," Arriette said, "Chemicals aren't my department—the Four Saviours might if Reiko isn't around. I think Ruby's the chemicals girl."

"How did ya hear 'bout Brollirium, then?"

"A book."

Dion flashed her fangs. "How else? In a greenhouse, it would act as plant food. Bit smelly, maybe worth it."

Arriette tossed a spare paper mask at Dion. "Can't be as bad as that fog. Put it on. You're making me nervous."

With an amused expression slicked across her rosy, delicate lips, Dion rolled her eyes, then hopped off the stool to catch the mask.

"Vampyrs don't have to breathe," she said, laughing.

Arriette raised an eyebrow. "Humour me."

"OK, then ya should wear one, too," Dion said.

Dion's fangs were protruding into her lower lips, and two tiny spots of red had appeared, causing her friend to squirm.

"Can't you put those away?"

She covered her mouth. "Sorry, happens when I feed;

ya *know* I don't eat humans!"

Arriette pointed at the scars on her neck and shrugged. "Awful memories. Start looking for more Brollirium or Irami," she instructed, grinning as Dion set about finding the ingredients at lightning speed, "or any alternatives."

When they had found a few matches, Dion escorted Arriette through the halls of their headquarters, grateful for the photochromic skylights and the overcast weather. Arriette was grateful for the signage—each corridor looked the same.

The gas plumed against the locked glass doors, forming a snowy curtain. She doubted their findings would make the slightest dent, but staying busy made her feel useful.

"I don't like this. Not one bit."

"Me neither." Tobias appeared at her side and wrapped an arm around her. He took a list of solutions off Dion's hands. "It's eerie, like something from a horror story. This is your idea, Arriette?" Flicking through the pages, he added, "It won't be easy to mix a potion to counteract so many causes."

"Dion suggested we try Irami."

Tobias shook his head, deflated. "There are villagers still in Enzo. If it's destroying plant life, how can we be sure it's not killing everything else? Irami won't fix *that*. Ideally, we need the spell the student used. Not meddling at all *just yet* is the best course of action."

Another piercing scream caused Arriette to jump, drop the ingredient jars, and crash into a fleeing follower as they rushed to their nearest corridor. They knocked Arriette to the ground and ran off. The jars smashed and pieces scattered across the marble.

Tobias hauled her up and dusted her off.

"What was her problem? I'm bloody flinching at everything," she grumbled.

"You're not the only one," Tobias said, scowling at the fleeing follower who hadn't bothered to apologise.

Dion helped Arriette regain her stance. "Uhm, Arriette... problem."

"What *now*?"

"Uh, it's *undeniably* too late for Irami."

Dion pointed over Arriette's shoulder at a group of bodies crawling through the mist. Slowly, their mutilated forms slithered across the gardens towards HQ's glass doors.

Her mouth hung agape. "This can't be real," Arriette rubbed her eyes. She whacked Tobias's arm. "Tell me I'm hallucinating. Oh, what we can do with an over-active dreamer's imagination. Mine's all over the place right now."

Tobias protested. "I can't create something this twisted, let alone fix it. This wasn't *our* doing."

Arriette backed away, crunching over the glass. "Can any form of dreaming fix it? How about if we gathered a bunch of us? You said last year there's that spiritual element to the gift."

"Doubtful. Dreamers jumping into the psyche of other dreamers is a great *visual* tool, but not for much else."

He cringed as the slam of an angry, desperate fist on the window jolted him out of his frustration.

"Open the doors!" Baby A cried, appearing from a corridor and fighting through the gathering crowd. "Let them in. We can save them."

"No!" Tobias snatched Baby A's speeding body and

clung to her tiny waist, spinning and releasing her away from the villagers with ease. "Look at them. They're crazy. They can't speak, they can barely walk, and their skin is—" He swallowed hard. "This is way beyond our capabilities. Did you find Reiko?"

"He's coming." She gasped. "They're suffering because of us, Tobias, aren't they?" Her ocean eyes filled with tears. "We can't let them die. The Recruit are supposed to be *saviours*."

Eager to please her best friend, Arriette moved nearer the barricaded doors to survey the damage. Tobias was right—the villagers weren't themselves in the slightest; their bodies were crumbling, peeling, flaking, and melting, revealing raw pink flesh and sores beneath. Their eyes were clouded. Some were bruised and puss-riddled and their lips had cracked, now bleeding. Few seemed to acknowledge any pain, though.

Arriette noticed some were missing limbs. Monsters.

"They're infected with something, Baby A. They're just animated corpses. If I open the doors, I'll risk the lives of everyone in here and the lair. The fog is poison... *has* to be. We're the only ones left in Enzo who can reverse this or stop it from spreading further; we should concentrate and preventing others from getting sick."

She brushed a palm over the itchy skin on her arms— could *that* have happened to her if she stayed out there longer?

"Arriette's right." By the doors, Reiko stood with his palms flat against the glass, hoping to soothe the women on the other side or at least ease his guilt. Arriette sighed with relief when she saw him.

"We can't help them yet."

Tobias pulled him away, afraid of the glass breaking.

"They can't get in here. It's too thick." Arriette reassured them. "We're safe until you can find a solution. Just in case, Baby A, can you go with him to the lab? Check as many exits as you can on your way. Dion and I were discussing the possibility of Irami and Brollirium working, but I dropped what little we had left, so that's a non-starter."

Baby A nodded. "I'm on it, Arriette, and I'll find someone to clean up this mess." She smiled as a final thought.

"Oh, no, do a headcount instead!"

Baby A led Reiko away and waved to get Tobias's attention as she passed both incoming telepaths. He nodded, his eyes following Pouki and Paulei until they disappeared behind the main reception desk. The retainers' cheeks flushed and their fingers entwined nervously.

Tobias scowled and nudged Arriette. "Something's going on back there. Is it your turn or mine?"

"I'll go," she said. "You get the next one."

"I'll hold down the fort and clean up the glass."

Arriette pushed her way to the desk and on her tip toes, peered over. The telepaths were crouched in a foetal position with their hands covering their ears and their eyes tightly closed. Tears streamed down their cheeks as they took comfort in the safe mental space of the other, like a subconscious panic room.

"It's... awful," Pouki managed through grinding teeth when he caught Arriette's eye.

He reached out to take hold of Paulei's hand, sharing the pain; their two minds combatting invasive images and sounds.

"The voices—we can't stop them. Painful, dying, tormented, trapped, hungry. *So hungry*!"

She swallowed. "Hungry?"

"*Revenge*," Paulei confirmed.

Arriette chewed what was left of her fingernails. If they could hear the monsters' thoughts, they couldn't technically be dead... could they?

"Can't you block their thoughts?"

"Too... many," Paulei grumbled.

Pouki added, "Too... powerful."

"Powerful?"

Bloody trails and fingernails smeared across the once sparkling glass as the Enzoian women clawed at the entrance, desperate for relief. Arriette found it equally uncomfortable to witness her friends in mental agony. She shoved aside two high stools to squat by their side.

"How can one slight mistake do *so much* damage?" she gasped. "A student couldn't have done this, surely? We're not prepared. What could he have mixed?"

Reversing wounds like theirs would be impossible. The women outside were shells of their former selves, with no personality or rationality. They trampled their fallen neighbours. Arriette feared the solution would be extermination. Blinded by her fear, she grabbed both telepaths by their shirt sleeves and dragged them to a stance, screaming for her followers to get out of the way. They parted as if in battle formation, some skidding on the marble as she barrelled through, towing Paulei and Pouki to the basement door. She used her skeleton key to gain access, leaving it open so others could join them. Her plan to evacuate had to be their next step.

"Both of you should go to the lair until this is over. If we need you, we'll send a messenger. You're of no use to us like this. You won't be alone. More will come."

"The wormhole is untested and—" Pouki began, but

Arriette slammed the door in their faces before either could protest, relieved by (and jealous of) their temporary escape.

FIVE

In the lobby, the rotting stink of death engulfed the new headquarters and, despite most of the Recruit wearing gas or face masks, it seeped into their skin, clinging to their clothes and hair. Some had to dash to their bathrooms with sickness.

Susan's eyes burned and watered as the stench entered her nostrils, sending her vampyric senses into overdrive. Her fangs protruded, puncturing her lips and leaving thin red trickles in lines down her chin and neck. Several human followers fled in fear of her and Arriette couldn't blame them.

"Don't you appreciate a nice, juicy dead body?" she said, turning up her nose as she used her thumb to wipe Susan's mouth.

Her nostrils flared and her eyes narrowed as she fought her instincts. "We don't eat the dead," she stated flatly.

"Certainly created a few, though," Arriette grumbled, depositing the blood into a tissue and shoving it in her pocket.

"There are..." Susan paused as she swallowed a mouthful of her blood, "...consequences."

"To what?"

"Eating the dead," she confirmed, disgusted. "How is that smell getting in here?"

"It's worrying me too. If the stench of their flesh can penetrate the structure, does that mean the fog has? Why didn't any of us change before, though? You should go to the lair too, Susan, if this is affecting you."

"No, I can help." She shifted uneasily. Then, catching sight of a wound on Arriette's arm, licked the rest of the blood from her lips. "You're hurt."

"Am I?" Arriette followed Susan's line of sight to a small graze above her elbow and fumbled in her pocket again for the tissue. "A follower bumped into me earlier and knocked me down. I broke some glass jars, so I must have nicked myself. I'm fine. I can't even feel it."

Susan reached for a first aid kit lying open on the reception desk and knocked the dirty tissue away. "Arry, it needs cleaning."

Arriette retreated. "Save the supplies. Feed, Susan—there's synthetic blood brewing in Reiko's lab. I'll catch up with you later."

The vampyr nodded solemnly, then shoved her way through the crowd toward the lab's corridor. Once she was out of sight, Arriette exhaled in relief. The rest of her friends were gathering in the foyer, ushering lingering panicked followers to safer offices, their residences, and the canteen, where they would be hidden and out of the way.

"Tobias, do you know of any way to share a telepath's images with another person? Is there a spell or something?"

He frowned and shuffled toward her, stepping over a scattering of discarded files and stationery.

"Why?"

"It might help if I understood the mindset of these women. I mean, *creatures*. Find out what they want and how we can get them to leave."

He said, "Pouki and Paulei would've discovered a way already. They may be able to show you, though, but I've never asked them anything like that before."

"They're consumed by the women's thoughts. I'm strong enough to take the weight from their shoulders. I'll ask them."

"Stronger than experienced telepaths?"

Arriette narrowed her eyes at the attitude behind his challenge. "Pandora gave me half of her spirit for a reason, and I *am* the most powerful supe on this planet, Tobias."

Tobias quickly added, "Don't remind me. What I mean is you're *one* pregnant person, Arriette. Pandora or no Pandora."

She raised her brow, flinching as the women brayed the glass again. "I receive images from Zìnnyi all the time. Few of *those* are pleasant."

"You don't need access to their thoughts to know they intend to break in and eat us... or something."

"It's the *something* that worries me."

Arriette hadn't wanted to admit it aloud, but as the glass was beginning to vibrate and the hoards were growing bigger, she was starting to imagine the Recruit's downfall.

Taken out by a bunch of, for want of a better word... zombies *after everything we've been through? No. There* has *to be a way to fix this.*

"Something caused their accelerated rate of decomposition, but I wouldn't say they're dead because Pouki and Paulei could still hear them," she reasoned. "Perhaps reading their memories can show us how or why —what that student's mistake did? It's a lot of damage and, to be frank, Tobias, I can't see a potion being the *real* trigger for all this. Can you?"

Tobias ran a hand through his dishevelled hair. "You suspect someone set this up to look like an accident? Purposefully tried to wipe out an entire village?"

"Don't you? That student was quick to bolt, and he's just a kid. Do we ask for credentials when they enter the building? Was he really a student? Most of our supplies are missing, too. I couldn't find any Brollirium. Odd, given it's the first thing we thought of using. Even *I* couldn't mess up a spell-casting or potions class *that* badly. He had to be under an influence or hired by somebody. You said Falkon Lou had supporters still in the city."

"Grasping at straws," he admitted, sighing.

"It's all I've got. I'm going to catch Pouki before he exits through Baby A's wormhole. He might be able to offer some clarity."

Arriette dodged the last of the followers and headed to the basement, leaving Tobias to tidy up the foyer. Luckily, Pouki and Paulei had joined the queue to exit but were still waiting for their turn. They seemed calmer and detached down in the basement. Arriette was sorry to be raising negative thoughts again.

"I'm glad I caught you. I need one of you to show me what you witnessed up there. Can you do that?"

They looked from one another to the wormhole, then back to Arriette. Helping others and using their energy for something positive and productive was giving their minds focus, and they had skipped safe passage through several times to delay having to leave.

"You saw what it did to us," Paulei warned.

"Just show me. Give the memories to me if you can, without having to view them yourselves. Is that possible?"

"But the baby—"

"I'm asking nicely," she said, cracking her knuckles in frustration. "You know I hate playing the bossy saviour card; don't make me pull rank."

Pouki ground his teeth. He gestured for Arriette to move aside, allowing those in the queue behind to take their places, then tugged her dress to suggest she ought to kneel.

"For what I am about to do, Zïnnyi forgive me."

Out of the corner of her eye, she saw Paulei back away and return to helping by the wormhole. It was at the opposite end of the basement to the vault where Pandora's box now lived; it took Arriette all her might not to go to it, or to answer its silent beckoning through the wall.

Pouki cupped her face. Intense pain coursed through Arriette's muscles as they went into spasm, instantly dragging her from the temptation. Her blood boiled. Images began to flow from Pouki's mind to hers, giving her a migraine; each vision lingered for an eternity before the next vicious memory replaced it, eager to destroy her sanity and for the first few seconds, Arriette hated him for obeying her order. HATED him. She despised how easily he'd given in, but it was clear to her this pain was unique to the monsters. She could hear their cries and screams, moans of agony and frustration. She shared their swift change as flesh rotted in proximity to the fog, eating all sense of right and wrong, love and humanity.

It was then she heard that familiar scream.

Pouki released his hold and Arriette crumbled, gasping for air and knotting her hair in balled fists as if to tear it from the roots.

"Your baby is *powerful*," he told her, helping her up.

"*She*," said Arriette. "The wiccan said she's a girl."

Out of breath, Arriette whispered, "She *saw* that?"

"No, she made it easy for you to share my vision."

"How can you tell?"

"Her consciousness reached out when we connected. She relieved some of the pressure. Zïnnyi has blessed her with *unimaginable* strength and courage. She's so... brave. And she must be part angel to achieve it."

Arriette smoothed a hand across her stomach and forced a smile. She thanked him, and without saying anything else, hurried back upstairs, still wobbly, too weary to check on the box.

Did she have the inner strength to deal with such a prediction, too? Despite seeing how the women were reacting and witnessing their change, their motivation remained unclear.

In the laboratory, Reiko and Baby A were arguing over measurements of a dark orange liquid when Arriette returned and asked, sweating, "Any luck? There are so many of them out there, more than I estimated lived in Enzo. We'll be surrounded soon."

"We're making progress," Reiko said and raised his brow at how dishevelled her orange dress was, "but without a back up supply of Brollirium, we'll hit a dead end."

"You're going with my theory?"

"We're going with lots of theories. Unfortunately, that's all they are right now until it's safe to travel outside of Enzo to locate the sap we need."

Baby A asked, "Still no sign of the student?"

"None," she said, defeated, "and I've seen Pouki's visions. It didn't offer any further insight into what these women want, but I did see their change. It was quick. I'll find the carpenters, so we can fix that window within the hour. If the hoards outside realise that there's a way in, we're dead anyway. I'm wondering if this window is the reason we can *inhale* their demise."

"We'd all be affected by now, Arriette," Reiko assured her. "And the carpenters left. If not, they're probably dead."

"*That* escalated quickly," she mumbled, hands on her hips. "Thanks for spreading the joy, Reiko."

"I'm realistic. I'm a human after all! At least it seems that although we can breathe in their rotten flesh, we're unaffected by the poison."

"Which supports my theory that they were targeted. The fog was designed to affect those surrounding HQ, not within it. To keep us trapped here for some reason."

Baby A gestured at Arriette's grazed arm. "Want me to take a look?"

"It's nothing. I didn't even notice until Susan asked me about it. Was she here because I sent her to feed?"

Baby A confirmed she'd been by for a few sips, but Susan left swiftly afterwards as the stench was overwhelming her. Arriette opened the broken window enough to inspect the grounds. The women of Enzo were congregating mostly at the front, but as more joined, those at the back were being forced around the sides to windows and other exits.

"You'll get yourself killed!" Baby A tugged Arriette inside and slammed the window.

"I'm sick of people telling me I can't use windows!"

"We're not wrong about the risk of an assassination," said Baby A. "But this time I'm more concerned about you letting in that fog!"

"Reiko just said the smell won't hurt me!"

"The smell, not the *cause*."

Arriette sighed. "For the love of all that is..."

"*Careful*," Baby A warned.

"Sorry. Look, last year when Susan and I went to investigate my vision before we found Pandora's box, we saw a road leading through the woods to Drakonta, starting at the temple. The rear exits are safe, but they won't be for long. We could run for help along that road."

Reiko squirted liquid onto a thin piece of glass and grumbled as he inspected it beneath a microscope. Arriette scowled at how little attention he was paying to her plan.

Finally, he said, "This doesn't look right."

"Like how?" she asked.

"I don't expect that kid did this, at least not all of it. Wilting flowers and smelly fog, I can comprehend, but flesh-eating mutants? There's *nothing* in this laboratory capable of such cruelty. I've tried every concoction, and all have failed."

"All of them?"

"Never say never," he mumbled, shrugging, "but it would take an experienced rulecast to conjure something so deadly."

"A rulecast. You mean an everlast's sorcerer?"

"Yes, one hired to serve only the highest of classes."

She gulped. "Makes sense, I suppose. A dreamer isn't capable for sure and none would be so cruel, anyway. I saw the fog early this morning by the cliff. Could it be linked?"

Reiko assured her, "What you were seeing was most likely the beginning of this nightmare."

"Maybe an evacuation is our only chance, then. Some are already leaving, but I can organise something more concrete."

Tobias appeared in the doorway, panting.

"Anything?" he asked. His hazel eyes were wide and bloodshot. "The foyer is almost clear, but there's a crack in one of the glass doors and I'm not sure how long my power can hold it, not with that stench, and not from this distance. It's clouding my head; my vision and strength are all... fuzzy."

"Get the other dreamers to support you," Reiko suggested, and Tobias's face crumpled as he tried to remember which of the residences he'd need to visit to ask for help. Not all of the Recruit's followers lived at HQ; many travelled from neighbouring villages or the city.

"Arriette wants to continue with the evacuation plan instead," Baby A told him. "We can make it out the back without being spotted. To Drakonta."

"We can send the vampyrs at least," Tobias suggested. "Because we shouldn't just abandon HQ."

Arriette snapped her fingers. "The dead don't eat the dead. You're a genius—I *love* you for it!" She kissed him firmly on the lips and grinned. "They're not feeding on each other. I haven't seen them attack the livestock, either. What they're after is us."

"As in humans?"

"Humans and supes," she told Reiko. "Susan said vampyrs won't eat the dead in fear of consequences, so Tobias is on to something."

"They do for a short while, though," Baby A argued. "Isn't that why headstones exist?"

Still distracted, Reiko added, "Bodies don't stay fresh for very long, Baby A."

Scratching his stubble, Tobias considered the possibility of the evacuation being successful due to the state of the lair. They were working against the clock and the longer it took for Arriette to make her decision and give the official order, the less chance of survival they had. The lair was a mess, but far safer than one building in the middle of nowhere.

"Do it," he said. "If Dion or Susan can find some Brollirium out there, perhaps Reiko could make an antidote for the land at the very least. Meanwhile, we'll concentrate on the monsters and finding out what caused this." Tobias opened the window an inch and checked the back of the building. "They're slow, so Dion and Susan can outrun them; Susan can walk in the daylight. We'll just have to find a way to protect Dion, or send a shifter if they're not interested in animals?"

"They might be able to tell." Baby A offered a counter-argument. "Out is easy. What about getting back? What if we're wrong and we're putting their lives at risk?"

"They're already *dead*," Tobias said. "What's the worst that could happen?"

Baby A, once again, said, "They'd be dead-dead."

"It's our only hope," Arriette told her when Tobias had left the room. "We should warn the Drakontans and Mousiquians. If we can't contain this, neighbouring villages are all in danger. If the vampyrs can send a messenger in passing, we'll be saving hundreds of innocent lives."

"And giving them all reason to hate us," she said. "Or terrifying them with two vampyrs charging around."

"They can make it," Reiko uttered. "Knowing Susan, she'll kill anything in her way, but she's persuasive."

"You bet I will," Susan said, taking them all by surprise. She strode confidently past Arriette and Baby A to assess the situation, not bothering to greet Reiko or ask how the antidote was coming along. Likely, she suspected his failure from the beginning. Disappointment was her usual attitude.

"I'm *not* giving you permission to murder people," Arriette said and folded her arms. "If we can change them back, we will."

"Self-defence?"

"Do what you have to, Susan, but *only* if you have to. Keep yourself and Dion alive and do your best to get to one of the villages and warn them. But do us all a favour and *don't* tell them this was the Recruit's fault."

"Instead I should say?"

Arriette groaned. "Uhm, that we're fighting an unknown threat in the village of Enzo."

Susan nodded once. "If it makes you feel any better, Arry, I do not believe this was our fault. Reiko may need to give Dion something to survive the sunlight."

"Now *that* I can do," he chimed.

***

At the rear door, Dion swigged from a long, thin test tube. The vampyrs sprinted to the tree line, careful to avoid being seen by the monsters advancing on the broken window, and Arriette was thrilled not to see any wisps of smoke from Dion's skin. Soon they were a blur in the distance.

Arriette made sure the exits were bolted behind them before she returned to the lab to wash the empty test tube.

"They made it. Dion didn't burst into flames, so whatever you gave her worked," she reported. "No carpenters. I think you're right, Reiko—they've gone."

"Can you blame them?"

"No, but do you think we can fix the window ourselves? Tape or nail it shut? Even a barricade of some kind?"

Baby A nodded, trying to remember where she'd seen some spare building materials. Perhaps the basement. "There's not much more anyone can do until the vampyrs return, but I'll give it a go myself if you'd feel better."

"Will Dion be safe?"

"If she's back in twenty-four hours, she should be," said Reiko.

"Are the Four Saviours in the building?"

"Somewhere," Baby A told her. "Who knows with wiccans? They're so flaky." She grabbed Arriette's wrist as she turned to leave. "In case you haven't noticed, you're about to pop and there are mutants outside desperate to tear us apart. This isn't up to *you* to fix on your own."

"Relax, I'm not going far." Arriette removed Baby A's tight grasp. "I'm not due yet and the Saviours' office is only down the hall. Walking down a corridor isn't going to take a few weeks, is it?"

Baby A frowned. "Aren't you worried?"

Duh.

"Of course I am! In Pouki's absence, they can offer some advice. They *are* Recruit trainers, and they worked with him. We should consult them if they're not already finding a solution. You know what they're like and they specialise in this sort of thing—chemicals, elements, weapons."

Reiko looked up from his beakers and burners. "Since when were they stationed at HQ?"

"Since the lair became a war zone," Baby A said, then paused. "They were supposed to be returning this week, I think. But now?"

Arriette nodded. "It's decided, then. I need to make

myself useful. I'll be back soon."

"With good news, I hope," said Baby A, and closed the door behind her.

SIX

Sapphire, Dianne, Ruby and Jade, known to Arriette and her friends as the Four Saviours or the *Elite Four*, were standing in the centre of their office when Arriette entered without knocking. It was an uncomfortably small room, but warm and homely decorated with a rug, woollen cushion covers and the walls painted a deep red. The curtains were drawn to block out the sunlight and the view of the Enzoian monsters, but the skylight shone what appeared as a halo upon them.

The quadruplets had formed a shield knot and were muttering a repetitive Haeyloian phrase she couldn't understand, though her knowledge of the language was vastly improving. From their tone and intent, it sounded like a protection spell and through their concentration, they hadn't noticed her arrival despite the creaking door and her impatient, conspicuous coughs to gain their attention.

Sapphire (or Saph to her friends and colleagues) broke the connection with her sisters and looked up from their trance first. Her face brightened,.

Arriette forced a smile and held up her hands.

"Sorry to interrupt."

Saph wrapped her arms around their leader's tense body, squeezing the anxiety from her muscles. Arriette breathed in the wiccan's midnight hair doused with aromatherapy oils and tried not to sneeze. Each inhale calmed her and offered a comfort she hadn't felt since her nightmares began.

"We need your help," she mumbled, spitting out a lock of black curls.

"We were expecting you."

Saph fumbled in her pocket for an elastic band and tied her hair in a high bun, revealing a triangular runic tattoo at the base of her neck, symbolic of her wiccan influence. Arriette noted how Saph's water triangle was the standard shape but upside down, whereas her sisters each had variations for their charms. For Ruby's fire knowledge, her triangle was a standard shape and upright. Dianne's air symbol looked a little like a snow-peaked mountain with a line across the tip, and Jade's earth symbol was its reverse.

"I sent Pouki to the lair," Arriette said. "He and Paulei are suffering. I was hoping you might have some ideas in their absence."

"You need more information about the baby? We already confirmed what that wiccan said. She's a girl," Ruby said. "What about her weight, or her hair colour?"

"Not right now," Arriette said. "I'm here about... them." She gestured at the window and shivered.

"Ah. If this was caused by a potion," Ruby advised, "I guess we could offer an insight."

"*Was it?*"

Perhaps there was some good news after all—an easy explanation with a straightforward solution.

Saph shook her head, though. "Honestly? No. There are few chemicals with the ability to change both a physical and mental state in their entirety, no matter how you mix them. I can't imagine Reiko would keep chemicals like that on the premises."

"He said he'd tried all the combinations and nothing had replicated the symptoms," Arriette told them. "How about a spell?"

She scowled at the other women, silently conferring. "Most spells would leave a trace of who the victim used to be and they wear off, eventually; there's got to be a return state. In this case, I can't see how those women will be normal again."

Arriette sighed. "Not a spell either, then."

"Unless performed by a rulecast," she replied, and her three sisters all nodded in unison.

"You're not the first to suggest a rulecast's work, which means an everlast is behind this. How do we know this isn't an illusion?"

"Whatever did this re-wired their core values and personalities. Wiccan spells don't do that, neither would an illusion," Saph explained.

Dianne asked, "Has anyone been outside?"

"No, Di," Arriette said, using her nickname to keep the mood light, "and nor will they. I can't risk it."

Di added, "Good, as it's highly unlikely. Unfortunately, whatever this is, it's irreversible."

This confirmed Arriette's worst fear; she would be unable to save the women of Enzo and may have to resort to genocide if they posed a threat to the wider community.

"The damage to the crops *is* consistent with a potion or spell, though," Arriette argued. "There's only one potion still in the lab and it's for stripping powers."

"That's Susan's?" Saph asked.

"Yes. The vampyrs are out looking for some ingredients at the moment. Brollirium or Irami would at least save the land."

Saph shrugged. "Probably pointless, in my opinion."

"Gee, thanks."

"Sorry." Saph cringed. "A power-stripping potion would kill crops and create a fog, but *mutation*? Truly dangerous chemicals would also need *super* high doses, and we just don't store those volumes here. For this reason, actually."

"I found a few chemicals and I didn't recognise any of them despite my research. Susan is studying wicca. I've been helping, so I'm sure after all these months I'd be able to identify something so toxic." Arriette sighed. "If you think any of them are a potential cause, we'll investigate."

"Well, there's Andopelhi, which is a chemical produced by Dream Lynx sharks in our oceans. It's in their saliva, helping them digest prey," Saph explained. "It causes a breakdown in flesh and is highly poisonous to humans."

"Do they swim in Enzoian waters? Possibly a fisherman caught one and brought it ashore by accident?"

"Our fishing grounds are too shallow. If the shark dies, the chemical would be rendered useless after a few hours anyway—it has to be extracted by a marine biologist in the proper conditions."

Di then added, "Besides, they're endangered. Isn't there a law against hunting the Dream Lynx?"

"You're asking *me*?" Arriette tapped her foot.

"You're the law around here."

Jade interrupted before Arriette could offer a snide reply. "Cryzilnam is in Drakontan lava. When it cools and hardens, the chemical causes it to crystallise. There are two or three Cryz ports within riding distance up the mountain, but it's notorious for causing some nasty physical symptoms like hallucinations, confusion, memory loss, sweating, dehydration, boils and dizziness, to name a few. When the volcano erupted last, the area was evacuated for that reason, but it hasn't blown in hundreds of years and the city's brightest retainers do not predict it ever will again. It's dormant."

Arriette hummed, pinching the bridge of her nose. "The Enzoian women are experiencing lots of those symptoms," she argued.

"Basically," Di said, "a potion or spell-casting accident within HQ is not the cause. You're looking for an external factor. If this was a targeted attack, it was made to look like the Recruit's fault. Like a set-up. That's our conclusion—take it or leave it."

Arriette gasped. "*Terrorism?*"

"We shouldn't rule it out. We're still in possession of Pandora's box and you just discovered you're a royal. There's a chance someone's after your power."

"My powers?"

"No, *power...* as in your status," she corrected.

"The box is locked away," Arriette said, checking for the key hanging around her neck, which dangled safely.

"Oh, I don't doubt your ability to keep the box safe. Nor do I blame the box itself. It's valuable, though, and so are you. Someone could be after either. There *is* a third, rather wacky, option. It's a long shot, but supe women produce a hormone during pregnancy." Di glanced at Arriette's stomach, then met her narrowed eyes. "It's a natural pain relief and numbs the mother's supernatural mind to some extent, preventing any of the parent's powers being passed through to the foetus too soon. Once in the bloodstream, it binds the baby's gifts temporarily until they've developed enough to deal with the responsibility."

"Pouki told me about that earlier. How soon would it take effect?" Arriette asked.

"It expires gradually, usually around two weeks before birth," Jade told her, "and then it would naturally dissipate so the baby can learn to use their powers. Works a bit like a power-stripping or binding potion."

"Like Casper's?" Arriette sat on a wooden chair and slumped. "I think Pouki used a similar one to mask my human pregnancy. My unborn daughter helped me receive a vision from Pouki earlier, which suggests she has some of her powers, and I'm due in a few weeks. Is this *my* fault?" Arriette bit her lip, hard. "If I wasn't born supernatural, would I still produce the hormone?"

Jade looked at the others and awaited their nod of approval before she advised. "More so than any other. You're one of the most powerful souls in existence, Arriette, and your body will be working hard. There have been a few recorded cases in the past where the mother's body under-produced the chemical. The consequences were unfortunate. With your daughter predicted to be so powerful, maybe it was never going to work to begin with."

"How would we know if my body was under-producing or had stopped completely, like naturally?"

"Shall we do a blood test?" Jade suggested.

Arriette held out her arm and gestured for Jade to take the blood she needed with a tap at the crook of her elbow. Jade didn't need a spoken or written agreement; she immediately began the process.

"Did my unborn child do this accidentally because my body isn't producing the hormone as it should be? Or because it *never* affected her? We were advised a dreamer wasn't capable of such destruction alone, and she's part

Tobias.”

"It's better to be safe than sorry. If she helped to funnel Pouki's telepathic vision, we are underestimating how capable she already is." Saph cringed. "You and Tobias are both active dreamers. With access to your powers in the womb, accidents *are* a possibility. She's the product of light and love, though, and to assist a vision like that from the womb, I wouldn't place my vote on her being the cause. She sounds angelic."

She shrugged like it was no big deal, causing Arriette to groan and shake her head.

"Wouldn't I realise if my body wasn't producing it?"

"Only *you* can answer that," Ruby said. "*We* have never re-produced, so we cannot speak from experience. We don't know anything for sure. Speculating is pointless, and there's still a chance this is all a set-up to make us *think* you're to blame, or the Recruit as a whole."

Saph pulled out a second chair and sat beside her. She tapped her arm again to find a vein, then took a blood sample.

"You saw a palm reader," Jade said.

Arriette hissed as the needle pierced her skin.

"Tobias and I wanted to be sure the baby would be healthy. We visited a variety of healthcare professionals. Most said the baby would be born a supe but the wiccan woman said not. You were able to confirm she's a girl too, so we thought—"

"I'm asking because... did she perform any rituals or give you any potions to drink? Anything that could have interfered with the hormone?"

"She just held my hand." Arriette's face went pale and her jaw dropped. "Wait, *she* didn't give me anything but Pouki did; he said there was an unlikely chance of such side effects when he masked my pregnancy." With her free hand, she patted her flat physique and sighed. "We thought it would be best to continue my Recruit leadership duties and protect Pandora's box. Tobias didn't want anyone outside our organisation to know we were going to be parents; he said it might make me a target."

"We'll know soon enough, but it's unlikely the issue," Saph said, placing a tiny bandage on the spot where she'd taken Arriette's blood. "This should heal fast. Let's get the sample to Reiko's lab. Until then, you should rest."

"Not until we have a plan or an explanation, at least. What about the dying plants? Could a spell or potion have killed the plant life and my baby's powers mutated the women?"

"Two different causes of two different simultaneous accidents?" Di almost laughed.

"Why didn't this happen to the Enzoian men in their temple, or to any of us? Why only the women in that village?"

"The men live far away. A targeted event missed them, or wasn't intended for them," Saph said, gesturing out the skylight at the mountaintop.

"I met some of them," Arriette admitted. "Doesn't it strike you as odd or suspicious, even? Susan and I met one of the Enzoian women. She had a symbol painted on her forehead."

Arriette demonstrated where the symbol was on her body and drew the circular shape with her finger.

"The Enzoian symbol on the forehead," Di said, nodding. "It's a perfect circle drawn with one smooth stroke."

"That woman warned us about the fork in the path."

"How strange," Di interjected. "Enzoian women don't speak. Much of their history is written on parchment, stored in the homes of the eldest women in the village. I believe silence is part of their religion; devotion to Zïnnyi and a promise to speak only to their creator through prayer, at least for so many months of the year."

Arriette thought this to be an interesting fact, because in the time she'd spent exploring the village she'd never held a complete conversation with the Enzoian women. A few hurried words, perhaps.

"How accurate is our knowledge of their culture? Ever seen the scripture or spoken to their elders—could their change be part of the religion, a reason *why* the men live on the mountain?"

"We haven't been here long enough to gather any information. We have no right to intrude on their beliefs. For all we know, their records are sacred and sealed. Why would they allow *us* access?" Di said.

"If this *is* our fault, they certainly won't after today," Ruby said, confirming Arriette's fears. "Just as we wouldn't immediately reveal everything about ourselves, nor should we expect them to trust us completely."

Arriette groaned and stood abruptly. "If the men live up there and the women live down here, how can their civilisation function efficiently?"

Jade laughed. "*Please* tell me your mother had 'the talk' with you, Arriette?"

"Spare me the lecture." Arriette pointed to her pregnant belly.

The ladies all laughed and blushed.

"I haven't seen that weird woman since Susan and I spoke to her," Arriette said.

"Are you sure she was Enzoian?" Jade said.

Arriette scrunched up her nose. "She wore the symbol."

"Anyone can paint their forehead," Ruby said. "How old was she? Because so far I have only seen girls not yet of age with that marking. It identifies their, uhm, *innocence*."

Unconvinced, Arriette scratched her chin. "She was older. I've been back to the well and even walked through Enzo many times with Tobias and Susan, but she's never re-appeared. Why warn us back then, only to avoid us now?" she asked no one in particular. "Who *was* she?"

SEVEN

"Well, it's official," Ruby said, as she handed Arriette a thin strip of parchment. It looked as though it had been dipped in her blood. Arriette growled and slammed the stained piece of paper against the laboratory wall.

Ruby peeled it off and passed it around her sisters. "Your body is not producing what it should to bind the baby's powers."

"We were so stupid, Tobias!"

Tobias closed the door behind them and shook his head, confused. "I'm sorry. I don't remember poisoning half the Enzoian population before reanimating them into murderous corpses. *We* didn't do anything, and I'm not convinced our daughter did either. Ladies, you said so earlier that we are underestimating the control our child already has after she helped Pouki and Arriette to share a vision, and Pouki would *never* give Arriette anything to risk her health, or the baby's, or the safety of our people."

Arriette wanted to reach out and kiss him for supporting and defending her. Doubt niggled as it always did in the back of her mind, but the leader in her soul screamed this was not something the Recruit predicted. Nor controlled. Though not a telepath, Tobias may as well have plucked that speech from her mouth.

"The spell Pouki put on Arriette to hide her

pregnancy may have backfired," Reiko said, "preventing her body's natural defences from binding the baby's powers correctly. Test results show there's no trace of the hormone at all in Arriette's bloodstream. Naturally, there'd be something this close to her due date."

Tobias asked, "Like the baby has used something she's seen inside Arriette's mind and then turned it into an active dream?"

Arriette shook her head frantically, slamming her fist on the counter and jingling a bunch of test tubes.

"Tobias, I've been shielding my mind as Pouki and Paulei taught me, I swear. I don't understand and can't believe Pouki wouldn't have considered this. I feel *fine*. I'd know if my baby was mutating the neighbours."

Tobias took hold of her shaking hands. "I pushed for this spell. If it's found to be the cause, then I'll take responsibility."

"Pouki was trying to protect me," Arriette urged. "I won't entertain this idea. He knows what he's doing; and the Four Saviours can vouch for him, too. They've worked with him for years. Trained with him. He's an expert! It's more likely my body was never going to bind the baby's powers, and if so, then it's for a reason."

"Everything supernatural happens for a reason," Sapphire confirmed and gently bowed her head at Arriette.

Her leader was right.

Pouki's mind and practices were solid.

"Nobody is placing blame," Ruby assured them both, "and there's *nothing* you could have done to prevent this, even if we were aware sooner. Inside your body, your baby has unlimited access to your worst nightmares and past experiences, with or without that hormone."

Tobias bit his lip and groaned, imagining the

possibilities. She saw her friends mutilated and massacred on the battlefield, fought a lava-breathing dragon and was only now, finally healed of those scars. She rescued her vulnerable mother from an orc, got bitten and almost sucked dry by vampyrs, was stabbed by her ex-boyfriend thousands of feet in the air, was betrayed, chased, embarrassed, and threatened too. There were so many painful, torturous memories in Arriette's mind and they were all readily available for their daughter's viewing pleasure.

"We need to figure out which vision or memory is being amplified," said Di before she cautioned, "*if* this is the cause. We should get a head start."

Tobias folded his arms. "I don't believe any of it."

Lost in her thoughts and drowning in guilt, Arriette said nothing. With her head lowered between her knees, she inhaled deeply on the stool she perched upon and closed her eyes to prevent a wave of unexpected panic. Already, her chest was tightening, her limbs tingling, and her heart pounding. For the first time in months, the scar following the length of her spine severely ached, as if her wings were threatening to surprise the room.

"The screaming woman," Tobias said suddenly. "Arriette has been hearing voices in her sleep; one woman in particular is always in pain like she's dying." He turned to Arriette. "Did you learn her name?"

"I don't know who she is, but Pouki said it was just doubts about becoming a mother," said Arriette, her voice quivering, "but I heard something similar when Pouki shared his visions in the basement as if he'd stumbled upon a secret and *amplified* it."

Tears streamed down her pale face. They teetered on her nose and chin, glistening in the lab's harsh clinical light. Tobias cupped her cheeks and wiped them gently away.

"Maybe Zïnnyi *was* trying to warn us," he told her as he lifted her chin and wiped away the droplets with his thumb. He knelt beside her stool. "You told Pouki you were afraid the sound was our baby."

"The screaming *isn't* our baby, though."

Tobias smiled and replied, "No, but our daughter has perhaps been amplifying an audio warning from our creator. She's been doing her utmost to get this message to you; urging us to listen to her, to take note. That's... incredible!"

Arriette squeezed Tobias's hand, unsteadily. How could their unborn baby already be so powerful? So *good*?

"So she's using His warning to activate what He warned us *she* was going to do? Is that... does that... how is that even possible?"

Half-laughing, half-choking on his surprise, Tobias said, "No, this wasn't her, Arriette; she was merely warning you it would happen. She didn't... *we* didn't cause this."

"But we're not ready for such power, Tobias. I can barely control *my* gifts. How can we fail at parenthood before we've even started?" Arriette started to cry again, withholding the ache in her chest to sob and stamp her feet and scream into the void. "This is such a mess. We're supposed to be protecting Haeylo!"

"There's nothing wrong with your parenting," Dianne told them firmly. "Sounds like a strong-willed and confident child. And no different from any other supe baby, I assure you."

Arriette wiped her dripping nose with the back of her hand. "Isn't there anything we can do to bind her powers until her birth, for her benefit... just in case we're wrong? Casper's potion?"

"Do you really want to?" Tobias asked.

"Whatever we do next, we cannot reverse the damage done, but there's no harm in trying to prevent further accidents. Powers can be unbound."

Tobias squeezed Arriette's hand and led her to the laboratory door, hoping to remove her from the temptation of binding an incredible power without a full understanding of its capabilities.

"Her power did not create the fog. If we do this, we are interfering with Zïnnyi's messages. Don't punish our daughter for something a reckless everlast and his rulecast did to get back at us for Falkon's imprisonment."

"Is that what you assume happened here?" Dianne asked.

Tobias nodded. "Falkon is imprisoned because of us, and I *know* he had a following in the city who will have been biding their time to get revenge."

"What if I'm supposed to do this?"

Tobias glared at her, bewildered. "You're not."

"The wiccan we visited said our little girl would be born human."

"And Pouki, the man you have just valiantly defended, told you that futures change because of free will. What you decide now, Arriette, could be what sways things."

Arriette offered a weak smile. "I hope you're right."

EIGHT

Arriette's patience was running thin. More Enzoian women gathered around the building and the mass of putrid flesh and broken bones drifted to the unlocked window in the laboratory, rattling her nerves.

Hard at work mixing potions, Reiko used what supplies they had left, whilst Arriette scrubbed relentlessly at the walls and glass, attempting to remove any scents that might attract those creatures, or allow them to see it as an access point. She sat to wipe the sweat from her brow with the back of her hand and peered cautiously at the line of trees in the distance.

Out of instinct, she reached for the healed vampyr bites on her neck.

"They'll be back soon," Reiko said.

Arriette hummed. "You read my mind."

"I'm many things. A telepath isn't one of them."

"You're worried about her?"

Reiko flinched. "Who?"

Arriette smirked, then carried on. "I already told you, there's no point mixing potions we *know* won't work."

She gestured at the pots and tubes scattered across Reiko's desk, but he shrugged and continued.

"I need to keep moving. You know?"

She knew.

Of course, she knew. Why else would she be

pointlessly scrubbing a laboratory on her hands and knees?

"The Four Saviours said there isn't much we can do. Some*thing* did not cause this ordeal. We can counteract this way."

"I'm only trying to reverse the environmental effects," he said. "I believe you and Tobias when you say your unborn baby was not the cause. And I agree that binding her powers is not the answer."

She scrunched up her face in thought. "You do?"

"We might need her at this rate."

"There is still doubt. If so, Susan and Dion may be out on a needless mission."

He cleared away the items he'd been using, following Arriette's lead that a clean lab would enforce a clean mind.

"If they can warn the neighbours, it's not pointless," Reiko reminded her. "Here, come help me. It will take your mind off their return."

Arriette dumped the cleaning equipment in a bucket, confident she'd done her best, then joined Reiko behind the desk with her protective gloves on and a face mask. Test tubes lined the shelves behind and every so often he'd reach back, pluck one at random, and add it to the boil. After a few minutes, he gave her a nod and gestured for her to open the faulty window for him. With as much force as she could muster, Arriette yanked the temporary wooden barricade Tobias had hammered up away from the pane and discarded it, hoping whatever Reiko had brewed would drift through.

"If this works, we'll owe you one."

"Keep your mask on," he told her.

"Is this stuff dangerous?"

Reiko shook his head. "Quite the opposite, but you are pregnant. Precautions, always. I'm not afraid of what's going out..."

"Only of what might get in. I understand."

She winked and did as she was told, then took the solution from the burner. It emitted an unusual yellow gas, fogging the room as Arriette shoved her hand into the open air. Slowly, they watched as it ate the smog. Arriette shook the solution a little to dissolve the remaining particles, emptying the contents in the long grass, then pulled the tube back inside and closed the window.

Shifting her right hand into a hammer, Arriette re-secured the wooden barricade.

"Did we salvage enough from those broken jars in the lobby?"

"Well, I hate wasting useful ingredients," he replied, not answering her question. "If anything, we've passed some time."

Reiko shoved Arriette's cleaning supplies aside with his foot and pulled a box of thin cream paper strips out of a bottom cupboard. He held one up and watched as it turned red. But he didn't stop there. Reiko emptied the box until the strips turned first grey and finally, they didn't change at all.

"You can remove your mask," he said. "The air in here is fine, so nothing got in. Now let's hope I brewed enough to cut through all the smog in Enzo, not only what lingers around HQ."

It *was* working, though, on a basic level.

Arriette was pleased to see the beautiful landscape again; the shape of the trees in the orchard a few hundred yards from the stable and, beyond that, an outline of the Drakontan mountain. But with their strapped resources until the vampyrs returned, would it reach any further?

"Any sign of them?" he asked.

"Not yet. You've done a great job, Reiko, with the limited supplies we had on offer. I'll leave you to it. Tobias will be worried."

Reiko bolted the laboratory door behind her.

Headquarters had calmed a great deal. She noticed more of the office doors and living quarters were opening —people were realising the women outside were unlikely to break in and were going about their business again, though not as usual. Some had already exited through the wormhole and, with fewer people in the building, the creatures outside were showing less interest. The glass hadn't shattered yet; the dreamers still in HQ were doing their job, collectively reinforcing it. So supes emerged and mingled, interacting semi-normally again, but staying out of the foyer where the bulk of the creatures were visible.

Baby A bumped into her and Arriette explained what the Four Saviours assumed about her baby's powers, plus how she and Reiko had initiated the first stages of 'Operation Clean-Up'.

"That's amazing," Baby A said, running a hand over Arriette's stomach. "She's capable of such stunning alchemy, all from the womb. Thank Zïnnyi you're not binding such purity."

Arriette grumbled. "I feel so guilty."

Baby A sighed. "For a child to master her powers before officially inheriting them is incredible. We can't deny that, and you have nothing to be guilty for."

"Unmastered, though," Arriette snapped.

"What do you mean?"

"There's a chance she didn't just help me see what was coming, but had a hand in causing it. Though her usage was accidental, if that's the case. Tobias and I were stupid enough to mask my supernatural pregnancy and the procedures my body should have followed. If I ballooned like I was supposed to, we'd have avoided this."

"*You* don't believe she's the cause."

"I don't want to. But what if she continues to damage the environment and kill more people? She's supposed to be good, not evil."

"Arriette, she's not evil." Baby A hushed. "Even *you* struggle with Zinnyï's visions. How can you expect a baby to understand what to do with them? We have to stand strong—your baby cannot do such a heinous thing, even accidentally."

She swallowed hard and blushed. "Neither does Tobias."

"So, what's the issue?"

"What if we're wrong and she hurts *me*?"

"She won't. Can't. She's part dreamer too, and ordinarily—not counting the werewolves' ridiculous power-switching debacle you experienced last year, of course—dreamers can't harm other dreamers."

"The Four Saviours are about as sure as I am. It's a theory right now. Pouki knows magic; he'd never make such a serious mistake," Arriette announced confidently. "They said someone could frame us; a terrorist set-up to make me look like a villain."

Baby A crossed her arms. "We need evidence before accusing anyone of anything. However destructive this experience has been so far, it'll only get better. But I believe *that* theory more. Your baby is a gift, truly. I'd give anything to be pregnant again, Arriette, no matter who the father is or how it happens. The thought of being a godmother thrills me completely, but there's something special about being a mother." Arriette offered half a smile, so Baby A added, "Your agreeable face is not very convincing. Practice. You'll need it when she's born."

Before the angel walked away, Arriette said, "Hey, I have an idea, but I'm afraid people will deem me a complete lunatic."

"*Intrigued*," she said, frowning.

"It occurred to me I haven't properly explored my time-travel ability yet, and I thought maybe if I could go back, I can say no to Pouki's suggestion about a magical birth."

Baby A's jaw dropped. "No!"

"Why?"

"*Don't* try something like that in your state. Let the situation be. You're about to pop, are emotional, and we need you *here*. If you disappear, what will we do without you?"

It was Arriette's turn to fold her arms. "You were fine before me and you'll be fine after me. Those were *your* words."

"Twisted words. Please, Arriette, listen to me. Don't do anything stupid. You had plenty of practice returning Ira Wilda to the battlefield. You said it went perfectly."

"It did." She nodded... unconvincingly.

"You need to work on your agreeable face," she grunted, then stormed away.

Arriette suddenly felt useless and moody. Everyone else had an important part to play in fixing the chaos. She only seemed good at creating it. Reiko was on smog duty, and the vampyrs were out in search of allies and chemicals. Pouki and Paulei were safe in the lair, but Arriette was simply lingering like that disgusting smell, waiting to hear anything further from the Four Saviours. Either that or to go into early labour.

In previous weeks, she retreated to the stable to find

comfort in Ira Wilda's company whenever she felt this way—unspoken secrets between them through a steady, reassuring silence always calmed her. Ira had never hurt her, and in the short time they shared before she returned him to help her past self, he'd even saved her life and guided her home along the river bank once.

Unicorns were known for their strength in water and their sense of direction. Now, Ira only provided comfort through fond memories. He symbolised what the Recruit stood for and his wonderful presence in their time had healed her soul—helped her to find some peace... for a while.

She wished she could be with him right now.

Instead, she decided to task Jet with an invisible trip to the stable to ensure the other animals were unharmed, well-fed, and coping. Jet's power to turn not only his physical form invisible but also his scent and his voice—effectively rendering him an untraceable ghost—would finally have a use after all. His unique but unpredictable gift baffled most of her team. Even Jet, as he once admitted.

Mostly, he spent his time in the infirmary trying to figure out what he was. Afraid of pretty much everything (including his strengths, never mind his weaknesses), Jet often expressed concerns he may be the only one of his kind. If that were the case, what use would he be, and how did he come to exist? Where did invisibility originate? Where was he destined to end up?

Arriette told him a heart of gold was difficult to find on Haeylo, particularly during their war against evil and Falkon Lou's battle for Pandora's box; Jet had impressed her.

Zïnnyi had a plan for him. She was sure.

She approached and rapped on his bedroom door.

Arriette heard a faint 'come in' called from one of the other rooms in his quarters. She pushed it open. The bedroom was like most other Recruit spaces—plainly decorated but welcoming. Nothing had been properly furnished yet, and the colours were all boring. In her orange dress, she was the brightest thing in the room.

"I'll be right out," he said from the en-suite bathroom, then appeared a moment later wearing brown trousers and a white shirt. His black spiky hair was still dripping from his shower and water dribbled down his neck, soaking the collar of his shirt.

Arriette pitched him a towel from the bed.

He turned his head upside down to catch the drips. "Thanks. I'm sorry that I'm hiding in here."

"It's fine, but I now need a favour you won't like."

He had reason to be worried. If those beastly women caught him, they'd devour him—shred his skin and snap his bones like twigs. Arriette feared for his life, particularly because of a temperature fault he'd previously experienced with his power. If he got too hot or too cold, his power flickered, switching his magical light on and off. She'd seen it herself, escaping the werewolves' imprisonment.

"They don't appear interested in anything with over two legs. But the horses haven't eaten."

"What do you need from me?"

"You need to check on them."

Jet laughed out loud, assuming this was a practical joke or part of her human humour, which he'd never fully understood. He straightened and stammered when he realised she was serious.

"It's usually my job," she said, "but I'm part human

and pregnant and still slow despite the camouflage. You can turn invisible and they won't detect you. You're the only one I can ask."

"It's cold outside, right?"

"It's... pleasant," she said. "I went into the garden before the women arrived."

"Is it safe?"

"The vampyrs did alright and animals have been running by their feet all day—deer from the forest, and I think I saw a hare bolt through. They never bothered. But us, well, that's another matter. Your power makes you immune, Jet. I'd have asked you to warn the villages too but the vampyrs are faster."

"I can try, but on my terms."

Arriette was pleased they would be soon drinking fresh water and getting something to eat. At least she'd save *some* lives today, even if they were not human or supernatural.

"I want to go through the loading bay at the back. It's quieter there so there's less chance they'll see me. Temperature affects my powers, but anxiety never helps. Can you have supplies waiting for me so I can make a quick dash?"

Arriette nodded. "Make sure they don't spot you, Jet. They'll ram the loading bay doors. There are a few weapons already outside from my last ride with Ira Wilda, in the shed attached to the stable." She opened the door to leave. "I understand. I'm asking a lot."

"It's my job, right?" He smiled, if a little awkwardly, then startled at a ruckus in the corridor when flashes of blonde and red zoomed by.

The vampyrs were back.

Arriette kissed the jagged s-shaped Eiwaz rune

beneath Jet's eye and winked, causing his power to flicker through embarrassment.

"I can always count on you."

NINE

Fed up with being in lockdown with no solid solutions to their problems, Arriette met Jet Carter at the loading bay and handed him the supplies as they'd agreed. The bay was cold and vast—empty except for a few bundles of hay, some barrels, and firewood. Her footsteps echoed as she carried bottles of fresh water and wraps of bread, cheese, and crackers.

"This should keep *you* going if you get stuck."

"Will I be out there a while?"

Arriette swallowed hard. "Better to prepare for the worst-case scenario, isn't it? If you feel it's all clear, head back when you're finished but stay invisible until someone can lift the lock. I'll ask Sebastian to watch for your return. His quarters overlook the paddock."

Jet nodded but said nothing else. He reached out and grasped her hand briefly, then shimmered into nothingness, taking everything he now carried with him. The doors opened and closed again, and Arriette replaced the bolt and exhaled.

Early evening was upon them. With a growling stomach, she scurried back through HQ to the lobby and almost ran head-first into Baby A heading in the opposite direction. Her soft peach cheeks were vibrant and sweat dripped from her forehead.

"Slow down. What's happened?"

"She escaped my sight. I've gone and caused more trouble. This is *all* my fault!"

Arriette scowled, unsure what Baby A was insinuating by 'more trouble'. None of what they'd experienced so far was anyone's fault, except perhaps her unborn baby's. Aware followers might overhear their conversation, she shoved Baby A through the library door and inhaled the musty, comforting scent of old hardback books.

"Tell me, what's going on?"

"I lost Angelica!"

Butterflies scattered in the pit of Arriette's stomach. An innocent but powerful child, lost and alone. One in the centre of the worst and most dangerous supernatural accident the Recruit had seen in over 100 years, too. Arriette had to remind herself just how outstanding Angelica's powers were. Despite her age, the kid could take care of herself. They had known one another over a year now after Arriette, Jet, Tobias and Susan rescued her from Falkon's werewolf experimentations. Like Susan, she could astro-project—split her spiritual and physical self in two as she slept.

"Which version did you lose?"

"Does it matter?" she balled into her sweaty fists.

"Of course it does," she replied and passed her friend a tissue to blow her nose. "Maybe she's gone through the wormhole?"

Angelic Baby A was beautiful and maintained her heavenly glow, no matter her mental or emotional state. Arriette was jealous. When she cried, her eyes puffed red, her face bloated, and she looked around 20 years older.

"The physical version," she mumbled eventually through the tissue. "She's here somewhere. I checked the list of names—everyone that leaves is signing Pouki's parchment, so we can document who may still be here and who we can use if needed."

Arriette angrily asked, "Wait, is *he* still here?"

She shrugged.

"Why were *you* responsible for her? I thought Susan... *oh*."

She shook her head, forgetting the vampyr had only recently returned from her supply run with Dion.

"Where was she last seen?"

"She went to the bathroom."

"Have you checked them?"

"Duh! Susan *loves* that kid; she's going to suck the life out of me."

"No, she won't." Arriette rolled her eyes and led Baby A to a rickety wooden chair. "They have been supporting each other using their astro-projection; she hasn't exactly *adopted* her."

At least not officially, Arriette thought.

Baby A chewed her nails. "I'm dead."

"Her irrational response to stuff is just a vampyr thing. Susan will not hurt you. I won't let her."

It wasn't the first time Baby A had raised Susan's lack of empathy, and it wouldn't be the last.

"If it's a vampyr thing, explain Dion," said Baby A.

"Dion's soul is human."

Baby A leaned forward on her elbows and sobbed into her palms.

"She can't have left the building if it's locked down, right? I checked the windows myself." Arriette hummed. "Where else might she go?"

"I'm *so* worried. What if—"

"Oh, Zinnyi, don't say it." *And tempt fate,* Arriette

thought as she hushed her friend. "She's not with Jet because he's at the stable. Those two are like best buddies since the werewolves. And the vampyrs went to the lab with Reiko. The telepaths are in the lair, or are *supposed* to be! So that leaves maybe Tabitha, Joy, Tobias, or Sebastian."

"Tobias is in the lobby finishing the clean-up with Sebastian. I just came from there," she said.

"Alright. Stay here and compose yourself. I'll find her and bring her to the library. It's probably the safest place for her, anyway."

"I can't sit here and do nothing!"

She handed Baby A a tissue. "You're no use to anyone like this."

She hurried to the foyer where Tobias and Sebastian were sweeping with their backs to the glass doors—on purpose, she guessed, because the sight wasn't pretty. They re-directed her, sending her off along another corridor to the canteen, where Tabitha and Joy were supposed to be reading the grimoire notes she'd accumulated so far.

Arriette wasted no time calling their names and barged in through the swinging doors with force. Instead, she found them counting and documenting medical supplies, surrounded by bandages, creams, safety pins, and other packaged, sterile items.

"Have either of you seen Angelica?" she panted, out of breath.

"Not for a few hours," Tabitha replied. Her tongue poked out the side of her mouth as she attempted to squish packets in an over-flowing white box with a green cross painted on the front. "Why, what's wrong?"

"She's missing. Baby A's in the library; she's scared

the kid got lost outside... or worse."

"I'll help you look," Joy said, shoving the remaining items aside. She stacked the loose grimoire papers and placed the box atop them so a draught couldn't blow them away.

"Tabitha will keep Baby A company."

They split up and methodically searched HQ from the reception desk in the foyer, the bathrooms, every bedroom, on-suite facilities, offices, conference rooms, storage cupboards, and the loading bay. As a last resort, they stopped by the laboratory on their way to the library, hoping Susan, Dion, or Reiko had been in contact. There was no sign of her anywhere.

Susan's eyes flashed and her fangs protruded when she found out Angelica was nowhere around, but she didn't get up to challenge who'd been caring for her.

"We should tell Baby A what's going on," said Joy, tucking her dark curls behind her ear as she bent to tie a loose shoelace.

"No, she already lost one child and I will not let her be driven insane after losing this one. Did you check any closets?"

Joy imagined the building as a basic floor plan— they'd all seen and offered their thoughts on HQ's design, so most knew the map off by heart. There were many closets and even an attic on the top floor for storage. She assumed the upstairs was empty and locked, but for a frightened little girl, could it make a peaceful hideout?

She voiced the concern to Arriette, who immediately rummaged in her pocket for the skeleton key to unlock the stairwell.

"I will assist," Susan said, appearing suddenly behind them and startling them both.

"No, we need you here. Joy, if you find her, don't come looking for me. Just take her to Baby A; she's worried sick. I'll search upstairs."

Arriette shoved the key in the lock after several clumsy, anxious attempts to open it in a hurry, only to find it was already unlocked. Though a massive security risk, somehow this comforted her—it gave her a likely location for a frightened child. She bounded up the steps, taking them (awkwardly) two at a time, suddenly grateful for her supernatural pregnancy and the boost it allowed her. Though she tired quickly, adrenaline kicked in; she barrelled through the door at the top, sending a wave of energy through her—it raised her heavy eyelids and forced both throbbing legs to keep moving.

Other than the door to the stairs, every other door on the second floor was open all the time. There wasn't anything to hide or protect up there anyway because the offices (and, of course, the magically protected vault containing Pandora's box) were on the lower levels.

"Angelica! Are you there?"

"Arriette?"

She panned at the sound of Tobias's deep voice and sprinted to the end of the corridor, following as he called to her. She rounded the corner. A door at the end was ajar. Light spread across the dull corridor, where Tobias sat cradling a terrified red-headed child.

"Oh, thank Zinnyi!"

She hunched over, resting her forearms on her knees, and sucked in oxygen.

"A follower in the lobby said they heard a child crying, so I came to check it out," Tobias told her, placing his own skeleton key on the floor beside them. Only the eleven individuals assigned to leadership during the ceremony last year had them, plus Arriette's spare.

Arriette exhaled a sigh of relief and reached out to take Angelica's hand.

"I've been looking everywhere for you. Baby A is worried. How did you get up here?"

Angelica pulled Arriette's spare key from her pocket and offered it to Tobias, blushing.

"Where did you get that?"

"The library," she uttered.

Arriette kept it hidden in a hollowed-out hardback book within her desk drawer. After the hours of basic schooling she'd received there, it made sense the child would know *exactly* where to find the key to her freedom.

"It's alright if you're afraid. We are too. Come on," he said, rolling his eyes at Arriette. "Let's get you back downstairs."

Tobias walked Angelica safely to Baby A's side in the library, giving Arriette time to knock on Sebastian Sky's bedroom door as they passed.

She needed his sorcery to write spells and apply his magic to the building's structure, because despite Tobias' best efforts, he was too distracted to keep the glass in the lobby from cracking again, and the dreamers needed to evacuate with everyone else. Also, the Four Saviours were busy trying to come up with any other solution to their predicament.

First, she'd request a protection spell to free people from having to wear those hideous gas masks, something written in Haeyloian for strength and resilience. Arriette had long since taken hers off, confident that Reiko's tests were accurate, but others were not so trusting.

"It's Arriette. Sebastian, are you there?"

Footsteps neared the door, and it swung inwards. He

ushered her in, glanced down the hall both ways, and locked it behind them.

"You're going to need a pen and paper," she said.

Sky nodded, understanding her request. "Is Angelica safe?"

"She was hiding. Can we blame her? I'm here because I need you to watch for Jet through your window, and I also need a favour."

His face dropped when she explained the spells she wanted to perform. To her surprise, Sebastian Sky had only written three of his own spells since re-joining the Recruit officially under Arriette's rule. An experienced, although young, sorcerer like Sebastian should have been practising techniques and rhymes daily, but after the war and re-building those magical wards, his skills were needed elsewhere.

"What I can offer you is limited. I'll try, but I'm out of practice."

"You've done it once before. You protected the lair! I believe in you."

Sebastian and Arriette had a special bond; Harriet Foley introduced her to him first. He was the supe to greet her, made her feel welcome and appreciated, and taught her the meaning of Indalo. Sebastian fought fairly in the battle for Pandora's box. He deserved his place at HQ, experienced or not.

Arriette didn't want to make a big deal of his lack of practice as it was partially her fault. Any additional help he could offer was better than none.

"All I ask is that you do your best." She smiled. "The Four Saviours are still here, so you can always ask them for help. They're basically doing the same thing, anyway." Arriette sighed. "Jet is at the stable. Please monitor him from your window if and whenever he shows himself so you can let him back in through the loading bay. You have the best view of the paddock."

Sebastian smirked. "Of course, Arriette. I saw Jet briefly, but nobody else seemed to. He's OK. I've been able to study the mutants, trying to monitor their behaviour. I made notes in the foyer and since I returned to my room."

That was more like the supe she knew, eager and excitable. His auburn hair glowed before the evening sunlight from the window, and his interest in the mutant women outside could easily be read in his eyes. His body was suddenly straighter as he held his head with pride.

Arriette brightened too when she learned he had research that could help them defeat this new threat. His notebooks were filled with observations, presumptions, and plenty more to help monitor the unusual beings. Arriette flicked one open curiously, the cover soft beneath her fingers as she did so, and the ink smudging from her oily skin.

She wondered if Sebastian might be a better candidate for the grimoire job.

"You have some interesting things in here, sketches and diagrams. How long has this taken?"

"Well," he said, scratching his prickly chin. "Since I first laid eyes on them. I'm sorry I have ventured out little except to help Tobias sweep, but I noticed the way they move is usually in sequence so I noted my findings. They stand in rows, and they move forward as a cavalry, planned and organised. It's like they're being *controlled*." He mimicked the jerky movements of a robot. "I presume they communicate via body language or telepathically, as we've never overheard them speak or yell orders. There are no leaders."

"Controlled? Pouki and Paulei can read the women in some sense, so perhaps their orders and discussions *are* telepathic? He allowed me to listen for a few seconds. It's painful and disturbing, but there were no words, only visions and sounds. The Four Saviours tell me the Enzoian women never speak much anyway, partly down to religion."

He hugged his shoulders, unsettled at the idea of the mutants plotting against the Recruit, searching for ways to drink their blood like a new species of vampyr.

"Are we any closer to resolving this and changing these poor souls back?"

"Assume, for now, this will end in tears."

Her negativity shocked him. "Why give up *now*?"

"I'm not," Arriette protested confidently. "I'm simply saying we should predict the worst. If we have too much hope and things go wrong, it'll hit us harder than ever."

"That's *on* the record?" he said, watching as the bodies continued to drag themselves across the sprawling lawns. "What about off the record, like on a scale of one to ten? Can we fix this?"

She hummed. Ten being positive and zero being no chance on Haeylo. She gave five, partly to annoy Sebastian for never providing a straight answer to any of *her* questions, and partly because she honestly did not know.

"We'll make it through," he said, sighing.

She patted his shoulder. "Reiko is clearing the air right now. Our vampyr friends have returned with further supplies, so he's going to use them to remove the rest of the poisonous smog that's killing Enzo's plant life," Arriette assured him. "We're doing all we can, and so far it's working, at least in part."

"Do you have an antidote for the women?"

She shrugged. "Not yet. They're not dead, though. At least, I hope not. Can you tell me more about their biology? I can pass it to Reiko and the others."

"If one moves, they all move. The mind is better explained by Pouki and Paulei, but they crave the basics. Their instincts are to stay alive, even if this means eating one another, which I've witnessed."

"Me too," she groaned, feeling queasy.

"I don't expect your baby did this either, Arriette."

Her eyes brightened. "You don't?"

"No. Tobias filled me in. These women are now an army, and an army has to have a general. None of these are. *This* general has a dark motive. A few now lack limbs, but they can still hold their weight. Given their mental state, they don't seem to realise their potential as fighters. Their feet are webbed now, as are their fingers—so swimming underwater might be a new skill. If we flee to the ocean, I think they'll follow. That's intentional. I saw one fall in the pond earlier and she paddled out in the same direction the others were moving. Their movements seem random, but they're marching together when you watch them for more than a few seconds."

"Perhaps, then, Tobias is right when he says this was an everlast's rulecast inflicting their revenge."

"It's someone high up the HPS that's behind this plot. Can you also see that their skin isn't fully scaled? But I *have* noticed it shines and glistens in the sunlight, almost reflective, where it's not torn. If we can capture one, experimentation may be the only way—"

"These were women," Arriette interrupted. "Human women—why would we need to experiment? Their biology beneath the surface will be like ours. Tests sound like something *Falkon* would do."

"If their exterior has changed, why not their interior?" he argued. "This isn't just a quick, sad excuse for a spell. It's *evolution*."

TEN

Arriette pondered Sebastian's observations and stroked the cover of a notebook he'd given her as she folded into Tobias's arms. The glass held, but there were no fewer mutants outside than there had been after the evacuation, only spread around the grounds, and they had no obvious solution to their dilemma.

"How are you holding up?" he asked her.

"My feelings are irrelevant. Just look at our friends."

She squeezed his hand, seeing a collection of Recruit followers gathering around them in the foyer, pointing at the women outside. She sighed and pushed through their bodies where she could now see the landscape clearing of the grey smog—Reiko's potions had a small, but positive effect, at least.

"It's a start," Tobias said. "The vampyrs warned the authorities in the neighbouring villages, and we're doing all we can."

"Are *they* evacuating?"

"Oh, yes. Susan was... *adamant*."

"I don't think Susan's vampyric glaring and hissing is going to be enough. But the Four Saviours might bind our daughter's powers still. It'll end this nightmare."

Tobias bit his upper lip and scowled. "I will never agree to binding her powers, Arriette."

"I don't like the idea any more than you do!"

"Alright. Let's speak to them."

He walked with her through the building until they could hear themselves think again. Arriette followed close behind through a clear path, pleased when the corridor fell quiet and the door to the Four Saviours' sacred space appeared. They wasted no time knocking and let themselves in to find the women standing around a long table that consumed most of the room. Candles flickered, incense burned, and a soft cloth and cushions draped over the makeshift bed. Dotted around the room, rocks and crystals sat in various colours, all sparkling in the candlelight, most with a polished surface.

In the year since the battle for Pandora's box, Arriette had studied some precious stones for their use in wiccan remedies, and she'd done so alongside Susan. There was no official 'Introduction to Wicca' class either of them could take, but enough wiccan followers lived in the lair and now worked within HQ to teach them both which stones held the highest value to the craft and what they symbolised. She'd also witnessed the Four Saviours using different kinds of agate, then looked them up in the library in the days following to quench her thirst for supernatural theory.

Saph had introduced aquamarine to travellers' canteens to cleanse their water of any toxins or poisons, and Arriette had a large one plopped in the bottom of hers. Ira used to sniff her beverages and tell her. Unicorns were skilled in and around water. Now if she shook her canteen hard enough, it rattled. Then Jade had suggested (after their losses during the battle) that Recruit soldiers should adorn their armour with hematite or carnelian; hematite to strengthen it, and carnelian for courage and protection of their breastplates and helmets—or anywhere their enemies would likely strike them. Most rejected the idea; sparkly and fashionable armour would not strike fear into their enemies, nor would it keep them camouflaged on a bright day. But Arriette was pleased to see some slipped them into pockets or on a piece of leather lace around their necks.

Dianne had always worn a moonstone on a pendant around her neck anyway to enhance her psychic abilities, specifically if she used a crystal ball or anything to predict a scenario's outcome. Arriette spotted two in her eyeline just in that room. She hadn't noticed until Casper's death that Jade wore a green stone sharing the same name on a beaded-style bracelet every single day, and had the stone present even more so since Arriette fell pregnant.

She'd asked Tabitha about the connection, and she explained that in proximity to a woman in labour, jade supposedly eased birth. A less painful delivery sounded good, but Arriette's interest in the stone peaked when Jade tried to hide the symbolism of an amulet she'd shoved down her blouse. Only a few days after Arriette became the Recruit's new leader, too.

"It's nothing," she'd said and waved Arriette away with a loose wrist. "Decorative."

Lies.

"It's an unusual shape," she'd commented. "Is it a snake?"

Jade replied, "A pretty swirl."

LIES!

So Arriette retreated to the library and discovered that jade represented knowledge and education. As she worked as a Recruit trainer, it made sense, but she also wore anklets with dangling charms and other pendants of greenstone in that specific stylised shape. Arriette dug deeper; she learnt it wasn't a snake but a bird, and it had links to Manaia.

Our forest is named Manaia after a white bird, Arriette remembered. *Said to be the first creature Zïnnyi created.*

Then she realised.

Andrew Kaines had been the first soul to walk this planet; technically, Zïnnyi's first creation. Had Casper initially shape-shifted all those years ago into Manaia? Jade was wearing the amulet in his memory, and didn't want to hurt Arriette's feelings.

Lies. But acceptable ones.

There wasn't much jade in the room other than on the Saviour herself, but visible near Saph's workspace was a lapis lazuli, symbolic of childbirth and fertility. Given Arriette's condition, it did not come as a surprise.

At this point, her hands shook.

Pouki's spell was supposed to ensure a supernatural birth; how would binding their unborn baby's powers in the womb affect Arriette's appearance and ability to do her job? She still wasn't one hundred percent confident with the Haeyloian language, though she understood enough for trading and plenty to wind up her mother (who had no time for 'such nonsense'). Haeyloian words were immensely powerful, and high-ranking everlasts tapped into them easily, as did their rulecast advisors. So could the Four Saviours manipulate it in the same way?

"Any news?" Arriette asked.

"No, but we have another suggestion," Jade said. "You'd need to get on this bed."

"The bed you've placed not-so-slyly in the centre of all these fertility symbols and stones?" She raised her brow.

Jade fiddled with her bracelet. "Busted."

The bed looked a lot like the table in the infirmary's morgue where she and Tobias had fought, only adorned with soft, beautiful fabric. She swallowed hard as she remembered trapping Tobias against a door with one of those solid slabs.

"Will whatever you've come up with take long?"

"Patience," Dianne said.

"No time. There are hundreds of women out there lusting for our blood. They're going to find a way in here, then we're all dead."

Saph remarked, patting the bed, "We are in no imminent danger behind these walls."

"And there are creatures already in this building lusting for blood, yet you do not fear *them*," Jade added quickly. "You're more than capable of dealing with this crisis; all you need to do is trust us."

"Susan is my friend," Arriette uttered, trying to breathe through her anxiety as she approached the bed, "which is *not* the same thing."

"This will be easier if you relax. We wouldn't do anything to put you or the baby at risk."

"That's what Pouki said," she muttered, laying back. "What are you going to do to me?"

Ignoring her question, Di spoke in hushed tones to her sisters, who scurried to grab various other items from the room, including incense sticks, a handful of the stones she'd already identified and some fine-smelling oils.

"Can I stay with her?" Tobias asked.

Di nodded. "Are you ready, Arriette?"

"Ready for *what*?" Arriette looked at Tobias. "I suppose I'm as ready as I'll ever be."

In silent contemplation, Tobias blinked slowly, then

nodded. They were both running out of time and ideas, and anything the Four Saviours could do to improve the women by restricting her unborn baby's out-of-control powers had to be worth a try.

"Do whatever it is now before I change my mind."

The Four Saviours flicked a sweet-smelling oil across Arriette's bed and lit an incense stick, which instantly calmed her and lifted Arriette's spirits. They boxed her in with a shield knot, similar to their formation for the projection chant. Arriette recognised the symbolism as Jade murmured in Haeyloian. Each woman joined as the sentence began again; their voices increased in volume, becoming more demanding and assertive.

"Reverenda ze de'va. Tran, Aeir, Flam ze Walne sïen emosia. Prim'ae're litte. Reverenda ze de'va."

Something kicked inside Arriette—her stomach tightened. Then, it inflated. She gasped, craning her neck to examine her sudden human pregnancy, with a wriggling baby inside of her, uncomfortable and probably distressed by the Four Saviours' magic.

Tobias placed his palms on her exposed skin, watching as rose-coloured uneven lines formed around her bellybutton. "This... is... incredible."

Arriette groaned and rolled her eyes. *He* didn't have to bear these scars. "Stretch marks... *really*?"

"They will heal," Saph grumbled, then continued.

He stepped back in horror when an imprint of the baby's foot met his fingers.

Jade broke from the formation. "Arriette, you're safe to sit now if it's more comfortable."

"Whoa!" Tobias gasped.

Ruby aided her upright, then continued the chant's repetitive words in a bare whisper.

"Reverenda ze de'va. Tran, Aeir, Flam ze Walne sïen emosia. Prim'ae're litte. Reverenda ze de'va."

The blood coursing through Arriette's veins tingled. She itched and twitched as Ruby's whispers penetrated and warmed her. Her cheeks flushed and her palms became slick with sweat.

"It's so hot in here, and my muscles are *contracting*."

She suddenly cried out in agony and hunched over. Cramping consumed her lower half, and corresponding lightning bolts of pain shot in short, electric bursts down her spine and thighs. None of her battle injuries, nor the claws of the dragon almost blinding her, shared this level.

"What have you done?" Tobias asked Jade. "She's in agony!"

She leaned in to take Arriette's temperature with the back of her hand. Then she continued, but didn't answer Tobias's question. Whatever they were doing, he knew it was reversing Arriette's supernatural pregnancy, perhaps even tempting labour.

"Reverenda ze de'va. Tran, Aeir, Flam ze Walne sïen emosia. Prim'ae're litte. Reverenda ze de'va."

Arriette's stomach continued to grow. Her frame became heavier, clumsy, and her breathing turned to rapid panting. After missing so much of the natural pregnancy, the way the experience *would* have changed her body stunned them. Arriette held such gratitude, witnessing it for mere seconds before she lurched forward, unable to control her lips from releasing a primal scream.

Tobias grabbed Ruby's arm. "Something's wrong!"

From the waist down, Arriette turned suddenly and instantly numb. "You said this was safe!"

"It is," Ruby assured her, gently nudging Tobias aside. She took hold of Arriette's clammy fingers. "This is what we expected."

The chanting continued. Arriette thought it echoed around the room, bouncing off the walls until she lost track and with it, her balance.

"I'm dizzy," she groaned.

Her skin was hot. On fire.

It has to be.

But deep in her heart, Arriette already knew this would not kill her. It was fixing her, reversing Pouki's work and turning her supernatural pregnancy into a human experience. Bones and organs were shifting, senses heightened. Emotions rising. Except, instead of it happening over months, it was happening in minutes.

"Are you using... black magic?" Tobias asked, but Arriette barely heard him over her shallow breaths.

Her mouth moved along with the chant, too, as if possessed by the language.

"Arriette? What are you doing?"

She turned on her side and curled into a ball as far as her body would allow, then sobbed through the words, trying to encourage Tobias to join in.

"Reverenda ze de'va. Tran, Aeir, Flam ze Walne s'ien emosia. Prim'ae're litte. Reverenda ze de'va."

The Four Saviours slowed their ritual and stepped back, releasing the knot. Arriette's lingering upper body pain subsided and the throbbing in her skull stopped. Feeling returned to her legs in a wave.

Tobias shoved between Jade and Ruby.

"What the *hell* was that?"

"I think it worked," Di told the others. "This is the reality of her pregnancy, Tobias. The way she looks and the pain she feels is, in a small way, like labour. We attempted to reverse whatever dream created the beasts but as you predicted, there wasn't one. It reversed the mask Pouki gave you instead."

Tobias shook his head. "Dreams can only be reversed by a dreamer, anyway."

"Unless you have *our* knowledge," Ruby sniped. "Thankfully, your baby is not the cause. There would have been more evidence."

"Her powers are bound now?" Tobias asked.

Saph advised, "No! Arriette did not permit it. Pouki's spell *did* cause some minor issues, but your child certainly did not create the mutations out there. Whatever happened targeted HQ. *An external attack.* Your child expanded its reach only to warn Arriette, the way an angel receives messages from Zïnnyi; you wouldn't have heard that woman screaming, Arriette, if not for your baby. The hormone was being under-produced, but your daughter is still in control."

"How do you know for sure?"

"Magic leaves a trace. There was nothing to follow."

Arriette coughed and groaned and shuffled onto her back. She could no longer see her toes, as her stomach hung in the way. All she wanted was to shower the sweat from her skin and curl up in bed. She couldn't care less what the ongoing argument by her side was about, or be bothered to take part in it.

She just wanted to *breathe*.

"What is the translation of the spell you used?" Tobias asked.

Jade answered, "We asked our creator to reverse the harmful spirit within Arriette's body—your unborn child's supernatural inheritance *if* it was causing problems. We addressed the elements we represent and asked for their protection and their help to trace the magical pathways to any causes of this disaster. They fuel us. As there were none, it simply reversed Pouki's mask. Arriette is now as she should, naturally, be."

Di added, "A test, and she passed."

"Haeyloian is a *powerful*, flexible language," Ruby continued, "so our intent and Arriette's subconscious did the rest. Would you like us to put you back, Arriette? Now we know the baby isn't at fault and there's nothing else sinister going on."

Arriette reached out to touch Tobias's arm, causing him to jump and lean over her.

She coaxed him closer to whisper in his ear, "She's screaming again." Arriette threw her arm towards the window and started to cry.

"Nobody's screaming," he said, urging Ruby with a 'get on with it' gesture to re-apply Arriette's supernatural pregnancy.

Saph strode to the window and peered through the curtains to check. She ragged them closed and, as if in fear, took several steps cautiously back into the room.

"I don't *believe* it."

ELEVEN

With Tobias's aid, Arriette struggled down the corridor to the reception desk. Her back ached and her swollen feet were sore.

It was quiet. *Too* quiet.

The air outside was clearing beautifully thanks to Reiko's efforts. A strange and eerie mist was drifting from the laboratory's side of HQ, which Arriette assumed was a freshly brewed potion using the vampyr's collected supplies. It was a fine, reassuring sight.

Tobias helped Arriette to the glass doors, and she placed both palms against it, glaring out at the crouching women. Some leant against trees and walls, others were sprawled on their backs, panting. Blood and bile soaked the surrounding grassland, splattering flowers and dripping like red ink into the pond beside, staining the once turquoise water maroon.

"The glass held," Tobias sighed. "Thank Zïnnyi."

"This was an *epidemic*," Arriette said to herself.

Though most of the women were decayed beyond repair or already dead, some were still alive and writhing. Their lacerations, broken bones, and even missing limbs healed at an accelerated rate. The survivors vomited up whatever had been in their systems, and one woman was hunched in agony, screaming through her transformation —the scream Arriette was drawn to.

Arriette flinched at that sound. "Our daughter tried to warn me about this. The screaming. Was she channelling Zïnnyi?"

Tobias nodded. "Whatever *this* is—we were too late, anyway. You weren't meant to stop this one."

"Couldn't if we tried," she admitted sadly.

Lingering in the lobby were several of the Recruit members drawn in by the cries outside against the sullen silence. Joy came to stand beside Arriette—the everlast reached out to take her leader's hand. She glared at Arriette's visible pregnancy with wide, curious eyes, and motioned to gain Tabitha's attention. Neither commented.

"Why only the women, then?" Arriette voiced again.

Tabitha arrived beside them. "Should we open the doors?"

Arriette shrugged and turned steadily to locate the Four Saviours standing in the corridor. "The elemental spell you performed fixed their bodies *and* mine... but how?"

Saph inhaled deeply before she admitted that it baffled them, too. "They need working organs and blood flow for our spell to repair their bodies, and some of them looked like the dead walking, Arriette. I'm... not sure this had anything to do with us."

"Coincidence?"

"Suspicious, but I guess so? We can interview the surviving women once their transformation has finished. Perhaps they can tell us more."

"How, if they don't speak?" Tabitha interjected.

"Write." Arriette scowled. "One spoke a long time ago in Enzo, remember, so if we can find her, then maybe she can tell us?"

Amid the crowd, she saw Susan's shining blonde hair.

Her friends were drawn to the centre of this recent activity. Gliding would have been an understatement. As the vampyr's movement through the mass of heads was so delicate and perfected, Arriette imagined her more of an angel than a blood-sucker.

"One of those women spoke to us, Arry," she confirmed, paying no mind to her new shape. "Riddles aren't all she might be capable of. We should find her."

Her baby jammed a little heel into her left rib. "Beaten from the inside and out," she uttered.

Arriette groaned and rubbed the spot. Her mind was still fitting pieces of information together and attempting to log additional facts and suggestions amongst everything else she'd been through.

Susan, although dead and dangerous, had been Arriette's best friend once upon a time; she trusted her judgement even in death. She still wished one of her own inherited powers was to retain knowledge like Tabitha, though. Then she wouldn't be so dazed and confused all the time, or have to dash to the library to research something. But Arriette hadn't yet registered their horror at the sight of her suddenly human body, and before she could protest Susan's suggestion, it hit them all abruptly.

Joy took her fragile exterior by the shoulders and led Arriette to the nearest seat. She jumped, bumping passers-by and grabbing their attention when the baby kicked her again, and chuckled at how nervous the events of the day had made everybody.

"A human birth?" Joy mumbled, "and in less than... two weeks? I'll tell Angelica and Baby A we've made some progress," she said, handing Arriette's care over to Tabitha Hope.

"The wiccan who predicted our baby would be born

human was on the right track," Tobias said.

Arriette grunted, "Pouki will be *pissed.*"

"I can't trust those are the same women out there," said Tabitha, pulling them both back on topic. "Don't open the doors yet in case it's still not safe."

"But they can't hurt us now and you might be able to help with their wounds," Arriette said.

"The Enzoian women were always low on the Haeyloian Power Scale, on par with humans. Are we to assume they are no longer that?"

Tobias agreed with Arriette. "Sebastian has evidence they're different. Those wounds are healing themselves. We have *never* seen that before, even with angelic blood."

Arriette massaged her temples. "As painful and nauseating as the mutants' thoughts were, they existed only in visions rather than conversations—there's more to separating the women from the men. Haven't any of you stopped to consider why the men only visit to reproduce? If you truly love somebody, you spend all the time you can with them, right?" She glanced up at Tobias, still proudly by her side. "Why not for the Enzoian monks?"

Tobias shrugged. "Different cultures have their ways, and we must accept them. Just because *we* live together doesn't mean they should."

"Tobias is right," said Tabitha.

"Did the telepaths get anything about their past lives before the epidemic?" Tobias asked.

"None. It was as if they didn't exist before today. Either they have no memories, or something is blocking them—preventing them from showing us."

Ruby slid between two followers to weigh in. "Whilst we can give these women a temporary sanctuary tonight to ask them some questions—via the rear entrance, for safety

—somebody should go to the temple. Can we find out from the men what happened today?"

Tabitha scratched her chin. "What do you four guess is going on?"

"Until we have more evidence and have spoken to these women tomorrow, we wouldn't risk a guess. I am confident the ritual we performed for Arriette was not the trigger, though."

Tabitha frowned. "What ritual?"

"Tell you later," Tobias mumbled. "And you're not going, Arriette, before you get any ideas."

Disappointment overwhelmed her. Now her opinions and orders were overruled because of her physical state, which was exactly what she wanted to prevent with Pouki's spell. Expressing her disapproval only triggered an unwanted argument, so she quickly backtracked and hoped she could at least help the people remaining at HQ— perhaps play a valuable part in interrogating someone.

"We should gather everyone together first," said Tobias. "We're scattered, and all need to agree before anyone ventures outside. It's too dangerous. I'll call Paulei and Pouki back from the lair, and Sebastian should try to signal to Jet that he should return if he hasn't already."

Arriette agreed. "The Enzoians will want rid of us after this."

"They can't force the Recruit to move and if we can prove we had nothing to do with this, at least not directly, they may *want* us to stay. The Recruit is powerful now and known across Haeylo from Mousique to Drakonta, to the city and beyond. You're the keeper of Pandora's box and a royal. Nobody will want to anger you," he said. "You've proven you can take care of this planet, and Casper believed in you. They will too."

"They are no safer having us on their doorstep."

"Our daughter didn't cause what happened," he reminded her, stern-faced. "They have already tried to break through the glass doors to bite our flesh and drink our blood. We're even."

"They were under the influence of something. We can't blame them for their actions," Tabitha reminded him.

Tobias hummed. "That's true. Epidemics wipe out communities. We've only been here a year, and that's not long enough to uncover everything about the locals, but Enzo *has* to have been targeted because the Recruit is based here. Before we arrived, it was a tiny coastal... nowhere."

"Or perhaps I'm the target? Or Pandora is? I'm supposed to share this body with a part of her soul and during this crisis and that painful ritual I just survived back there, she's still *nowhere* to be seen. But our enemies don't know that. They might assume we're keeping both Pandora and the box to ourselves."

Tabitha squeezed Arriette's shoulder. "What happened under the Drakontan mountain is a Recruit secret. It's unlikely word has spread so far. If it had, there would be supes flocking for pieces of that dragon."

"I guess only Zïnnyi knows," Arriette said. "Either way, this happened. We must find out why."

They made their way to an office, taking steady and deliberate steps so Arriette didn't trip over her own hidden feet. Each corridor looked the same, with brown and cream designs, few paintings or portraits and a wide, open layout. Once they were all settled in their residential suites, Arriette would encourage her followers to paint, decorate and express themselves. Their HQ should be a home, not just a place of business; somewhere they could all enjoy safety.

They walked the length of the main corridor connecting the foyer to the canteen and were hand-in-hand as they arrived to find there were still a few Recruit members yet to arrive. Susan had her feet on a desk at the back, whispering with the Four Saviours who talked her through the ritual they'd performed on Arriette. Joy Johnas was eavesdropping.

"Arriette," said Joy, "I found Baby A and Angelica. Sorry, I didn't make it back to the foyer this evening. I got sidetracked."

Arriette smiled, greeting Baby A and Angelica at the same time. "How are you both?"

"Hopeful," said Baby A, yawning, "and fairly confident. Angelica is still a bit scared, but she knows HQ is safe."

"Good. *I'm* nervous too. It's normal."

Tabitha laughed. "At least you're honest!"

Baby A told them that Reiko and Dion were still in the lab, and Jet and Sebastian were on their way—he had to open the loading door to let Jet inside before they started anything with the surviving women, and then Sebastian had to gather the rest of his notes. Paulei and Pouki were back from the lair and heading their way. They were taking a few moments to listen in on the women's minds, now they were relatively human again.

Strolling in late, Reiko and Dion took their seats at the front, pleased with themselves for fixing the air and hopefully restoring life to the plants, trees, and atmosphere. They bickered, and Arriette smiled at their success throughout all of this—it gave her a beacon of hope at the Recruit's dedication and intelligence. It also confirmed her suspicions that the two of them may have a thing for one another. They were two of her dearest and most loyal friends; she wanted them to be happy and Dion needed some stability.

"Is there any of your potion left for storage?"

Reiko beamed. He assured her he'd already filled some new beakers with the potion for future use. The lab had been locked, and the window had been re-secured.

Paulei joined the group fifteen minutes later with a notebook and pen. Arriette noticed he had some things jotted. He cast himself to the side politely and focused on his notes where his silver sideburns caught the dying light. After that, it didn't take long for everyone else to arrive and take their seats.

As Arriette was breathless and self-conscious, Tobias patted her knee and made the announcements on her behalf. Everyone that passed her had to double-take, then forced a compliment that the human side of pregnancy suited her.

"You're glowing!"

Lies!

Arriette could see it in their eyes. She looked like a boulder, and she felt like a beached whale.

Tobias began, "Whatever changed those women back wasn't an instant cure, and the land has only been partially patched up."

"They're healing themselves," Tabitha countered. "Something we've never seen before other than slowly with angelic blood. This is accelerated. If they self-heal, can the land if it was affected by the same disease?"

"They didn't mutate themselves, so we can't be sure what's going to happen when they're back to 'normal'. Until we leave HQ and investigate, we won't see the extent of the damage elsewhere," said Tobias.

Baby A raised her hand to intervene. "We deserve to celebrate some success, and we need time to recover from this nightmare. Can we not get a good night's sleep first?"

She cast a side-eye to their leader, and Arriette groaned that once again, she was the reason they couldn't simply get on with it.

Many others agreed, and they hummed or chattered in unison, filling the room with a warm vibration. They were tired and frightened and crashing from a lack of sleep and an overdose of adrenaline. There were plenty of rested followers who could tend to the women for a while instead. Arriette didn't want to argue with either side—she was too exhausted and too heavily pregnant.

The meeting had been called to resolve the mystery of the mutated Enzoian women, *not* to decide if their progress was worth a pat on the back.

Arriette said, "Tobias is right, but so is Baby A. Regain your composure and sleep. We can call another meeting then—I can't see how a few more hours will make a difference because it will take that long to rescue the survivors and get them somewhere comfortable. Perhaps the attic, as the entire top floor is empty or used for storage. *Definitely* not the basement. The vault and the wormhole are down there."

Reiko didn't see things that way. He snapped his fingers at Baby A, then at Tobias and Arriette, with grinding teeth.

"I didn't just slave over chemicals and potions for us to sit back and relax," he grumbled. "It happened in minutes. We can't afford to spare a few hours."

"Firstly, you didn't *slave* to do anything. This was a joint effort. Secondly, we're doing better than we were an hour ago. For now, *that's* what we should focus on," Baby

A told him.

Instead of fuelling the fire between Baby A and Reiko's opposing views, Arriette suggested Paulei and Pouki should discuss their notes for a little while, allowing her to sit and listen. She pondered how convincingly she could nap during the whole thing with her eyes open, and catch up with Tobias later.

This is going to be one hell of a long debrief.

As if hearing her thoughts, Tobias rubbed his face and let out a throaty sigh, so she reached for his hand.

There were things Arriette knew about her friends' personalities—their ticks and triggers—she'd figured out for herself over the past twelve months by living beside them in HQ. They were things that perhaps didn't matter so much on a battlefield, but meant everything when hosting a meeting like this, or at least trying to.

Combined, they liked to talk. Most of them, except for Susan, liked the sound of their own voices, so talk was what they did best, rarely agreeing on anything and preferring to argue, banter, and generally annoy Arriette to the point of having to pull rank. She never enjoyed having to be bossy and on this occasion, she didn't have the energy or the answers they were expecting, anyway. All she could do was be present and mediate; her job was to listen and observe, then decide when they'd had the rest they all deserved.

Though she loved them dearly, they all had big egos, believing in their opinions and movements so strongly that, despite the many amazing contributions, nobody would listen to anyone else's voice unless backed by their leader. She chose them as Casper had chosen her—of *course* they were going to express themselves strongly. It's what she expected of them.

Can't run a planet and not develop a bit of an ego, she reminded herself, smirking. They had all earned their place ten times over, and hers could probably be brought down a notch or two sometimes as well.

Forget the HPS, you'll demolish it, is what Casper had once told her, and she'd had to professionally inform people in her way a few times. She may as well have announced, 'Hey, don't you *know* who I am?'

But the most notable of all; her friends loved one another so much that protecting their organisation and those within it would take priority, sometimes even if that meant corrupting a fairly decent or proven plan of action. Of all the things she'd discovered, this was her favourite. Flawed, yet *beautifully* faultless.

After cursing and shaking fists at one another, Arriette decided enough was enough between Reiko and Baby A. They were individually too stubborn to agree. If she didn't have the guts to step in and tell them to shut up and respect one another, then Arriette knew the group *deserved* to be eaten alive by those women outside, or what remained of them.

And her hormones had, frankly, had enough.

On one side, she had Reiko willing to continue with their clean-up efforts. On the other, the person hoping for rest and recuperation to return the Recruit to their operational balance was the do-gooder angel, Baby A.

"What do *you* suggest we do?" Arriette asked Tobias instead, taking the others by surprise.

Faces turned their attention to the most powerful member of them all besides Arriette, and awaited a serious and useful response. If Arriette was their queen, then Tobias was her king.

"Reiko is the only one who thinks a time-out is a bad

idea."

"Because it *is*," he interjected. "Diving head-first into more trouble to investigate this epidemic is our best bet."

Arriette narrowed her eyes until the bald-headed hunter held up both hands and backed away.

Dion, she noted, stayed out of it.

She wiped beads of sweat from her brow with the back of her hand, then re-adjusted her seated position on the uncomfortable wooden chair and shifted to the right to free her baby's foot, yet again, from her ribcage.

Tobias swallowed hard. "If we leave this situation any longer, there won't be anything to bounce back to. It might bring us more harm. We're all tired and in need of a break, but those willing to work longer should. We can introduce shifts until we're safe again."

"They've been cured, though," Paulei told him. "Our responsibility is to investigate how they mutated, how to prevent it from happening again. To get out of trouble is what we're here for—the Recruit represents the resolution of such situations."

Reiko nodded. "I agree. We know *how* they mutated, because looking at them gives us all the data we need. Sebastian has extensive notes—you've all read his observations. What we don't know is *why* the women of Enzo only? Our responsibilities are much deeper than information... we need to take action. Right now."

"We're going to," Arriette said. "When we open those doors, we're inviting a threat inside, so we're not arguing over whether taking action now is a good idea, are we?"

"Then what *are* we arguing over?" Baby A groaned, folding her arms and slumping in her seat.

"We're arguing over if we're strong enough to do this full stop."

Paulei raised a hand but didn't wait for Arriette to gesture at him. "Arriette and Baby A have our best interests in mind when they tell us to rest, and on a rota system, as Tobias suggested. I was going to suggest one, but you beat me to it. Our judgement as a team is clouded by our exhaustion."

Arriette stopped Reiko before he could retaliate. "For now, we'll take this investigation steadily. When you walk out of this door, I grant everyone optional... what shall we call it... *leave* for twelve hours, so do with that what you please. Want to rest? Fine, rest. If you want to work, then work. If you leave HQ for any reason, wear your mask and be careful."

Reiko attempted to protest, but Dion's caressing arms wrapped around him. Her harmonic voice soothed his anxiety, and she led him away without offering an opinion knowing Reiko would head straight for the laboratory instead of to his bedroom, and he'd need her influence. She winked at Arriette as they left, which was enough to know she'd made the right call.

Baby A thanked Arriette before everyone, except Reiko and Dion, pressed on with other issues. She suggested Arriette might like to take her own advice.

"Forgive me for intruding on such personal business, but we can't help noticing a change in your appearance." She gestured at her enormous stomach and swollen ankles. "Tobias says this was unplanned, and I wanted to be sure you weren't, uhm..."

"Compromised?"

Baby A sighed. "I would *not* put it like that, but if we're going to talk about it, we may as well face facts. Are you going to manage like this?"

Tobias's eyes widened, and he shook his head,

suggesting Arriette ought to lie to the angel. The last thing the Recruit needed was for over half of their leading powers to be under any unnecessary stress and worry.

"I might look dreadful," she said, "but I'm fine. The only thing that's compromised is *my* safety. You have nothing to fear, though. Tobias is taking care of me and Tabitha and Pouki combined haven't left me alone in months. The Four Saviours did this to make sure there wasn't anything more sinister afoot, so it's a positive thing. If I thought for one minute any of you would suffer or be affected by this, I'd ask Pouki to re-apply his masking spell immediately."

Baby A seemed satisfied. "So twelve hours?"

"And not a minute more."

TWELVE

For three of her allocated twelve hours, Arriette sat at the desk in the foyer with her head in Haeyloian history books. These were mostly texts by the deceased Harriet Foley, a wiccan ex-member of the Recruit and Casper's estranged daughter. This made her Arriette's biological aunt, though she hadn't known it at the time of her death, nor would she ever have expected Casper of being willing to end his own daughter's life to prove his allegiance.

Harriet spoke little of mutations in her work, but there were rare and difficult spells capable of temporarily resurrecting something. That was to be expected after thousands of years of supes practising alchemy. In Harriet's reports, she'd witnessed the resurrection of a wild forest bird, a pig from a neighbouring farm, and even a rat, but they were controlled incantations performed by rulecasts and experienced wiccans. The experiments lasted seconds, but the spells were a definite success.

Arriette was thankful she hadn't needed to go to such extremes to fix the women of Enzo. The Four Saviours' ritual had done that for her somehow.

It was difficult to concentrate because despite the later and darker hour, there were now lots of people around—passing comments were thrown about the survivors which she couldn't yet answer, and they raised questions about her due date (which she didn't *want* to answer).

Harriet's history pages were a long shot, and they did little to aid her knowledge, but scanning them made her less guilty about sitting on her butt and contributing little to the investigation.

Physically, all Arriette could do to defend herself in this state was throw her weight around and look scarier than she was; she was truly vulnerable, slow, and knew she would be useless in a fight. She had her magic though and wasn't afraid to pitch a fireball or spread her wings and drop someone from a building.

I've done it before.

There were thousands of books in the library, gifted to the Recruit from various neighbouring villages, Charles Melovich and his daughter Rihaana in the city, and books from her mother's cottage and Rosewood Cottage. Too many stacks for Arriette to get through from the Indalo store's archive and the lair's town hall.

The latest box she had excitedly collected herself after being summoned to Charles's office for a meeting via their pendants. It illuminated and vibrated, then materialised her beside his desk in the same way her wings appeared. She'd instantly been sick from the sensation, but Rihaana already had a bucket and a tissue ready for her, anticipating it might throw Arriette's stomach the first time.

So, instead of reading (because for once the task appeared overwhelming) she added to her grimoire project for a while. She made sure Paulei's notes were in there, and Sebastian's observations, too, shoving them into the folder and annotating them. Temporarily, she filed them under M for mutations and monsters and Z for zombies. But it wasn't long until Arriette's scrap-booking was interrupted by Paulei.

"Arriette, you have visitors," he said, resting a palm on her shoulder and turning her slowly to the glass doors. A dreamer she didn't recognise was in the process of fixing the crack for good.

She scanned the grounds. In the gloomy distance, the figures of three broad men were approaching and beside them prowled wolves, some grey and black, some silver, stalking towards the building on all fours, their eyes glinting in the moonlight. Arriette immediately got to her feet and warmed her palms, preparing to pitch one of those fireballs, but Paulei tapped his head.

"Friends, not foes," he said, "I checked."

He couldn't blame her for being tense, because the last time the Recruit had been face-to-face with a shape-shifting werewolf, they'd almost become lunch. To join forces with them after the battle for Pandora's box was a pleasant surprise, as was their visit to HQ now if they intended to offer help.

The dreamer ushered them through quickly. Paulei remained by her side in Tobias's absence, still unsure he trusted the weres after they had so easily switched sides once before, especially after being the one to introduce them this time as *friends*.

"Master Kid Kyle, are you well?" Arriette asked, flexing her fingers.

He smiled, shaking her hand gently, then cupping it with both his palms. If he noticed the heat emanating from her discarded fireballs, he did not let on.

"Yes, Arriette. I see your baby is developing. When are you due?"

"Not long," she replied, and she would have extended her answer had he not interrupted to ask if he needed to greet her formally.

Arriette shook her head, blushing. "I'm the leader of the Recruit, not royalty," she told Kid. "A formal greeting is unnecessary."

"I hear otherwise," he whispered, then winked.

"You did?" she scowled. "How?"

"We have watchers in the woods."

So spies, then.

Reluctantly, Arriette allowed him to proceed with an ancient werewolf tradition, mulling over the implications of the weres having skulking spies on Recruit property.

When speaking to somebody of a higher rank, as a mark of respect, it was custom to address them as such to prove you meant no harm, and to lower your head beneath theirs to show inferiority. Like a salute or a bow in other cultures. Arriette noticed the pack had remained outside for this reason. When they'd met the first time, the masters were still unsure of her status, so this would be the first time they'd delivered the official greeting—they had crafted something specifically for her, too.

Arriette flinched at the thought of them bowing before Falkon Lou.

"Ze verefrow ira ze armeh, en prim'ae're ze elitia, clen Shou."

Arriette frowned, attempting to translate his speech using the Haeyloian she'd learned, but he spoke too quickly. Eventually, she rolled her eyes and Master Kid Kyle put her out of her misery.

"The werewolf clans watch over the leader and protect the chosen one. We offer courtesy and respect for one so great. On behalf of the Shou clan," he said.

"Your use of our ancient language, manners, and everything about your customs is so rounded and beautiful," she said. "I struggle to understand Haeyloian when it is so fluently spoken, even now."

"I'm honoured you should think so," he said and released her hand. "It comes with practice. And be assured, Arriette, our watchers are strategically placed for your benefit. Your news is secret safe with all three clans," he added, before stepping aside so the two other pack leaders, Izzy Charter of the Shoku clan and Kaleb Solumn of the Tri clan had room to do the same.

These three wolf clans were the last spiritual were creatures known to remain on Haeylo, each with a unique supernatural gift and their rituals and personalities. Some Arriette feared more than others because of their nature. These weres were unlike the wolves she had encountered in Manaia Forest. Those were castaways and rejects, neglected by other clans and smaller, less ritualistic packs, or so she hoped.

The Shou clan believed their god with the same name controlled their human halves when their bodies took the form of the wolf, whilst the Tri clan believed they had to control both halves themselves, and nurtured each of their three faces before every transformation: human, wolf, spiritual. Their symbol was a triquetra: the power of three —the symbol comprised three ovals forming a triangular design, joining in the centre.

The Choku clan, blessed with unnatural strength and speed during a shift, were not religious, though respectful of authority. Under normal circumstances, only with caution they would be approached.

Kaleb Solumn said, "The Choku Clan are honoured to meet you again, Arriette Monroe. We are here to offer the Recruit our services. We received word from your vampyrs that there was an attack at HQ."

"And, I imagine, from your watchers."

Arriette chose not to offer Kaleb a handshake. On a good day, his personality was prickly, so Arriette much preferred dealing with the Shou leader who always dressed so humanly compared to the other clan leaders. Today he wore a suit and tie, with polished shoes and fang-shaped cufflinks. The Choku and Tri clan members dressed more traditionally in loose-fitted clothes to accommodate shifting, and had allowed their facial hair and nails to grow. It seemed the Shou leader wasn't so worried about ripping through expensive fabrics.

"As you can see, I'm in no physical state for hands-on work, and we have been dealing with a crisis. I'm pleased Susan and Dion found you."

Arriette gave them the short version.

"Anything for the woman who allowed our continued existence," said Master Kid Kyle. "Are you aware that we clan wolves believe weres were placed on Haeylo to protect the forests? We have been doing so and watching this area from afar for a long time, but didn't want to risk approaching HQ until now."

"Wise, and kind to risk it at all," she said. "And I didn't know that. Sick women litter our grounds—Enzoian women, made ill from an unknown threat that also destroyed some of your forest territory. I need to find a specific woman for interrogation amongst them, too; it's very important as she's the only one believed to speak openly. There's so much we don't know about their community. We were hoping she'd tell us more."

"Do they blame you for this crisis?" Kid asked.

"Not to our knowledge, though Enzo was a target to attack the Recruit."

"You wish for these women to follow your beliefs?"

asked Kaleb.

"No, merely share their own with us to enable a deeper understanding."

"I see," said Kid, nodding.

"Are you wanting these women moved or killed?" asked Izzy Charter, and Arriette gasped.

"Moved. Not killed." She exhaled sharply. "Most of the women sadly died during the outbreak, so their bodies will need to be moved and burned, but we're sending some of our people to speak with the monks first and learn their preferred rituals, as they may need to be buried."

"We will help in any way possible," Kid said.

"Thank you. We'd like any survivors to be brought inside, but to a secure room, perhaps upstairs, where they can cause no harm. We can give you a description of the woman we need to talk to. There are retainers on duty assisting with their medical needs."

He bowed once again to dismiss himself and his peers, and exited the building through the glass doors to give the orders to his companions in their wolf form outside. The wolves immediately sprang into action to assist the surviving Enzoian women to their feet, walking them carefully around the rear of the building to the designated areas. Some clung to their fur and others rode on the backs of the larger wolves like horses. Their immediate response to their orders was militant.

Kid returned to collect some water an hour later, and after taking a swig from his canteen, asked, "Arriette, how are you going to interrogate all these women? There must be at least fifty."

"This is a large building. We can fit them in."

"May *I* make a suggestion?"

Arriette hoped he would say that. "I'm all ears."

"Why not use the Recruit's lair? It's huge and, at the moment, unused. If you write a list of the questions you need answering and provide pencils and parchment, my wolves can interview them for you and note their reactions. That is, if you would permit our passage."

"And the other packs?"

"Will remain behind to assist you here, and some will remain in the forest as always. We can house them in the castle."

"Hmm, well, it's not a pretty sight in the lair. We're still cleaning up from the battle last year," she told him.

"Our packs partially caused the mess," he said, "and so they will not mind a little extra chaos."

Arriette was speechless. Before he disappeared, she thanked him awkwardly and asked the two other wolf masters for their co-operation. They were now to re-direct survivors to the basement for a safe exit through the wormhole. And the werewolves would not hesitate to rip somebody's head off if they stepped out of line or threatened Arriette and her people, so she wasn't worried about the Enzoian women's presence in HQ or the security of the vault.

The only key still dangled safely against her chest.

With the investigation progressing, Arriette decided it was time to get some guilt-free sleep. She pushed her way through the wolves to her bedroom, thanking them all as she did so, then bolted the door for the night.

****

Entertaining werewolves was the last thing Arriette had in mind, but as her hand reached for the doorknob after a restless hour of sleep, she realised that other than water, the Recruit hadn't offered them anything, not to eat or a place to sleep.

And her time off was almost half-way over.

She had barely turned the knob half a centimetre before Paulei Leigh knocked and startled her. His usually pale face was now grey and his motivated smile had faded, replaced with urgency and fear.

Arriette rubbed her eyes and groaned. "I gave you leave."

"I need your authority to take some tissue samples."

"Paulei, I can't do this at the moment. I'm not feeling well, and I need Tobias."

"Do you need me to call for Tabitha too?"

She shook her head. "I'm just heavily pregnant and bored with it. I have a stomach ache and feel a little light-headed. What else is new?"

"Better to be safe. And the samples?"

"Sure, whatever. I don't care." She sighed.

"I'll find Tobias for you."

Arriette closed the door again and moved her hands in gentle circles across her stomach. Would her child one day have to deal with these atrocities—be this tired and stressed every day because of a job she one day *fell* into? Why had they chosen to bring a baby into a world as broken as Haeylo, when it would never mimic Earth as their creator had intended? Their technology and their cultures and their ideals and beliefs... Haeylo was supernatural, and its people used magic to get the things they wanted when, like the wolves said, supes were supposed to *protect* it. The everlasts had allowed no further developments in fear that history would repeat itself, drip-feeding society. Unlike human beings, they had not struggled for their evolution and were reluctant to surrender it as Arriette had learned after dealing with Falkon Lou. They were lucky in HQ to be able to use their history books for a greater purpose.

There was a sharp hammering on the door again. Tobias and Tabitha hurried in.

Arriette rolled her eyes. "I told Paulei I was fine."

"Is it the baby?" Tobias knelt and placed his hands on her stomach. "What's wrong? Are you ill?"

"I'm fine!" The baby kicked. Arriette tensed. "Ooft!"

Together, they aided her to the bed. She sat for a few minutes with her eyes closed, trying desperately not to cry. Her muscles throbbed and there was a terrible pulling sensation in her pelvis.

Arriette was paying little attention to the conversation happening outside her head. Once again, though she did not sleep, the screaming woman was haunting her.

"Arriette?" said Tabitha.

Tabitha's voice lingered in Arriette's consciousness, and as she tried to open her mouth to tell her, that consciousness slid.

"Arriette?" Tobias sat beside her on the bed and gently shook her. "What's happening?"

"I think something's wrong," Tabitha said. "Can you get Pouki?"

Heavy footsteps all around.

An indoor thunderstorm of voices and clanging and panic. Arriette's vision clouded and her eyes wouldn't fully open, but faintly she could still make out concerned faces and see their auras even through closed lids. They were flitting around the room like bolts of lightning. Occasionally someone would bump the bed and jolt her awake for a few seconds.

The outside world wasn't her chief concern; the

screaming, faceless woman in her dreams called out, and Arriette reached to chase her.

Her efforts were futile.

She tried with all her might to pull the screaming woman to her with weakened telekinesis, but failed. To bring this nightmare to the forefront of her mind, potentially to reality, dreaming should have been her best bet, considering Tobias also held this ability and their baby would, too. But after several attempts to use it, Arriette gave in and prepared to try something else. The human labour had weakened her powers.

Ownership of an everlast pendant wasn't about to get her anywhere fast, and shapeshifting, though fun, was also pointless—she would still be pregnant no matter her shape and have to go through the same natural pain. Nor would taking her comfortable feline form do anything. Wings would not find the voice within her unconscious mind either, but her angelic connection with Zìnnyi would... if she could contact him.

"Arriette, can you hear me?"

Tabitha's voice tickled her consciousness, and a light blue aura crossed her vision. Arriette wanted to answer her, but her mouth wouldn't move.

The aura quickly turned dark, replaced.

"Tobias, I think she's passed out."

"She's breathing though, right?"

Tabitha barged him to the side and took Arriette's pulse with her fingers. They were cold against her skin, but nothing compared to the blood-curdling howl of that woman in Arriette's memory.

She trembled, seeing the stranger's silhouette in her mind's eye. The figure wasn't crumpled on the grass outside HQ like the others, whose wounds healed on their own. She stood tall, faceless, in the centre of them.

"*Why* did I perform that ritual on our leader?"

Pouki's voice drifted through like a breeze as Arriette searched harder for Zïnnyi's influence to boost whatever signal she could find to identify this screaming silhouette of a woman.

"Supe pregnancies are different, and after my spell and the stress of her job.... oh, whatever happens, she *must* live."

"You're signing her death certificate!" Tobias yelled, his booming voice exploding across the room and through to Arriette, who jolted again, but didn't wake.

"She can hear us, that's good," Pouki said.

"Tabitha, is this normal for a human birth?"

"How should *I* know?"

Tobias grabbed her shoulders. "MAYBE BECAUSE YOU'RE A RETAINER!"

Arriette's unborn baby burst to life within her.

"Something's happening," Tabitha said, breaking free of Tobias's grip and kneeling beside the bed. "She's *got* to be in labour. I've never witnessed a human birth, and I don't know what to do if the mother passes out."

Tobias dragged a chair to Arriette's bedside and held her clammy hand. She appreciated his warm breath on her neck and his smooth skin against her frame as he prayed. Deep in her heart, Arriette knew he needed her to promise him she and the baby would be fine. And she wanted to, but something about that screaming woman once again locked her within. Her connection to Zïnnyi was basic and pathetic—absent images of those beautiful clean white robes or floating heavens.

Something or *someone* stood in their way, preventing their angelic communication.

Pain shot through Arriette's abdomen and up her spine. It was a familiar sensation whilst mastering the materialisation of her wings. So she braced for them, grateful when nothing happened. Instead, warm fluid soaked her dress and the bedsheets.

"The baby's coming," Tabitha said.

"I thought she still had a few weeks," Tobias said.

Pouki shoved a pillow behind Arriette's head to support her, then wiped her forehead.

"Babies can come early, but this reaction to labour isn't normal," he said. "She shouldn't be asleep; this is something supernatural."

"But it's a human birth." Tobias squeezed Arriette's hand harder. "Tabitha, *I mean it*. You save her. Save her if it's the last thing you ever do. Save her if it kills *you*!"

"I love Arriette as much as you do," she reminded Tobias, swatting him away to give her room to work. "Calm down, we just need to wake her up."

"I can't lose her."

Pouki placed his healing hands on Arriette's stomach and inhaled deeply. Opening his mind, his presence pounded on the walls of her prison, drilling through the barriers to reach her with his gift. But this wasn't something Arriette had planned, nor was it a defence mechanism, and she couldn't control it. The screaming woman's voice slipped, and in its place came a whirlpool of emotion and sensations. So much physical pain: burning, drilling, tugging. The baby would be born soon and Arriette would have missed it. So she wept internally, feeling her bones creak and her muscles contract, but trapped and unable to express her fears.

The mysterious presence backed away, leaving Arriette to fight her losing battle. Her wings unfolded, firing her upwards as they sprang free and flopped over either side of the bed. The skin containing them unzipped, revealing their unique light.

Then Arriette's eyes snapped open.

Her wings thrust everyone forward at once, lifting Pouki off his feet and throwing Tobias across the base of the bed. He and Tabitha dived back over her, pinning Arriette's arms and legs down to lock them in place.

"She's awake!" yelled Pouki. "Let's make sure she stays that way. This needs to happen *now*."

"It... hurts!" Arriette growled through gritted teeth.

Tobias sniffled. "What's happening to you? Where did you go?"

Tabitha grabbed clean towels and instruments to prepare for the delivery, but frowned as Pouki backed away.

"I'm a Recruit trainer, not a doctor," he said.

"And I'm a retainer, not a midwife! Get over here!"

"This isn't medical, this is *magical*," said Tobias. "Can't you feel that... *energy*?"

Arriette's breath caught in her throat. She coughed, lurching forward with each awkward inhale and exhale. There was something else at play here; something eager to be free of her body. Fighting to escape.

Something like a baby.

Some*one* like Pandora.

"Stop... arguing," she groaned, "you're... making... it... worse!"

Tabitha placed a cool flannel across her forehead. "Tobias, find Baby A. She'll know how we can safely restrain those wings."

But he couldn't move.

Pouki ran instead, slamming the door behind him.

Arriette's wings rustled and shifted under her weight. Tobias took off his belt and tied down her chest, trapping the feathered breasts beneath her.

"Tabitha... help... me!"

"I'm trying!"

Arriette ground her teeth. "Let... me... go... *please*."

"If I do, your wings will tip the bed over."

Baby A burst through the door, rushing to Arriette's side and wasting no time. Pouki followed but stood back, allowing the angel to take the lead.

"Keep the belt fastened to the frame," she told Tobias. "Arriette, the baby's coming, so I'm going to need you to push. We have to do this now before your wings snap the leather. Your body knows what to do and you have to trust it."

"I... can't!"

"Look at me," she said, turning her best friend's chin. "You're *Arriette Monroe*. You're indestructible. *What* HPS, remember?"

"I'll... demolish... it." Arriette smiled at Casper's memory. "There's... something... else… *someone...*"

"You can do anything!" Baby A encouraged.

"That... was... then."

"This is happening *now*. Come on. You can do it!"

Arriette nodded, taking sharp breaths, and then began to push with the next sensation, but her eyes were rolling and unfocused again. So Tabitha's rushed to the foot of the bed to help the infant along, and to witness the birth of their future leader, and another princess.

"Are you with me, Arriette?"

Pouki hurried Tabitha. "She's passed out again, Tabitha. You're going to have to do the rest for her."

Arriette's breathing was light but rhythmic, and the

call of the screaming woman was trying to take her again. The presence was back, blocking her channel to Zïnnyi, tempting her.

"Now, Tabitha!" Pouki urged, clasping his hands together and resting forward on the bed. "Zïnnyi, let this child be healthy."

Exhaustion consumed each cell; the sensation of tiny bubbles within Arriette's blood drove her to a seizure until the rise and fall of her chest came to a sudden halt.

Tobias placed a cool palm across her forehead.

He scowled. "Wait a second. Arriette? Arriette! She's not breathing, Pouki! SOMEBODY DO SOMETHING!"

Tobias panicked, shaking Arriette's shoulders until the cries of an innocent newborn girl filled the room merely seconds later.

Pouki closed his eyes with relief. "Thank Zïnnyi!"

Baby A tore Tobias from Arriette's side, passing him his daughter. "Clean her up and wrap her in a blanket."

"Baby A, I—"

"NOW!" She ushered him to the back of the room where a small basket awaited. "Let Tabitha work on her," she said, calming herself, swallowing tears and her own panic. "It'll be alright, Tobias. It'll be alright."

Her eyes streaming, Baby A crossed to Arriette and pressed two fingers to her neck, searching for a pulse.

***

Walking. I must keep walking.

The light calls to me, beckoning me toward my destiny. It glows. Burns brighter and hotter than I have ever known.

I pace barefoot, carefully, upon a darkened canvas.

Reflected in water lapping over my feet, stars twinkle, but there is no beach and no waves. When I glance back, I am leaving neon footprints that stretch into the distance, like I've been here forever.

Suddenly, there is a flash of red, and photographs of my life surround me, formed from dazzling constellations. I see my mother in her garden, and Casper on the porch of his cabin. Rosewood Cottage, now overgrown, is abandoned and dusty, but the village is thriving.

Desperate to call out for help, I open my mouth but cannot speak to the faces in those snapshots. Nor can I cry.

But I can SCREAM.

And the scream is familiar.

I am so afraid.

But then the golden outline of a figure forms ahead and extends its hand to me. Faintly, a second set of footprints appear beside mine, and they too stretch behind us.

They have been there a long time.

They are still with me.

Casper? Please, if you're with me, revive me.

I... I don't want to die...

THIRTEEN

Tabitha rushed to Arriette's bed, where she gripped her shoulders and shook as violently as her energy could muster. "She's not breathing!"

Tobias watched in horror as he cradled their baby. Her cries bounced off the walls, almost as if to try and wake her sleeping mother.

"What are you *doing*?" Tobias sobbed. "Baby A!"

Baby A hushed Tabitha who was screaming now, too. "I'm waking her up; she doesn't get to bail on us like that. I WON'T HAVE IT!"

Baby A wiped her eyes and sank to her knees. "She's gone, Tabitha. There's nothing you could have done."

"Arriette can't just *die*."

"I've been to the future. I've seen her alive," Baby A said in shock. "Arriette is *not* supposed to die today and..."

"And *what*?" said Pouki from the doorway, his hand on the doorknob and his eyes fixated on Arriette's lifeless body.

Behind him, crowds were forming in the hall. Whispers passed back to colleagues and friends, werewolves and followers, of their leader's demise.

"I... don't... *understand*." Pouki reached across the bed to cup Arriette's pale face, keeping his gaze fixed on Tobias as he tried to hush their daughter.

With the slightest spark of a brainwave, Pouki could

confirm there would be hope of a resuscitation; he wouldn't have to be the guy to announce their leader wouldn't be coming back.

"Her consciousness isn't in there," he told them. "I'm not registering anything at all."

He waited for several more minutes, focusing, praying. And he wasn't the only one.

News spread swiftly throughout the building, and in the foyer, Paulei suddenly found he no longer sensed his leader's presence, either.

He dropped his pen and set off down the corridor.

The atmosphere at HQ thickened until it turned choking and tense. But the werewolves and their masters continued to work with stern faces. If they ceased, the Enzoian women would stray, and Arriette's plan would fall apart.

On the inside, it did not stop Kid Kyle and his counterparts from falling to pieces, too.

Arriette's daughter suddenly stopped crying, sighed, and gazed up at her terrified father through glassy khaki eyes.

Her *mother's* eyes.

FOURTEEN

The days following Arriette's death passed hurriedly, and by the next morning, the realisation that she wasn't coming back knocked Arriette's mother off her feet. So Baby A asked Ma to spend a few months at HQ, with the freedom to return to Drakonta when emotions and the uproar had settled. It would also allow her a chance to get to know her unnamed granddaughter and to help Tobias with the late-night feeding.

On the second day, Sebastian visited Pouki's residential suite sweating and red in the face. Before he explained why he'd disturbed Pouki's grief, the telepath slammed the door. So Sebastian headed out to Arriette's coffin to *think*, taking a large canteen with him.

On the third day, Tobias, although without Arriette's love and support, realised he still needed to name their baby girl. He suffered each time he gazed into her grassy green eyes; inside of her soul, he saw Arriette gazing back, and Tobias knew, once grown, she'd be a bundle of joy and a handful of trouble all at once.

Exactly like the woman who gave birth to her.

The number of names put forth didn't matter, and the Recruit offered lots of beautiful suggestions, including Grace and Belle. The Four Saviours recommended Miracle or Lumina as she has been born in the eve, but none seemed to fit, and he couldn't bear to name her after her mother, either.

"It can wait until tomorrow," Tobias told Baby A, and she didn't—*couldn't*—argue.

On the fourth day, the Recruit held a meeting in the canteen without him, but not about the naming of his child. Soon, they'd be forced to elect a temporary successor to reign until Arriette's daughter turned eighteen and could, by their laws, take her place. Their current leader ceased to exist so most likely, the piece of Pandora's soul she had absorbed was also now gone. Baby A suggested they should gather to consider the implications and potentially use Arriette's key to examine the box for signs that Pandora had returned to it.

Paulei Leigh spoke first. "I think it's too early to assign anyone to her role," he said, "because we don't know where Pandora went and we can't open the box to check. It would release the gateway evils again. Has anyone tried to access the box from the outside?"

"No," Baby A confirmed, suddenly disgusted with how plain and boring this meeting room, like all the others, was.

Lifeless, like their leader.

Like her best friend.

"The vault is still secure. Nobody in or out."

"Then we should not assume that Pandora is loose upon Haeylo now Arriette's body is no longer her host—half of her soul still lives within that box, and it seems logical that it has simply and magically returned to join its other half. Or, it died with her."

Baby A was in no mood for this argument, so she said, "The box is sealed. The key is still around Arriette's neck."

Paulei asked, "Is a soul bound by the physical

realm?"

Baby A was about to tell him she didn't think so when Sebastian scurried in late and took a seat at the back.

"Sorry I'm late, I—"

"Forgot your priorities," Jet finished, sighing.

Baby A scolded him. "*Where* have you been? This is kind of important!"

"You can't keep going to see her," Jet told him, "because you'll drive yourself mad."

"You've been with Arriette?" Baby A rolled her eyes.

No wonder he looked flustered and exhausted. Why would *anyone* voluntarily put themselves through such emotional torture every day? There were crinkles in his normally pressed purple robes and they were dirty, sleeves damp and fraying. Ignoring how Baby A scowled at him, he shoved a cream-coloured folder across the table until it landed in her right hand, then sat back and removed his purple hat, defeated. Now was not the time to voice his concerns, and he'd already tried to raise the subject with Pouki unsuccessfully. But if Baby A read that file, she'd do something about it.

"You forget I welcomed her to this lair, and I can't help feeling it's not her time, so I went to check. Leave it alone." Sebastian shook his long auburn hair free. "The wolves have nearly finished interviewing the women, by the way, and I have their findings. Plus, they got me some samples for Reiko."

"The interviews are in this file?"

Sebastian nodded once. He narrowed his eyes at Jet. "Alongside other things. Seems *some* of my priorities are still in order."

The wolves deserved a permanent place in the lair for their labour and dedication; they had interviewed most of the surviving Enzoian women in just four days. Kid Kyle had estimated there would be fifty, so it pleased the Recruit the number of survivors had exceeded that and was so far at sixty, and Arriette would have been overjoyed to hear they saved those extra ten. Sadly, though, everyone else was dead.

"Enough moping, then. We all have work to do," Baby A forced, and Sebastian scrunched up his nose.

"Seems they are biologically still human."

"They are *now*."

He knew better than to tell Baby A what he was thinking: that she *and* Pouki could shove that folder and those results in an uncomfortable orifice.

Jet nodded, though he didn't agree either. He took over from Sebastian when he saw the disapproval on his friend's face, explaining briefly their conclusions regarding the interviewed citizens. They decided the talking female didn't live amongst them, as none of them matched the description she gave.

"Have any of them explained how this happened?"

Paulei raised a hand to chime in. "None of us can pick up on those same thoughts now. Pouki and I tried with no luck, and given our circumstances, we asked other telepaths to try should our grief compromise our powers. There's some kind of blockage."

"Pouki, can't you break down those barriers the way you did with Coyote?"

He made a sound a lot like a snort and shrugged his shoulders. As if he hadn't already tried that, but since Arriette's death, Pouki had been disinterested in any official Recruit duties, and instead cursed the world and their creator for choosing to take her from them at such a critical time. Baby A couldn't blame him; she didn't want to perform for their followers either, but if not her, then who would step up?

"We have to try. Arriette told us to find her."

"Well, Arriette isn't *here*, is she?" he sniped.

Paulei glared at him and the two exchanged a silent telepathic word, then he said, "We're going to keep at it, I promise. Anyway, they've all changed back now and are human again. Their wounds are healed, but they still won't talk. All we get are a few basic written responses, and most of them claim not to recognise how or why this happened, only the pain they experienced and that they were driven to attack our building by 'unknown'."

Baby A flinched. "Driven by 'unknown'? They used the word *driven*?"

"Yes," Paulei replied, also concerned, "by something unknown."

Magically powered refrigerators and vending machines hummed in the background, and as the sun had set on both Haeylo's surface and now in the lair—since the dreamers had synced the two for Arriette's memorial—most were retiring for the evening. Only cleaners and kitchen staff pottered about.

"Tonight we can rest," Jet said, "and I'm taking the first of the final three interviews in the morning bright and early. Baby A and Susan are going to take the second and we were hoping, Sebastian, that you might volunteer for the third?"

Sebastian hummed, "Of course, but Tobias said he wanted to be part of this, and—"

"No," Baby A cut in. "Tobias has been through enough these past few days, and I don't care what he says. I'm *not* having him take the weight of this on his shoulders, too. He has their baby to care for."

"On that note," Paulei said, raising his hand. "Has anyone noticed she's already getting... bigger?"

Sebastian lay his head gently in his hands and rubbed his face in agony.

"*Nobody* listens to me," he grumbled.

Stuck between the two of them, he grumbled under his breath, sat up, and stretched before meeting Jet's curious eyes.

"What?"

"You're knackered," Jet said.

"We all have a job to do, Jet."

Jet scowled. "Have you slept since we lost her?"

"Have *any* of us?"

The awkward silence answered his question for him.

"Let this go."

"Let *what* go, Jet? Sebastian?" Baby A flicked open the folder, suddenly curious. "Is there something going on, something about Arriette or the baby? If it gets back to Tobias or Ma and you—"

"Calm down, I'm keeping them out of it," Sebastian replied, and scratched the back of his head. "I can't be the only one who thinks there's something strange about Arriette's death and how fast her baby is developing already. I mean, study her body. Go outside and *look* at her."

"We have," Baby A snapped, "and it makes no difference how many times you visit her. She'll still be dead. Why are you doing this to yourself?"

"Is it because she still looks so beautiful?" Joy interjected. "I put some makeup on her, and I brushed her hair. It's unsettling; she doesn't look dead, but it doesn't mean she isn't."

Sebastian shuddered and said, "I've been wetting her

lips with water, using a spell to carefully lift the glass. I'm not a fool; I understand the funeral procedure. What else am I supposed to do but investigate this myself? *You're* not listening to me, and Pouki wouldn't entertain it because he can't hear her thoughts anymore."

Pouki groaned and stood abruptly, throwing back his chair in the process and startling Baby A, enough to rouse a gasp. "That's because SHE IS DEAD!"

"Yell at me all you want, telepath. Haven't you noticed something? I mean, don't the dead decompose? And Arriette isn't."

"Not *that* fast," Jet told him. "We are only to display her for a week; it's a ritual before a burial to prevent her from being turned. Then she'll go to the tomb where Casper is."

"The only vampyrs with access to her body are a vegetarian and her ex-best friend. Neither has any interest in turning her." Sebastian sighed and tried to explain his observations without shouting. "Her cheeks are flushed. That only happens when there is blood pumping. Her hair is still shiny. Her wings, too. The feathers of an angel's wings fall out when they die. Baby A, I'm right?"

Sheepishly, Baby A sat. "They do, but not always straight away, and only if the angel dies with them presented."

"Arriette did! I'm telling you magic is involved here. We *can't* bury her in that tomb."

Baby A reflected, then told Sebastian she would take it under advisement and visit Arriette's coffin again to check her wings, but she was unconvinced. Then she quickly changed the subject before Pouki and Sebastian could get into a fistfight over the file she now clutched to her chest.

"I wanted to be the one to tell you all that Tobias decided on a name for the baby," Baby A told them.

"Is it a Haeyloian name?" Paulei asked. "What does it mean?"

"He wouldn't tell me. Not yet."

"Why? Are there other names in the running?" Paulei hummed as he said, "I'll bet so, because she's the spitting image of her mother. He should name her Arriette."

Joy offered half a smile. "Tobias said she isn't showing signs of the gifts she presented in the womb yet."

"That's not abnormal for a supernatural child," Paulei said. "In fact—"

Through the doors burst two wolves of the Choku clan. They were pointing toward Arriette's coffin in the town, still sitting on the podium.

"Forgive the interruption, Baby A, but there's been a security breach," said the first.

Jet and Sky jumped to their feet and ran toward the window, glaring out at a sprinting woman in Enzoian robes.

"Who the *hell* is that?" Jet asked, his invisibility flickering.

The second wolf caught his breath and stopped Jet as he ran to the doors. "One of the Enzoian women," he told him. "She must have escaped. The castle's north watchtower spotted her heading toward Arriette's body, and Master Kyle ordered us to inform you immediately."

Infuriated, Sebastian stamped his foot and ordered the wolves to go after her with Jet. In case someone had tampered with the coffin, he told the others he would check Arriette's body personally. Again.

"I think you've found the woman you needed to speak to, Baby A," he said before he lifted his dragging plum robes and tapped his head and heart. "Illumina, Nes Sebastian Sky."

A whisk of wind caught at his feet, building a grey tunnel around his body like that of a tornado, and as it lifted, Sebastian grabbed the wand he'd chosen in the Indalo store: his purple pointed hat.

Only then did his rounded figure disappear.

The canteen was left feeling cool and isolated. This type of incantation took a short while to fade, especially one with power to remove the physical form of a sorcerer and replace them at another point in space, a little like the traces of a wormhole once a traveller had initiated a jump.

Using the wind to get around wasn't something Sebastian Sky had ever done either. He mostly learned theory alongside Arriette rather than actually practising. He could get away with it now the Four Saviours were becoming more involved in the Recruit's active duties, but this spell was not one of the more complex, and the Haeyloian language had sensed the urgency in his voice, giving him the boost he needed.

A lot could be learned in four days.

He reappeared beside Arriette's coffin, rustling lingering petals as the wind settled around him.

The stranger remained unmoving by Arriette's head.

"Back *away* from her," he warned.

His approach was cautionary, as the Enzoian figure lowered her cloak to reveal an old woman, watching Arriette's still chest and pursed lips through the glass.

"You shouldn't be here," Sebastian instructed, inching closer and preparing to grab her if she made any sudden moves he didn't like.

Reiko skidded to a halt beside him, closely followed by Jet and Baby A, and the two wolves were now in their shifted form. They snarled and hunched, preparing to pounce on someone's—*anyone's*—orders.

"She fits Susan's description of the mystery woman," Baby A confirmed, out of breath and confused. None of the remaining women did, though, she remembered. So who *was* this woman, and how had she masked her true appearance from them during the interviews? Had she travelled through the wormhole from HQ, or accessed the lair some other way, like the beach tunnel or the waterfall?

The woman grinned, showing dirty crooked teeth and thick red gums.

She uttered, "Arriette is dead."

"I'm assuming no thanks to you?" Baby A growled.

The woman hissed in response. "You will never know. But she *had* to die. It was... inevitable."

"Why?" Baby A cried, unable to remain calm. "Tell me why!"

"The... mistress... does not take lightly to failure."

The elderly woman placed a thin, shaking hand on Arriette's coffin then, and the fury in Baby A's eyes ignited her electricity. Reiko unsheathed Arriette's scimitar from his belt and held it at arm's length. It would be fitting for their leader's murderer to die by her blade, and he couldn't wait for it to meet the flesh of their enemy.

"Put that thing down, Reiko Port," the woman said. "In the time it would take you to swing it, you'd be too late."

Reiko's snarling lip upturned, revealing his missing teeth. His glare was menacing. "Tell us who your mistress is and how you know us, and I may not have to take off your head with this *thing*."

The woman leaned to breathe hot air above Arriette's face, then casually polished the glass with the sleeve of her robe. A false show of respect for the saviour she had conspired against.

"Everyone who is anyone around these parts knows of the Recruit," she said. "But *my* mistress? She is *unknown*."

She smiled then, forming a triangle with her thumbs and forefingers from each hand. Her ring and middle fingers formed a curved line across the centre creating a circle, and her pinkies poked up straight. She held it high in the air—the symbol of her mistress.

Pouki's fists clenched at this perfect risen sign.

Baby A's eyes brightened and sparks shot from her fingertips, lighting up the street and setting fire to the petals that gathered at the woman's feet. But none burned her skin or set alight her robes, or caused her concern at all. She waved one palm to put them out and casually slumped against Arriette's coffin with her right hip, facing a gathering crowd.

"You can switch off your angel now, Pouki Hallidae," the woman said, "as silly fireworks are of no threat to me."

"Who... is... your... mistress?" Baby A managed through grinding teeth.

"Stand down, Baby A, I think *I* know who she is," Pouki replied.

FIFTEEN

Arriette's body was vulnerable on that podium, out in the open street, and unprotected from any intruders or enemies. Despite Sebastian's concerns, Baby A hadn't given the funeral a second thought—they were in a secure underground lair protected by magic, and the only vampyrs present in the vicinity had zero interest in their best friend's dead body.

Reiko could see now what this woman was planning to do, and fearing the public defacing of Arriette's coffin, he nudged closer as she talked about her mistress having white skin and dark hair, like a witch from a fairy tale, all the while raising the symbol higher.

"Arriette's dead now. *Leave* her," Jet said.

Reiko sheathed the blade she'd already spotted and began, one step at a time, to ascend the podium.

The woman replied, "I'm afraid I can't do that."

Reaching behind her, the bitter woman started rummaging in her filthy brown robes. She pulled a dagger from the belt beneath and held it out. The blade shone as it caught the lair's moonlight, and its beams ricocheted across the glass, enchanted in some way.

"She's already dead, lady," Reiko told her, reaching the last step. "You can't damage her any more than you already have."

"I can. And I have to."

Appearing in doorways and windows, drawn by the commotion, Arriette's followers peered out. Reiko sighed at the sight of children she'd played with after the battle, who'd asked her what a real dragon looked like, and bit his lip at the idea of them witnessing her coffin, perhaps her body, vandalised.

"So you're going to stick a knife through glass to make sure you *got* her? You must care for this mistress of yours to lose your head."

Angered by his presumptions, the woman turned her weapon on Reiko, and something unnerving illuminated behind her eyes. But Reiko didn't move.

"Reiko, get down from there," said Pouki. "I know who her mistress is, and it's not worth it."

Reiko couldn't trust his ears. "Worth getting stabbed over? That's Arriette, Pouki! I'd give my life for her any day." He turned to the Enzoian women. "You don't appreciate the level of trouble you're in, lady."

Pouki warned him again, louder this time. "Reiko, *move away.* I can tell you everything, but this is too dangerous."

Reiko flinched slightly at the tone, but didn't turn to meet his friend's gaze. "What exactly *are* your orders?" he continued. "Put down the blade and come with us; there's no way out for you now, but you don't have to die. We can talk about this."

"I can't negotiate; there's no time," she spat.

Pouki bellowed, startling Reiko enough to cause him to move back to the top step of the podium. As he did so, the woman also dropped her guard, easing the blade to waist height.

"*Please* don't do this to her," Baby A pleaded with the woman, realising Pouki would not make any progress protecting Reiko. They were all too upset to take any orders. "Take *me* to your mistress instead. *I'll* talk to her."

Without warning, the woman spun on her bony heels and plunged the blade in. The incision was perfect, and as she inserted it, smoke rose from the glass. It carved its way toward Arriette's heart. Gasps and cries echoed through the streets, bouncing from building to building, and the volume was enough to force Reiko into action. He lunged and grabbed the woman from behind, then lifted her from the ground and flung her backward, away from Arriette's coffin, down the stairs.

Baby A shot toward Arriette and removed the blade, careful not to touch it, fearful of being burned. She held it at arm's length with the tip down and away from her, not trusting its seemingly intense power.

The woman hissed as she tumbled clumsily down the stairs from the podium.

"Idiots!" she cried.

"*Shut. Up.*" Reiko managed through a snarl. He dragged her up by her robes and led her across the meadow against her will, grazing her knees and elbows. "Interrogation room. Now!"

"She won't go easy, Reiko," said Pouki, running to catch up with them. "Her mistress is strong."

"Who the hell is she?"

"I'd have to confirm it," Pouki uttered, struggling to match their eager pace.

Baby handed the knife to him. "Here, Pouki. Perhaps you can use this to pick up Arriette's thoughts?"

"No," he said without trying, but he took hold of the weapon with two fingers, like a pincer. "This dagger is giving off strange vibrations—it's more connected to this woman and her mistress than it is Arriette. It's definitely...

cursed. Or something."

"Or something?" Reiko repeated, scowling.

Since when did their telepathic trainer second guess himself? He took out a clean handkerchief from his robe's inner pocket and wrapped the blade within it. Then, satisfied, he instructed Baby A to take it back to HQ, where it would wait in the lab for Reiko. But Reiko had other plans; he wanted to be the one to question this woman.

Baby A travelled one way with Sebastian and Jet. Reiko and the Enzoian woman in the other.

Pouki stopped between them and chewed his nails. He had a *lot* of work to do.

***

In the same room where the other women had been questioned, Reiko threw the woman so hard that her skull banged against the far wall. He entered after her and slammed the door behind them, taking deep breaths through his nose and out through his mouth to keep from wringing her neck.

"Next time, you won't get back up," he warned.

She rubbed her forehead and checked for blood, all the while cowering at the hunter's display of strength. The Recruit's bald-headed, heavily tattooed potions master was not to be trifled with.

"Please, I'm just an old woman."

Reiko laughed, disgusted with her attempt to beg him for mercy after what she'd done. "Lies! Who is your mistress? The blade is possessed, right?"

"No!" the woman said, straightening her robes. "It's useless now. The enchantment will have worn off."

"Tell me, witch!" Reiko raised a fist.

"I'm not a witch, and I don't need to tell you anything," she said, satisfied she wasn't bleeding. "Your telepath already knows who I work for, even if *I* don't." She sighed, then said, "And I have a name."

"Curses on your goddamned name."

"Rude."

Reiko dragged a wooden chair over to sit opposite her and lean in. "You have no idea, lady. How can you *not* know who you work for?"

"My name, though you don't seem to care, is Rain Irontome," she grumbled.

"Rain? I'm Borderline Psychotic. *Not* pleased to meet you."

She struggled and sat back in a chair, distancing herself from Reiko's narrow eyes and straight but flushed face.

"It surprised me Arriette appointed a human to her Recruit members," she began. "Known to be a weak species and yet... you seem so... capable."

"I didn't want to hurt you, Rain," Reiko interrupted, "but the more you talk, the more I want to twist off your lying little head and volley it."

"Then why don't you?"

"Arriette wouldn't want me to harm an..." he swallowed and crinkled his nose, then cracked his neck "...innocent."

The woman rubbed her skull where it had collided with the wall and rolled her eyes. "Little late for that. I already sold my soul. A long time ago."

"To your mistress?" Reiko quizzed.

"Yes."

"You don't have her name?"

"Unknown."

"You're Enzoian?"

The woman grumbled. "I was. Once. And I appreciate their plight. That's why it had to be *me*. Those poor women, their circumstances are unfortunate, and their history binds them to live in the shadow of their former selves."

Reiko had calmed somewhat, so he sat back and invited the woman to explain. It was the only chance he'd give her and he hoped this was the start of a long story, despite the brute force he'd used so far.

"Go on," he prompted, meeting her gaze, "because you're not leaving this room until I'm satisfied *I* know everything *you* know."

Rain groaned and shifted uncomfortably. "Why don't you just ask the telepath?"

"Oh, I will. But I want to determine all this from you first so I can see how many lies you tell me." Reiko cracked his knuckles then, which startled her enough to get her talking.

"An unnamed queen—so powerful that she possessed over half of Haeylo and dominated its people many, many years before Arriette Monroe—once attacked Enzo. Her reign never stretched as far as Haeylo's city, thankfully, probably because of all the first-class everlasts living there, but her taxes were high and humans starved because they couldn't afford to feed themselves or clothe their families. She came from the sea, where monsters are said to swim in the Depths."

"Monsters?"

"Yes, like water dragons. But they are not what you should fear. They called her the *first* everlast, an *unknown*, because she never declared who she was, her abilities, or where she originally came from. Nobody dared challenge her. It was a living nightmare, and she wanted Enzo because of the richness of the land. Your previous leader, Casper, knew of her... from his past... though their last encounter was brief and indirect. He left her alive and deemed her no longer a threat."

"A mistake?"

She rolled her eyes. "The Recruit forced her to pull back her reign and release certain territories in exchange for leaving her be, to live out her days at the Edge. Her rage is said to have transformed a stretch of land called the Fishtail into the *Barren* Fishtail, as she sucked the life from everything around her."

Reiko sympathised with this history. He experienced what it was like to be dominated by someone you so strongly disagreed with back in the tribe.

"The Enzoian women were still constantly fearful of what she might do next. And rightly so. Because she came back across the sea."

"Even after the Recruit's involvement?"

She groaned as she rubbed her head again. "Ah, they had moved on by then. The queen's daughter fell pregnant with a knight of her army and they ran away together, afraid of her mother's reaction and the identical sister princess's revolt."

Reiko narrowed his eyes at that. It sounded so familiar. "This queen had *twin* girls?"

"Probably still does unless she's also displeased her mother," Rain spat and dragged an imaginary knife across her throat. "They were everlasts, too."

Insinuation understood.

"Brutally, they were tracked down and the knight was murdered for betrayal. The daughter fled and built a life of her own. For a while, she stayed here in Enzo, or so the history books would have you trust, further angering the queen's ill-intent towards these poor humans, so the princess left and settled elsewhere, never to be seen again."

Though the story did tug on a distant memory, perhaps from a story he'd been told as a child, Reiko said, "I have never heard of this unnamed tyrant of a queen, nor any princesses of Haeylo... besides Arriette and she's new. Sort of."

Rain added, "You're forgetting how large our planet is, Reiko Port. Just because *you* have never seen this queen does not mean she does not exist. There are many kings and queens across Haeylo. Our known land is small compared to all we haven't ventured to find."

She paused and awaited Reiko's reaction, but none came, so she continued.

"Angered by her daughter's betrayal, the queen ravaged Enzo until much of it died at her hands. She believed *they* were harbouring the princess. Enzoian men would travel up the mountainside to the temple to pray. But also to re-lay the measures in place to protect their village from a beast bellowing within. A beast created by Zïnnyi. They created paintings and signs from their answered prayers, and made adjustments to the entrance to the mouth of the cave."

"The beast Arriette slayed to access Pandora's box," Reiko reminded her. "A dragon."

Rain chewed her lower lip. "Well, it was during their time away for this process that the queen attacked Enzo. The women refused to help her and denied knowledge of the princess's whereabouts—which was likely true. The queen didn't believe them, so she placed a hideous curse on the village, forcing the women to live as monsters; a mutant force of evil designed to act when the queen could not, to wipe out threats. A force unaffected by weapons or magic, and one that terrified the men of the village, forced to relocate almost permanently to the temple."

"They took the form of the living dead," Reiko asked, then quickly added, "because of the fog?"

"Zombies. Undead. Whatever you want to name them. Her rulecast releases a potion to reach as many as possible, and the curse within each woman does the rest. Like a trigger. When the two are combined, there can be no stopping them. It *must* run its course."

"So those without the curse, or who had not inhaled the fog, they would be unaffected? Is that why you've survived so long? You're exempt somehow."

Rain nodded frantically as she said, "It is terrifying for it to happen around you, and for there to be nothing you can do. The men choose only to return to the village for the continuation of the Enzoian people. You and I, we, might feel the effects of the potion—itchy and sore boils, headaches, that sort of thing, but we are not cursed. The other women will feel as the queen once did, and hate as she still does."

"Could there have been another woman hiding from the fog who did not turn into a zombie?"

"Potentially," is all Rain offered.

Reiko's fingers entwined as he leant forward on his knees, listening intently to Rain's story. A story, he understood, to be filled with lies and manipulation, but that intrigued him. Why would she lie to him now, cornered in a small interrogation room with nowhere to run and no escape plan?

"You are not Enzoian."

Rain's face remained emotionless, as it had throughout. This history was a practised retelling, maybe something she had recited to others in the past; not yet shared as a personal memory.

"My family was lucky. We were not present in the village when the curse fell, and so the Irontome line remains pure, though we feel the potion's sharp sting if it is released. We live in the forest, away from the wolves' patrols. The women never turn on us; we seem to have an immunity, do not die young like the others, and do not turn into monsters. And we are *not* controlled by the queen's rulecast."

"Then what do *you* have against Arriette Monroe, Rain? Why do what you did? Surely, you'd want revenge on this awful queen, and not on people trying to help this planet heal, or people who'd gladly have helped you rid this world of her influence, had you only asked nicely? Why not simply take your family and go?"

"Because there *is* a way to break their curse."

Reiko noticed a glint in the corner of one eye. Not quite a tear, but the closest to a human reaction she'd shown so far.

"I could not pass on such an opportunity."

"It involves destroying the threat to the queen; whatever makes the rulecast release the fog?"

Reiko assumed the Recruit building their brand new HQ on the queen's turf had prompted this response. A major overreaction, in his opinion. The Recruit were not there to harm or intimidate anyone, only to save and protect those in need, and to keep Pandora's box secure. The queen's rulecast, whoever they were, had deemed Arriette's leadership in this location potentially life-threatening to the queen (if Arriette had found out about her tyranny, it might have been!).

"A wiccan within the queen's court foretold there would be a woman—dangerous and powerful, more so than the queen," Rain said. "Her arrival was unknown, nor her form or her age or her intent. But the queen vowed to lift this village's curse if one of us—*any of us*—brought her the heart of the soul she feared most. Her undoing."

Reiko rubbed his face with his calloused hunter hands and groaned. "*Arriette's* heart, I take it? She will simply take the heart and leave you all to suffer, I guarantee."

Rain's face flushed. "I have to try! The women of Enzo are plagued but have not been forced to turn into those zombie-like creatures for many years until now. Arriette's presence here, and her capture of Pandora's box, it *started* something the rulecast did not want the queen to face."

"Her own death, probably, or his."

"Without that living, dormant dragon, Enzo has no defences against the queen if she returns." She slumped her shoulders.

"That symbol you formed is her crest?"

With shaking hands, Rain re-formed the symbol slowly and carefully to allow Reiko to study it. Her thumbs and forefingers touched and formed a triangular-looking teardrop. Her middle and ring fingers crossed its centre behind, splitting the circle into an eye with a triangular tip. Then her pinky fingers stuck up in the air like towers or, as Reiko would soon realise, the tips of a crown.

"I pledged allegiance to the queen in hope of freeing my people from her curse. I used her symbol out there not to bow down, but to show her I'm trying. If there is no curse, there can be no reaction to the rulecast's potion."

She paused and inhaled deeply before she said, "Arriette is dead now. It will cost you nothing to allow me to take her heart and take her head to the queen."

He gasped. "You want her head too?"

"Only to prove the heart is hers!" she blurted. "I *am* sorry for the show I put on, but I needed you to see this was important. And I needed *her* to sense my loyalty, even if it is... forced. If she did not know of my existence, she will now."

Reiko scratched his chin and sat back. "So what *are* you?" Rain lowered her eyes, and Reiko chortled. "Come on, lady, those flaming petals didn't touch you. Are you a wiccan?"

"No," she said flatly. "I'm like you. Human. But as being wiccan is a learned power, I studied enough to make my point. I wanted you to let me take it. I didn't want to have to hurt anyone." She paused. "A façade, smoke and glitter. Nothing more."

"I see."

She struggled for the first time against her restraints. "Please. You can help me. Make the queen see my people no longer need to suffer. Remove Arriette's heart and form the symbol. She will see it."

"Not in our lair she won't, sorry. It's protected."

Reiko leaned back and hammered a fist on the door. A wolf of the Tri clan in his human form entered. Reiko scribbled a quick note and slipped him the sheet of parchment.

"Take this to Sebastian Sky," he said.

The wolf nodded once before exiting. He took it straight to Sebastian, who ran to confirm Rain's story in the library. If the queen dominated Haeylo, even if it was on the other side of the world, the Recruit would have crossed paths with her, and Reiko's vague memory of a very similar tale would be revealed. There had to be some kind of documentation, even if only in one of Casper's old journals. And he'd make Rain sit here until every book has been studied cover-to-cover if necessary.

Casper wouldn't omit to give his people a warning regarding her nature, either. Where this queen was now baffled Reiko; if they had battled her before, she could be in hiding or dominating a far-off location to bide her time. Being pushed back by the Recruit had to sting her ego, meaning she lived somewhere beyond the Barren Fishtail land bridge. Or, he feared, she may reside in the Petrified Forest, where they suspected the rogue demons and vampires had fled. But perhaps the Enzoian curse would be lifted naturally if they killed her, or if they took out the rulecast, at least she'd be without her potions master.

Reiko sat with Rain for two hours until the wolf returned and let himself in. He nodded once to Reiko to show she was telling the truth, but then gestured Reiko should follow him out.

But first, he passed the parchment back. Reiko saw there was a new line added, but rather than in Sebastian's handwriting, it was in Pouki's.

One line read: *Ze Entit Sehde Eyeh.*

Impatient, Rain groaned and tugged her restraints. "You have telepaths here. I saw them. You should have them read my mind if you don't believe my story. It is documented in the scrolls at the temple. Read them for yourself!"

He re-read Pouki's note and chewed his lip. The All Seeing Eye. Arriette's grandmother and Casper's ex-wife, Christine Kaines. *She* was the unnamed queen? The unknown power they all feared? So he had heard the story before… from Arriette and her mother.

He said, "It's OK. I believe you."

Rain visibly relaxed, but her scowl remained. "Will you help me lift this curse?"

"Not yet," Reiko said. He paused at the doorway as he asked, "Why do your people not speak? Why didn't they just tell us all this when we interviewed them?"

"It's the curse," she told him, "to prevent anyone from doing exactly as I am now. When the event is over, their bodies heal so they can continue until the rulecast identifies an additional threat. They've built an army."

"The queen is unaware of your family's exemption, then. She thinks you're like the others."

Rain nodded frantically. "She *must* be, or I would be dead. If your lair is protected, she is still ignorant. And if I die, their chance of breaking the curse will perish also because they can't tell anyone else. All these years, I have waited to commit a crime that goes against *everything* Zïnnyi teaches. I've studied Harriet Foley's work to protect myself through sorcery. Honestly, I never wanted to hunt anybody. And doing what must be done—to take Arriette's heart—will cause her no pain, and nobody else any harm either."

"Not physically," Reiko uttered. But, satisfied she was telling the truth, and an innocent sent by Zïnnyi, he promised, "The Recruit will do all we can to help you, Rain, but Arriette's beating heart is not the solution."

When Reiko had closed the door, Rain writhed and screamed, then stopped abruptly.

She narrowed her eyes. "You said *beating*?"

SIXTEEN

Now Reiko had a past to trace, and a bloodline to track to find out why Christine Kaines wanted Arriette's heart so badly. Guarded, Rain waited in the interrogation room while Reiko followed Baby A and Pouki to her coffin, because he had to hear this direct from Pouki.

Ze Entit Zehde Eyeh. Really? Arriette's flesh and blood, her biological grandmother from Earth; how and why would she hate Arriette so strongly?

"Why would Rain not have the queen's name? Ze Entit Sehde Eyeh is a legend. You and Casper battled her in the past! I feel like such a fool," Reiko told Pouki when he arrived at the library.

The wolf excused himself, leaving Reiko with Sebastian Sky and Pouki, who were both eager to explain themselves.

"I told Rain I had never read of such a queen, but there was something familiar about her daughter's circumstances. She's talking about Ma, isn't she?"

"Yes but you hadn't heard of her in this context," said Pouki. "The Recruit faced her years ago, though we did not know who she was. She and Casper never laid eyes on one another. They've changed their appearances since Earth anyway. Casper had to, but the queen wore a mask. That rulecast is a figurehead that acts on her behalf."

173

"Rain called her an unnamed queen."

Pouki nodded. "To them, that's true."

"The queen wants Arriette's heart," he whispered, as though others outside the library's walls had ears. "If she's already dead, the curse will lift. Would Arriette mind?"

Sebastian seemed to stop breathing for a moment. "Of course... she would... mind!" he spluttered.

Pouki hushed him. "We'd need to be sure of her motivations. Arriette would want the best for Haeylo, but before can decide, Baby A has asked us to visit the podium and bring Rain. I think she wants to see what that woman will try next, if anything."

Rain, still restrained, accompanied Reiko, Sebastian, and Pouki to the podium where Baby A awaited. Despite the guards surrounding the coffin, Rain was anxious to get her shaking, bony hands on Arriette's heart and Reiko wasn't convinced she didn't still want to break free and use wiccan knowledge to try again. If the Enzoian trusted his word to help Enzo, though, perhaps she'd let the Recruit do as promised and help instead.

"I'm sorry, Rain, but I cannot allow you to take Arriette's heart," said Baby A when they reached the top step. She had her hand above the slot in the glass where Rain's blade had pierced the coffin.

"Reiko has promised to assist me in any way possible."

"And we will." Baby A asked, "Why was your family not in the village that day?"

Rain shrugged. "Perhaps the creator took pity; an opportunity to seek council and find sanctuary. I assumed it was my duty to free these people—it is, though not directly."

"I sincerely hope so," Reiko said. "And you were

right. Our telepath knew the queen's identity. She goes by *The All Seeing Eye,*" Reiko finished.

This shocked Rain. "The triangular symbol I formed. It's an eye?"

"Yes, beneath a crown, and the Recruit has crossed her before."

"We have not seen her in years," Rain told her, "but she must live as we are still cursed."

Reiko paced the length of Arriette's glass coffin, allowing Rain to be restrained but unmarked by a guard. He trusted her enough now not to attempt anything stupid or to run away.

"There is documentation in our library of the queen. Her real name is Christine Kaines," he told Rain. "And she's Arriette's biological grandmother."

Rain scowled, puzzled, and frantically shook her head. "How can that be? She's thousands of years old and Arriette is—"

"Christine was a wiccan on Earth, and with the help of her third daughter, Harriet, they cursed the family to allow them a promised passage to Haeylo. They were technically the first everlasts," Pouki said.

Rain was mute, stunned.

"Until we see this unnamed queen, we cannot be one hundred percent certain, but we are convinced she and Ze Entit Sehde Eyeh are the same, and that the Recruit did not quite silence her after all."

Baby A asked Rain if she was the woman who had approached Arriette and Susan last year. She had warned them not to take the dragon's path and tried saving their lives. "Why not tell them everything then, Rain?"

"For that vampyr to deem me crazy and suck me dry?" Rain gulped and took a step back. "She tried to mask her true nature with a hood, but living with monsters all my life, it is difficult to hide anything from me."

Satisfied, Baby A told Rain, "We are going to let your people go home. Now the queen believes Arriette to be dead, it is unlikely her rulecast will send a second wave."

"We have all we need from them. Tissue samples for the laboratory for The Chronicles of Pandora, statements however brief because of their lack of speech, and notes on their behaviour," Pouki added. "All given voluntarily, I should add."

Rain shuffled closer to Reiko. "Your other friends will not approve of me, and they will *not* trust me."

"No, but we do," Baby A said. "They are all rational people, and they desperately want to find out how Arriette wound up like this. If you can explain, they will understand, and our organisation can offer you all the compassion you deserve."

"Even after what I did?"

"*Because* of what you did," Reiko said.

Pouki offered Rain a seat beside Arriette's coffin, up by her head, and she took it, still bound at the wrists behind her back.

"The queen wants revenge on her bloodline?"

"I cannot say," Rain answered him. "If she truly is Christine Kaines and a direct relative of Arriette's, I would agree there is sense to the speculation."

Baby A heaved a sigh. "We will have to bring Tobias and Ma in on this."

Pouki picked some imaginary fluff out of his beard, catching Sebastian's concerned gaze, and said, "He's managing better than I was."

"If you still want to help, Rain, there is plenty more to be researched in the library," said Baby A.

Before she could answer, Reiko used a pocketknife to cut the ropes restraining her. "We can have an angel heal the friction burns and will return your dagger."

"Reiko, you and I will return to the lab to look at the tissue samples of the women. Maybe something in their biology will answer some questions? Magic, especially a curse, leaves a mark, so hopefully we can find the scars the queen and her rulecast forgot to erase from their DNA."

Sebastian promised he and the wolves would work to get the Enzoian women up to speed and home safely. This seemed to further relax Rain enough for her to stand and examine the coffin herself.

"We will have to get somebody to make the trip to the temple and ask some questions of the men," Pouki said. "They might remember the queen's reign, or may have other stories that could help us find Ze Entit Sehde Eyeh's current territory."

"Your leader does not look dead, does she?" Rain said suddenly through observation, causing Sebastian's attention to shift and his posture to freeze.

"*What* did you say?"

"Forgive me," Rain said quickly and turned her back, raising both hands to show she didn't possess another blade, and had spoken out of turn. "After what I did, it is not my place to—"

"No, please," Baby A prompted. "What were you going to say?"

"Well, she's still so... beautiful," Rain finished. "I have never seen a body preserve quite this well, even during mourning. Her wings are still bright and beautiful. And I have seen my fair share of... death. Is that, Reiko, why you told me her heart was still beating?"

Sebastian turned his gaze upon Pouki and Baby A. They were now all scrutinising the feathers on Arriette's wings, which were still silky and white and appeared freshly groomed. Baby A had already checked the seals around the edges to confirm nobody had forcefully tampered with her. Only the thin slice made by Rain's blade had exposed her to the lair's elements.

Reiko blushed and lowered his head. "I… forgot. Speaking of Arriette in the past tense is still difficult."

"I think we need to get this open," said Pouki. "Rain is not the first to observe this phenomenon."

"Agreed," said Baby A.

Sebastian exhaled with relief. "*Finally*," he uttered and patted his canteen.

Pouki sent his friends away to put their current plan in motion. He didn't believe in his heart that there was any chance of waking Arriette as Sebastian so strongly hoped, but he knew they would have to try for the good of Haeylo, even if it meant pointlessly disturbing Arriette's peace.

If Christine Kaines wanted revenge on her line, the Recruit needed to put whatever they could in place to protect Ma and Arriette's child from a future attack.

Once again, they would have to prepare for a battle they hadn't started. But it was one that, even without Arriette by their side, they had to win.

SEVENTEEN

Tabitha Hope ploughed up the path to the temple to the wishing well where it forked, offering words of encouragement to Joy Johnas despite them both being out of breath and struggling. They remembered the first time they had ascended with Arriette last year to fight the dragon and secure Pandora's box. Tabitha had almost fallen to her death, and Joy broke her wrist during the battle. Even with the memory and experience, they were tired and aching from the hike.

Haeylo was in bloom, but since Arriette's death it appeared disappointed and darker than usual; the way the flowers wilted slightly, the leaves were prematurely brown and the grass less luscious.

The planet was grieving.

"The path forks ahead. We should take the right road. The left goes to the ruins of the cave that we raided with Arriette," said Joy.

Tabitha agreed, "I don't need reminding. Did you hear about the outcome of the scavenger hunt for the dragon's remains? Reiko's team found some excellent ingredients."

"Ingredients for what?" Joy asked, scowling.

She shrugged. "Some kind of medication."

Part of Reiko's job as a potion master included extending the lives of the Recruit, but he hadn't got round to it yet with the clean-up effort, the build of their new HQ, and now the Enzoian crisis. But when Arriette discovered she was to become an everlast through the finding of her pendant in the Indalo store, she offered her friends a means to remain by her side for as long as they wanted. Joy would not need such measures being a third-class everlast, but Tobias and the others would age naturally, leaving Arriette without them in the future. A future she couldn't accept. On some level, she told herself it was to help them continue their jobs as Recruit members to ensure all their hard work was paying off, just like Pouki's ritual should help her pregnancy. But Tobias had warned her that life must take its course, and they hoped by getting married, despite her age, their union would void her everlasting life anyway, but leave her with the other benefits of owning an everlast pendant such as communication and protection.

Until that happened, Reiko was their plan B.

Now, at the mention of the dragon's carcass, Joy and Tabitha wondered if Reiko had already discovered how to make them all temporary everlasts and which of the allocated powers would agree to take such a medication.

"Don't you think it's about time we... gave up?" Joy asked.

Tabitha gasped, exercising her disgust at the statement, but internally she had questioned why their creator seemed to fight them at every opportunity. No matter the good they did, there was always more of the box's damage to clear and the potential for it to escape again.

"Don't say that aloud," Tabitha warned her.

They arrived at the top of the cliff and gazed at the arch, welcoming the Enzoian monks into their place of worship. There, they prayed to Zinnyi and hid from their female counterparts in the village below. They walked through the right-hand tunnel and eventually arrived in the temple's marble halls and gorgeously painted walls, pillars, and ceilings. Curious about their presence, a monk dressed in his traditional brown robes approached, bowed, and asked how he could assist.

"We're here to ask you about the curse," Joy said, "and to ask about your burial procedures as we have some terrible news."

"Oh," replied the monk, biting his lower lip, "then you should follow me." He handed each of them robes of their own to hide their more fashionable attire, and they complied so as not to draw too much attention to themselves. They pulled the hoods up and scurried after the monk.

"Please sit," he said, gesturing at a bench in one of the emptier halls.

"We want to ask about your women," Tabitha said, "because, as I'm sure you've heard by now, our leader died and we believe it's linked to the queen who cursed you. Our headquarters was attacked by the women of your village and though we did not fight back, some of them died. We'd be grateful for any information you can give us; our intention is to find this queen and stop her."

The monk inhaled deeply. "I cannot give you a year, nor a name of this queen, but I know of this curse. It was before my time, several generations ago. And there are some things even we cannot disclose—the curse prevents it. I'm… sorry you were targetted."

"We already have her name. *The All Seeing Eye*," Joy reassured him. The monk nodded, recognising it. "But there's a survivor of your curse. Rain Irontome. She claims there is a process to reverse it if we can satisfy the queen's need for revenge."

"That I cannot confirm, but I am surprised Rain is still living if this is true."

Joy scowled. "Why?"

"This queen possessed mysterious, unknown powers. She could read everyone and everything, control the seasons, the elements, and be one step ahead. She was a wicked witch. A truly *evil* queen," the monk explained. "Our women feared what she might do to us and sent us to live up here to pray for Zïnnyi's mercy. So far, he has not granted us a solution."

Joy sighed as she said, "I think your solution died with our leader."

Tabitha placed a hand on her friend's shoulder, then leaned forward. "You didn't leave the women out of choice, then?"

"They banished us here for safety," the monk said, "but we return when we have to. You should not seek this queen. If Arriette is dead, then the threat to your people has died with her. I would advise you simply... let it be."

"No," said Tabitha, firmly. "There's a way to defeat her, and *you* believe it, too, or you wouldn't pray for it every day."

"How can I disclose anything when the queen sees all? Ze Entit Sehde Eyeh was here at the beginning of Haeylo and she will be here at the end. This is fact, and our women will *never* be free from their monstrous curse."

Tabitha and Joy looked at one another suspiciously, sharing similar thoughts. They had known only one other wiccan woman to be born on Earth and transported to Haeylo because of her powers, but she had a single weakness. Harriet Foley had suffered the kiss of her true love. Her father, Casper. And besides Arriette's mother, the queen also had another daughter. Could it solve how to destroy her? Surely the love of her life was Casper, and Arriette had killed him.

Joy lowered her voice as she asked the monk, "Do you love your women?"

"Of course."

"Then *help* them. Tell us where to locate this queen."

"You don't need to," he replied. "She'll find you in time, especially if she learns Arriette Monroe has Pandora's box. It would be extremely foolish to attempt an attack in her territory, where she is strongest and most prepared. Draw her to you, and if you must, battle her in Enzo."

"So we'll wait for her to arrive on our doorstep and deal with her then? That would put Enzo at risk."

"That would be my advice." He hesitated but decided if the queen knew all, it was already too late. He sighed. "On Earth, before she became 'Ze Entit Sehde Eyeh' if that's what we are to call her, it is said that her husband betrayed her trust, and so as he dreamed of God and of agreeing to a new world, she dreamed of revenge on the woman who convinced him to do so."

"The creation of Haeylo was a marvellous thing," Tabitha said, but the monk shook his head.

"She saw his affair as a betrayal; an opportunity to leave her and their children behind to start a new life."

Tabitha gasped. "Andrew Kaines had an affair?"

"How do *you* know all this?" Joy asked him.

"Stories passed through the generations. That's all they are, though. Rumours."

"Or myths," said Joy.

"Perhaps, but they are all I can offer. The thought of

never seeing him again drove his wife insane. She wanted a chance to face him, and so she and her daughters followed him here. But on arrival, their village suffered. Desperate to grasp hold of hope, she elected herself to lead them. The village became a town, which became a city, and then a kingdom. But still without him, madness gripped her, and drove her to dominate and then destroy everything in her path to narrow down his location.

One of her daughters, against her mother's wishes, ran to create a life of her own away from royalty. The queen stopped her. But there were rumours the daughter escaped and gave birth to a daughter of her own, and that their bloodline continues."

Tabitha logged this version of the story in her retaining memory, and to add it to Arriette's grimoire when they returned to HQ so she could compare it to whatever they had discovered during the interviews.

The monk continued. "Overpowered by her mother, the daughter who managed to escape has not resurfaced. It is likely she lives as she too holds their gift of everlasting life in a way. But, she has done nothing to interrupt her mother's plans."

Joy and Tabitha stood. "Before we go, we must ask you where the escaped princess lived before she disappeared to give birth."

"Enzo originally, and then Drakonta, but there is nothing to document a residency."

Tabitha smiled and lowered her hood. "We can show ourselves out."

"Before you go," the monk said. "I must ask that you burn the bodies of our women. We would rather not know their identities."

"You don't want your friends to know if their loved

ones are gone?"

"It is better to be ignorant."

The monk bowed, then left them alone to their thoughts. So they walked back along the path between the temple and the Enzoian village in silence, aghast at the story they'd heard.

As Tabitha and Joy were travelling back to HQ, thankfully only having to walk downhill, the rest of Arriette's friends were busy trying to find out what exactly had killed her, and hopes were finally high since she'd stopped breathing. Hardback books and dust surrounded Susan, Dion and Rain in the library, and surprisingly, it had taken little for Rain to agree to share a room with them. Her neighbours were unpredictable monsters; two domesticated vampyrs couldn't scare her.

Several months back, Charles and Rihaana had already agreed to move some of the less important scrolls from the library in Haeylo City to HQ to fill their shelves, and they planned to flick through those next in search of stories about *Ze Entit Sehde Eye*.

"Found anything?" asked Susan, joining Dion by one of Harriet's older scrolls regards wiccan chants and rituals.

"I found the spell she used to give herself everlasting life, but it's less of a spell an' more a form of personal torture. It should be destroyed."

"Have Tabitha document that when she arrives back," Susan said, tapping her head, and Dion agreed it was a good idea to log that one for Arriette's grimoire, too. "We may need it."

"There's no other way to break the spell, though," Dion said. "Just a kiss, an' it's unlikely Christine would use such a mediocre antidote."

Rain bit her nails, frustrated that she had found

nothing of use in any of the twenty bound books she'd scoured.

"As the others are not here, can I ask you something?" Rain began, shoving another aside.

Susan pointed at herself, and Rain raised her brow. This question was directed at her.

"Why do you want to become human again? That's what the potion was for, right?"

"How do ya know 'bout the potion?" Dion asked.

"I listen. I observe," said Rain.

Susan cringed and softened her voice. "No wonder you've survived so long."

This building had ears. It seemed there was no such thing as a private discussion anymore.

"I was never meant to be... this," she admitted, pointing to her protruding fangs.

"Is Reiko's synthetic blood helping?" Dion asked.

"A little, and I like the taste; it's saltier than animal blood. Even Arriette said it was enticing."

"But less so than human blood?" Rain asked.

Dion exhaled and turned to Rain. "She and I are different creatures entirely."

Susan rolled her eyes. "She never blamed you."

Dion startled. "Who?"

"Arriette loved you as a vampyr, and if *you* went ahead with any kind of transformation, she would have loved you all the same."

Dion paused and slammed another useless book down, sending up a puff of dust. She grabbed a scroll that has been squashed beneath it.

"*Loved,*" Dion murmured. *Past tense.*

"Look at *me*. After everything *I* did to her, she still accepted and welcomed me to the Recruit."

Rain remained silent, but flicked through a few pages of a script written by Harriet a few months before her death. The paper was still thick and crisp beneath her fingers, torn from a diary or journal of some kind. She interrupted their conversation by pointing at the title of the script, and handed it to Dion, fascinated by her red locks and now intrigued with luminous eyes.

"I was beginnin' to think we'd be 'ere all day," she said, smiling. "Well done!"

The script was a last entry, written before Harriet passed away. Perhaps she sensed her time on Haeylo was about to end, or perhaps she'd had a moment of guilt, and a need to spill it across the page. Either way, it was a lucky find, and they would report it as such to Baby A and Reiko.

The text was in beautiful handwriting, and each letter 'I' was dotted with a sweet little heart—definitely Harriet's work. Even her penmanship was gorgeous. Dion unravelled the paper and flattened it on the desk, placing two paperweights at either end to hold the scroll open.

Susan's eyes were furious as she scanned over it. Dion placed a comforting hand on her shoulder.

"How could Casper not have mentioned this to you, or to Arriette?" asked Susan. "I am glad he and I were never properly acquainted."

"They were his family," Dion reminded her. "Even knowin', I don't think we could 'ave prevented this. Zïnnyi has a plan and we must trust it as Arriette did," Dion comforted.

Rain frowned, confused by the discussion taking place by the vampyrs towering above her. She stood to meet their gaze bravely and asked them in a polite tone to fill her in.

"Sorry," said Susan, "but this came as a shock. Read the script... if you wish."

"I... I cannot."

"Ya can't read? Alright. I'll read aloud, then."

Susan narrowed her eyes, but Dion dismissed her attitude as a reaction to the emotional strain they were both under. If she proposed to add future value to the Recruit and perhaps seek sanctuary with them, reading and writing needed to be a skill she possessed.

"It's basic," Dion told her, "an' it may mean more to us as members of the Recruit than you. Harriet speaks of our leader, who passed away upon Arriette's reign. For one leader to take over, another has to kill 'em. Harriet loved Casper, which unfortunately caused her death. Casper was distraught when he murdered her, but protecting Arriette was always his priority."

"He killed his own daughter unknowingly?"

"If he hadn't, I think Harriet would 'ave eventually attacked her. Casper wanted to prove his loyalty to the next leader, too."

Susan took over. "Over a family dispute, Harriet's mother cast her aside. Harriet wanted to learn to use her wiccan skills as she found some of her mother's old books, but her mother wanted it to remain a secret from Andrew. But not Harriet. In her writing, she names him as her father, and later says she wishes she had not left her mother and sisters alone when they reached Haeylo. It's like conscious writing," Susan observes, "as if she wanted everything out of her head suddenly. But, it's nothing we didn't already know, I'm afraid. It does, however, confirm Christine was a practising wiccan on Earth, and so there could be no end to her knowledge and power. Wiccans are low on the HPS, but Christine Kaines is beyond it now."

Rain scowled. "So Harriet walked away from an entire *kingdom*? And her family? She was beautiful and rich and she threw it away because she wished to join the Recruit?"

"Seems so," Dion said.

"Technically, she was also royal," added Susan. "My guess? Harriet craved a kingdom of her own. And she found one; she ruled in Casper's place for years."

Dion sighed and sat back down. "Until Arriette."

EIGHTEEN

Standing opposite Jet Carter's constant frowns of disapproval, Sebastian Sky continued to talk about the possibility that Arriette could still be alive, and he pondered an efficient way to transport her and the coffin off the podium and somewhere safer. Baby A and Pouki had agreed to examine her wings once they did so, but away from the public eye. They'd decided on HQ's top floor.

The coffin's weight distracted Sebastian from Jet's straining, complaining about the height of the podium. When Jet's invisibility flickered whenever the lair's artificial breeze swept across the square, it gave his emotions away, and again whenever Jet's eyes lingered for too long on Arriette's peaceful expression. He flicked his fingers frantically to hide tremors and returned quickly to the task at hand.

Sebastian paused. "Jet, is everything alright?"

The coffin's base was awkward but Jet hung on. "Seems such a waste. Arriette would have wanted people to move on."

There was no point brooding over what they had no power to change or control. But his gut feeling had never let him down, and he'd learnt from the best how it was always wise to follow your intuition.

"I miss her too," Sebastian admitted, sniffling, then

grabbing his end.

"Sorry for being so hard on you. It's soul-destroying. But we *can* go on without her," he said. "Arriette was our glue; we'll find another to trust in her place. Maybe Tobias until their little girl turns eighteen?"

"No," said Sebastian, "We searched for her for so many years, and Casper dedicated lifetimes to locating Arriette. Zïnnyi is not so cruel."

"A year of love and laughter, though. Worth it." Jet smiled, remembering the adventures they'd shared, and mentally shoving aside the battle for the box Arriette had since locked away. "I think about those times and my chest heaves."

"I do too, and perhaps you're right. Life will get easier," Sebastian said.

"Do you ever wonder where she is now?" Jet asked him. "I've been imagining her as his right-hand man." He groaned, then corrected, "I mean, woman."

"Oh, she'll be up there," Sebastian said confidently. "Her angelic ability ensures a passage, but Zïnnyi loves Arriette like he loved Adam and Eve in the very beginning. She's his favourite—an immediate pass."

"There's a test?"

Sebastian stopped mid-lift of the coffin. Struggling, he said, "Nobody told you?"

Jet winced. "Fill me in and do it quickly."

"Zïnnyi checks when your heart gets weighed that it's lighter than a feather."

Jet shuffled, then decided the coffin was far too heavy for the two of them to move alone. "Ah, that's just an ancient speculation!" In unison, they put the coffin ends down. "What is this thing *made* of?"

"Glass and gold, mostly."

Sebastian practised his sorcery skills once again to aid the transportation of the coffin from the lair to the upper floor of HQ using a spell and his sorcerer's hat.

"The heart and intent is what matters," Sebastian told Jet when he cringed at the sight of its fading purple point. As it was Sebastian's official and chosen wand, he rolled up his sleeves and placed the hat above the slot where Rain's blade had burned through the casing, resting it gently on the glass. He tapped it a few times, testing that sparks would flow freely and not fizzle out in the breeze.

He gazed at Arriette lovingly. "I hope this works, and we don't land on anybody."

But before Sebastian could chant his motion spell, his breath caught in his throat.

"What's the matter?" asked Jet. "Get on with it; it'll be dark soon."

"Did... did you *see* that?"

"See what?"

Sebastian pointed to Arriette's lifeless body and gestured for Jet to hurry to his end. "Her eyes. Watch!"

"Sebastian, this is getting ridiculous. You're seeing things because you want to."

Jet tried to walk away. Sebastian grabbed his sleeve. "No, wait!"

Then Jet saw it, and he startled. "Did you...?"

"I *told* you!" Sebastian cheered, "I *knew* it!"

Jet shook his head in disbelief. "Am I dreaming?"

"We can't *both* be dreaming. We can't move her yet. It's a miracle—she's not dead! NOBODY LISTENS TO ME!"

Jet hushed him. "Don't tempt fate. A flicker of the eyelids confirms nothing; bodies do crazy things in death. Perhaps her soul still lingers, or Pandora's? We never had that final discussion about where *she* went."

Sebastian couldn't hold his excitement in any longer. "She's not dead! She's, she's—"

"*Paralysed?*" Jet mumbled. "But... how?"

Jumping up and down on the podium and causing it to creak, Sebastian urged Jet to get Baby A and Reiko.

"Who cares how? Come on, let's get out of here!"

Jet followed him across the street to Town Hall, where Reiko and Baby A sat in the canteen. Jet barged through the double doors, alarming a wolf sitting at a nearby table, and slumped between his friends, with Sebastian behind him.

He never figured he'd say this.

"*So,* uhm, Sebastian's right. Arriette's alive."

"I TOLD YOU SO!"

NINETEEN

I open my eyes to an emerald haze. There are unfamiliar trees around me, but they're beautiful and giant, and crispy grass beneath my bare feet. I lay in tattered clothes; brown shorts and a white camisole, probably because it's hot here, but I don't remember changing. Haeylo's Manaia Forest isn't usually so close and humid this time of year, though it has always been unpredictable thanks to the box's original damage.

It takes most of my energy to get to my feet. Sweat drips from my skin almost immediately and stains the neckline of my top. I'm trembling from head to toe, and there's a migraine forming and pressure behind my cheekbones, or so it feels. The skin on my feet is sore and tiny slices coat my heel and toes, and one is bent at an angle on the left foot, likely broken as it's swollen. But there's little I can do until I find my way back to HQ, or until my angelic blood fixes it.

I slowly trudge through the moss and foliage surrounding me. I brush branches aside with my aching wrists and hiss as blood is drawn from my open wounds.

Overhead, clouds are forming. It's going to rain. I decide it might be best to find shelter for the evening as the sun descends. And there are *so* many noises surrounding me, it's overwhelming. At first only the rustling of the greenery and singing voices of talented birds, the species a mystery, then occasionally miscellaneous wildlife. But as I walk, there's a roaring and it's getting louder and threatening.

My body is twice as heavy. My muscles go into spasm, my legs twitching before they crumple every so often, and then my heart skips a beat. I can't afford to fall and break a leg right now even with my angelic blood. Before me flashes snippets of my past, but it's a blur, as is my vision, as my eyes fill with stinging tears.

I stop and close them for a second so I can focus. There's a crying man and the wails of a baby; I'm still but I'm in so much pain. My eyes snap open again as I struggle to control my emotions, so I break down in tears, angry with myself for becoming so lost and alone in a forest I should know like the back of my hand. But I'm confused, unsure how I showed up here, or why I'm alone.

Ahead, I spot a clearing, and hear the roaring of a beast I cannot name. Despite my fear, I keep moving forward because it's the only thing I can resolve to do. I might ask somebody how to get home. But in anticipation, I stumble through twigs, which snap between my toes, and hobble down to my knees, hoping to find somebody... *anybody*. Thick mud, ankle-deep, sucks my legs down. I'm sinking further and realising soon I will drown in what appears to be the boggy banking of a stream. Water flows to meet me, cooling my body and lowering my temperature. I welcome it because it's easier to swim here, but I'm not out of trouble yet.

My chest is tight. I reach up my camisole top, one I don't remember changing into, and stretch it, because I can't risk taking it off. I need air so badly, it's all I fixate on. My leaking blood seeps into the material, so I lower my shoulders into the water, forced to throw around my weight to shift my body out of the remaining sludge.

There's a thud, and some kind of creature approaches with only its stone-hard head visible. On initial inspection it's a small dragon without wings, but as it nears, I suddenly realise it's larger and faster than I am, swimming to get me from behind. Birds flap and flee the scene as the water shifts and splashes, and then I'm beneath the surface, fighting for air and choking on my fear. Needles strike and pierce my skin all over, like wicked daggers, and I'm dragged further down and turned over and over until I can't determine which way is up.

I cannot die here. I *won't* die here.

With the last of my willpower, I kick viciously and strike the scaly skin of this demon. There's a grey-green form and frothing bubbles as I swim to the surface, relying on my escaped air to show me the way. It swims far enough away, preparing a second attack, but it gives me just enough room to paddle on my back, keeping foggy eyes on it. Its mouth opens wide to snatch me again, but I've reached the bank with seconds to spare. Hauling myself up, the creature swishes its tail—I'm too high now; it would need to re-calculate its attack, and its long body disappears beneath the murky surface. So I take off running, wet leaves smacking me in the face as I flee limping, ignoring my wounds until I know I'm clear of its hunting ground.

Most of my clothing has been swallowed by the menace and my legs are bleeding, but I'll live. I'll need some clean water and bandages soon to avoid an infection, until my inherited blood can do the rest.

This place doesn't sound or behave like Manaia Forest. Light rain patters on the plant life, and I slow to allow it to drench my face until I can see. I must be elsewhere; a territory far, far away from all that I know. Was I kidnapped, or have I travelled in space rather than time, and if so, for what reason? I'm leaving a sticky trail of crimson behind me, which will attract every animal with a taste for human flesh no doubt, including the one I have just encountered. Vampyrs, too. If my exhaustion, thirst, or hunger don't kill me, then something else will. And soon. But I've lived through much worse than this and I'm not going down without a fight.

I can sense those painful memories again, but I'm unable to draw upon them to decide just how lucky my existence here actually is. Then the roar of that beast grows louder and more distinct, like the rush of a waterfall and the grumble of a dragon's stomach. The only way to get to it is to drop on my hands and knees and crawl, so I slither clumsily out of the woodland and guard my eyes from hundreds of beaming candles as they flicker past me. They hurry. I can barely glimpse their style of transport. And then I comprehend... they *are* the mode of transport.

It's the sweetest miracle I've ever laid my eyes upon, and I gasp, horrified and mystified by these mechanical creatures zooming below me. I drag my body up and crawl across a hard black surface, uncomfortable against my knees and my palms, but to my right is a railing I can grab hold of. I haul myself up and dangle my head from exhaustion over the edge, to gaze down at a swarm of metal animals and their chaotic race in opposite directions.

"This is... *unbelievable*."

Blinking, I clear the dirt from my eyes and wipe my face on my wrist. I'm stunned, and my mouth opens and shuts like a pouting fish before I dare to let go of the bar and view more of this realm from above. But I'm clumsy through the pain, and climbing the railing for a higher view is a task I fumble to achieve. There's an absence from my spine; I can't summon my wings, probably because I'm injured and tired. But it feels like I have a limb missing, which starts instant panic. My feet slip and slide, but eventually, I strain and balance.

"Miss, you should come down from there."

I turn to face a tall, mousy-haired man in jeans and walking boots approaching. His hands are out in surrender and concern crumples his face. He's abandoned his bags further down the path. My attire is inappropriate for his eyes, and so I attempt to cover up my chest and thighs, but because there are rips, it's impossible.

He sees my struggle and takes off a denim blue jacket. "Here, I won't hurt you. Let's talk. You don't have to do this."

I frown, but the jacket is appealing. I reach and snatch it, then tug it over my shoulders.

"Do *what*, exactly?"

He seems to balk at this and back down. I beckon him a few steps closer, which he's grateful for, but only so I can examine his features. I fondly recognise them, but my mind is a blank canvas and I can't recall his name. But he's kind and clearly concerned.

"What's your name?" he asks.

I'm afraid to offer the only information I can still remember. I must look like a crazy person, a lunatic.

"Come on down from there," he says.

"I'm sorry," I manage, "I'm... I'm Arriette."

"Where do you live, Arriette? I can take you home. Get you some help."

"I... I cannot remember."

"*Amnesia*?" He scowls. "Alright, well, my name is Andy. Can you get down off the railing? You're making me nervous."

"But I want to fly," I say, "so I can get a better look at these metal monsters. What do you call them?"

I point to the open skies above the roaring machines and their pretty twinkle lights.

"Fly over the road?"

"To look at this from the *stars*. It must be beautiful."

He shakes his head and offers me his hand, but I'm reluctant to take it.

"These strange animals." I gesture at the unknown creatures hurrying about their business beneath me. "They move so fast!"

"You're on an overpass. Those are cars, and they're dangerous at that speed. Please... come down."

"Cars?"

"This is the new highway. People are on their way home from work. Can't you remember anything about where you're from or the name of a family member? A husband? A child?"

I swallow hard at the word child, hearing crying again. I can only stammer, "I'm from H-Haeylo."

"Are you British? Your accent is... difficult to place."

"I'm *Haeyloian*," I tell him, puzzled and trying to pronounce my home as best I can. "Where on Haeylo is this place?"

"You're in America."

Andrew returns to reach into his bag and pulls out a large piece of paper. He unrolls it and inches toward me. I am paralysed by his beauty; his tanned skin and deep, sorrowful eyes become imprinted in my memory and I search for a match. Nothing yet, but I feel something creeping up as I study his gentle demeanour. That voice is so... homely.

There are names and drawings on the paper, and he carefully hands it to me. These are all names I vaguely understand, in a language I am used to speaking, but it's territory I have never walked.

"This is a map of your surroundings," he says.

"Wait, America? I... I am on... *Earth*."

He nods.

"*You* live here."

"Yes. You don't recognise me, either?"

I force a smile. I do, vaguely, but can't tell him how or why. So I say, "I *think* so."

"I'm on posters. See?" Andrew rummages in his bag for another piece of paper and holds it at arm's length. I squint to read the writing. He's running for something called a president. The document is asking people to stand by him and appoint him the leader.

He'll know the way, then, I tell myself.

"Can you take me home?"

"You remember where that is?"

"No," I say, "but I thought you might if you are the leader of the people."

Andrew shrugs. "I might be tomorrow evening, but until then, I'm just Andy. If you recognise my face, then it's a start; your memory loss can't be permanent." He inches closer again and this time, I don't stop him or flinch away. "What *happened* to you? Are you going to come down, and we'll see if we can find out where you live?"

I wipe the sweat from my forehead and fix my fingers around the railings to lower my body. My bones creak with every awkward step I take. Andy hands me a blanket from his backpack and I wrap myself in it, drying my face and hands on the soft fleece material. I see at the bottom there are food packets and bottles of water, and he offers me one of each.

"I live in Enzo village I... *think*."

"On *Haeylo*? You're injured pretty bad, and you've got a nasty head wound." He reaches to the crown of my hair and strokes, then pulls his hand away, revealing red. "And your legs!"

"A long green dragon tried to eat me."

"Oh, Arriette. That was probably a gator, there's been unusual sightings of them in this area."

In his voice, my name is musical. He whispers each letter to ensure he pronounces it correctly. This man, this *human* man, is magical in a way I have never experienced. Like me, perhaps he defies the HPS. But he obviously doesn't believe I live in Enzo, and if I'm on Earth, that's why. I'm not even sure I believe it myself.

"You look so..." I struggle for words, "so much like *home*."

Andy smiles and walks me along another, quieter roadside to a vehicle of his own. He opens up the car door and slides me in, warning me to mind my head.

"Mind my head?" I ask.

Is this a term for a fast and dangerous mission I should prepare for? Is something exciting about to blow my mind? It doesn't feel dangerous in here though, because the interior is soft. The outer shell has a light dusting of grey and silver sparkles, and it's high and mighty, with four solid wheels and a hole in the top, which Andrew opens immediately to cool us down. He collects his possessions from the path and hops in beside me, slinging it over his shoulder into another seat behind us. He turns a metal stick that jingles against others, and the machine bursts to life.

"Andy is short for Andrew."

He smiles. "Yes."

I grip his arm with force; I leave fingernail indentations in his skin. Andrew glares at me until I meet his thoughtful blue eyes, and he softens, understanding my fear. For me, this is a novel experience.

"I'm glad you didn't jump."

My head becomes flooded with images, sounds, and memories of the people I have known and my life before this strange happening. Before the vehicle can move, I touch his chin, turning those ocean eyes to meet mine again. So familiar.

"Are you OK?" he asks, but he doesn't pull away.

"Fine, A-Andrew..." I mumble, my hands shaking and my past bombarding my skull. Each memory hits me like an arrow.

"Well, *Arriette*," he smiles, "I don't know where you came from or where we're going, but please let me be the first to welcome you to the United States of America. Buckle up."

The journey from my pickup spot is smooth, and I caress the leather seat and squash my nose against the glass, glaring out at what Andrew calls America in awe. How the *hell* did I wind up here, in these clothes, and why can't I produce my wings or start another travel back to Haeylo? My gifts have been stripped, but I'm so blinded by the intense and colourful landscape.

"It's magnificent." I say this aloud without meaning to, but Andrew's lips upturn.

"I must disagree," he says.

Andrew doesn't offer me any further explanation. His eyes are fixated on the road ahead; he's overtaking other large vehicles and swerving between what he explains are lanes until we reach an exit. As we do so, there are two red lights ahead and Andrew hits the brakes.

"This is *incredible*," I gasp, waving at a young couple in the car beside me. They pull an unimpressed face and ignore me, but their eyes brighten when they see who's driving, and they wave back.

Andrew doesn't return the gesture.

"I wouldn't bother waving," he tells me, "because not everyone in America is as friendly as I am."

"*They* are."

He sighs and sets off when the light goes green. "It's a habit I don't want to encourage."

"Oh." I sink slowly into the seat. "So, what year is this?"

"Year?"

"If my memory is hazy, maybe a year will help me recall how I know you. It's returning slowly. At least I know my name and where I came from, right?"

"Right."

"So if I learn as much as I can about this place, then perhaps I'll remember how I arrived here?"

Andrew agrees, accelerating through a more built-up area, residential I think, and pedestrians are running with shopping. Some wear white masks over their mouths, and others wear what looks like a clear screen over their full face, strapped around the top of their heads.

The buildings are higher than those in Haeylo's city and everything is exaggerated with advertisements and enthusiasm. *Buy this! Now!* Every shop window has been designed to be brightly coloured in neon and huge block text. A looming road billboard advertises food and another displays clothing with sexy models and luscious living conditions. But looking out of the window at these houses, many are damaged and run down, and lots of the posters are torn.

"The year is 2139. You're in Washington, D.C." He points at the horizon. "The big white building you see *way* over there, behind the trees... the current president lives there."

"I assumed you were the president?"

"Not yet."

"Is it an important position?"

"Very," he sighs, "and sometimes I feel it's *too* important and not exactly what I need. I have children and if I win this job, then they'll see much less of me. What do *you* do for a living?"

I grumble. Another troublesome question. "I think I do a similar job," I tell him. "And I have a family, too, but I cannot be sure."

"It'll come back, don't worry."

"So 2139 is busy, over-crowded, and the people are not very nice."

Andrew smirks, and I know I've amused him.

"I've seen nothing quite like this. Genuinely." I exhale and fold Andrew's jacket over me as tight as I can manage without it nipping my wounds. The material is warm and comforting, more than the blanket over my knees. "I wish you would believe me."

Andrew pulls the car into a long paved driveway and turns off the ignition. His home is serene. The house itself is a huge cream mansion with rolling acres of green grass and oak trees. Pinned to the fence is a yellow poster with a strange monster printed in black, and beneath it in large red letters reads 'MUTANT FREE ZONE'.

I shudder and draw my eyes to a swing set in the front yard and a young girl playing there. She spots her father and waves. Andrew waves back.

"Is that one of your daughters?"

"That's Eme. Her sister Mya will be inside with her mother."

I smile. "I prefer to be outside, too. Thank you for helping me, Andrew."

"I wouldn't be a very good president if I didn't care about my people, would I?"

Andrew gestures for me to exit the car and I unbuckle my belt, excited to meet others like him, but I take a minute to figure out how to open the door. His speech is so informal and fluid, like rolling waves and gentle breezes. I notice my own is robotic and stubborn as I grapple with his twang. I must sound so alien, so I pretend I have nothing to say.

"Follow me."

I'm bewildered. The front door opens and out steps a beautiful woman of around my age and height. She is blonde, blue-eyed, and perfect in every way. Her lips are tinted like a red rose and her hair shines in the sunlight. She wears a golden headband like a crown or a shining halo, and it reflects the sunset.

"Andrew! Who is this? You look dreadful," she tells me.

I know I do. I bow in respect. "My name is Arriette. Andrew has been most kind to me."

"I found her," he tells his wife, "trying to jump off a bridge on the highway."

I gasp at his presumption. "I was *trying* to fly!"

"Christine," he says, grasping her hand, "I'm going to take Arriette to the hospital, as I think she's suffering from amnesia and she is homeless right now. Can you fix her a bed in the back bedroom for when we return and rustle up something for her to eat? We shouldn't be long. I just want to get her checked over."

"On *our* insurance," she grumbles. "She could be... infected."

I figure I have offended her by intruding on their life, and so I shake Andrew's hand and thank him for everything he did, then set off down the driveway, forgetting I'm still wearing his jacket.

"I can make it on my own from here."

"Arriette, wait! Christine, I can't let her loose. She has no idea where she lives or who she belongs to. She'll get mugged or killed or run over." He lowers his voice. "She didn't even know what a car was and she's got a nasty gator wound."

"She could be a criminal," she whispers. "Or infected with that disgusting mutant flu."

I hear her from the bottom of the driveway, reading her lips and frowning at her assumption, but I understand I'm a stranger, and she doesn't want to risk her children's lives by offering to help someone who can't remember how or why she ended up in this mess.

I walk back toward Andrew and his wife with my hands up. "I will not harm your family or your property. Andrew believes there is something wrong with me. I'd like to prove him wrong, but I also doubt my ability to survive on this planet alone. A green dragon tried to eat my leg." I point at my wound. "I escaped. I can escape anything else thrown my way."

"Did you just say this *planet*?" she asks.

"I come from Haeylo, and I'm sure I have family and friends who miss me, but how and why I travelled to Earth I cannot explain, just as I could not answer Andrew's question regarding my job."

Christine rolls her eyes. "Taking in another stray. This

has got to stop, Andrew. It won't guarantee a win."

"No, but it will keep me human!"

"You're lucky somebody didn't recognise you and try to assassinate you or something. Stop going off on your own to *save the world*."

"Please, if you permit," I interrupt, "I would like to be taken to your hospital. Anything to help clear my head and restore my memories. And you should leave me there, uhm... Andy."

Christine tells Andrew to be careful around me and retreats through her front door. She calls her daughter Eme inside, then slams it. I know she thinks I'm crazy, and perhaps I am.

Andrew steers me to the vehicle, embarrassed.

"I am not offended," I say, taking him by surprise. "I would be worried and threatened, too."

"It's not you, really," he says, reversing. "I'm supposed to travel with a bodyguard, running for this position and everything. It's nonsense. There are people who need help far more than me. I like my freedom and privacy. Plus, I've worked my *entire* life to improve this planet and the people on it, but still they baffle me. I fill these bags three times a week and feed the homeless."

"You were not always in charge?"

"At the moment," he explained, "I'm part of a political party that hopes to change the world for the better, but society hates do-gooders, and Christine fears for my safety. Our motto is '*save the people, save the world*.'"

"So you walk alone and offer to help crazy women?"

Andrew smiles. "I do what I can for those with less. Food and water. I help to build them basic shelters."

I hum. "That's why you could help me."

He nods. "There's a camp about half a mile from

where I found you. I thought you might have strayed. I want to make a difference. Things are getting worse here, Arriette. You're lucky you can't remember anything."

I frown. "You do not believe I am from another world."

"I didn't say that."

"You *implied* it."

"Then I'm sorry," he says. "Christine thinks if I get caught, somebody will take a shot at me. Like an assassination attempt. Having you here will increase that risk and start rumours."

"A shot?"

"Yes," he confirms. "People like to take out leaders they do not agree with with guns and knives."

"I see."

Something in the pit of my stomach flutters, like I've heard this warning before. Oblivious, Andrew speeds through the residential area and we emerge on another main road. In the distance, I see higher buildings with glass windows and mechanical devices flying even higher than their tallest floor.

My breath catches, and Andrew leans forward.

"You've never seen a helicopter before, have you?" I shake my head, and he continues, "We have planes too that carry hundreds of people to other continents."

"The only things that fly where I am from are the angels, shape-shifters and occasionally, hunting vampyrs."

Andrew shakes his head and tries not to laugh, but I see the disbelief. "Technology has improved a lot. I fear it will be the end of us."

"How do you mean?"

"Well," he begins, monitoring the road and a mirror protruding from his window, "our religious leaders have been preaching about a judgement day for centuries now and nobody listens to them. Recently, we've had earthquakes, land shifts, tsunamis, and volcanic eruptions all over the world. In this city, we've had twenty-three earthquakes this *month*. Places that never used to experience such disasters have daily occurrences. These machines you're so fascinated with, Arriette, they're poisoning our air because of the toxic fumes they produce. Computer technology and personal devices run practically *everything* and there are thousands of unemployed because mechanical instruments have their jobs. They work faster and better than humans, or AI that knows more about us than we do."

"What is AI?"

"Artificial intelligence, which learns things and controls things. But it's not the worst thing about living in 2139. Pollution and toxic waste are causing infection, and we now have mutations occurring."

"Like zombies?" My stomach twists.

"Not quite. There have been a few serious cases, but mostly it's like webbed feet and extra limbs, that kind of thing. Basically, humanity is dying, Arriette, just as our planet is. I don't think we have long."

"You and me?"

"The species," he corrects. "We're turning into something new in order to survive our new environment."

This news comes as a shock to me. I was so giddy from the new and the interesting things around me that I didn't spot the homeless people sitting beneath the billboards, or the cracks in the shop windows. I didn't see the woman behind the counter with an extra three fingers, or the division of society between those with and without money.

But as Andrew mentions this terrible future and I glance out the window at their environment, I witness the children scrounging scraps, litter tumbling across the road, and the grey smog hovering above the city we're heading toward. Andrew shows me the sky above the house painted white. It's orange, and the clouds are black. Every chimney and car exhaust he points to is kicking out a dark-coloured fog.

I shudder. Now I can see, plain as I see Andrew, that their world is in trouble.

"I *remember*," I begin, rubbing my temples, "reading something about Earth. I saw pictures, but I am shocked to learn they are incorrect."

"Not incorrect," he promises me. "Maybe just old? Times change. Humans change. We have destroyed the planet we call home, but it wasn't always like this. As President, I hope to make some slight changes that will in no way save humanity, but may buy us some time to come up with a long-term solution."

"But if this planet dies, you will also die."

He nods. "That's true."

"So why bother if you are due to meet your doom?" I ask. "You might fix it, only to die and another will undo everything."

"Somebody has to be responsible. I need to be a part of something greater. We have to try and save the people, because if we save the people—change their behaviour and their actions—we can save the world."

I'm saddened, but I can't explain why. "So, that poster on your fence?"

"Tells passers-by we are still human. We're clean. We're healthy. Many fear the mutants, so they won't deliver mail unless we clarify who lives there."

Arriette chews her lip. *If only he knew that being human was no longer an advantage where I come from, and these 'mutations' are the start of a new era; the rule of the everlasts, retainers, shape-shifters, time-travellers and angels.*

We turn into the hospital car park and climb out to be greeted by a pleasant brunette woman in blue overalls. Andrew shakes her hand and thanks her for any help she may offer, directing me to follow her into the building. I do as I'm told.

"Mr Kaines! It's a pleasure to see you. Where are your photographers and your *groupies*."

Andrew rolls his eyes. "Kallie, now is not the time to mock me. Your sister already disapproves of what I'm doing."

"Which is what?" Kallie asks Andrew, raising a curious eyebrow. "I'm struggling to see the sense in this, too."

"Arriette is injured and lost and I'm pretty sure she's got amnesia. Check her out, then release her for me?"

I jump because I'm overwhelmed and over-stimulated by the machines and members of staff, people crying and complaining, and the stench of chemicals. None of this seems to be powered by spells or potions.

"Don't say I didn't warn you," Kallie tells Andrew. "Christine called me the second you left. She's very concerned."

"She's always 'very concerned'," he grumbles.

Andrew takes my hand and squeezes it gently, making eye contact as if to protect me from the vicious words of his sister-in-law, which I'm also not surprised by. I remain silent and pretend I'm not filthy from swamp water, blood, and sweat. Nobody seems to bother, because they're all in a similar condition. Most of these people appear to have been at war.

"One of the mutant zones in the city is on fire," Kallie tells Andrew. He, too, has noticed the panic in the emergency room—more so than normal.

Over my shoulder I spy a man in black, his white collar cutting his skin at the throat. He shouts and balls, thrusting a little brown book at passers-by and begs that they listen. I halt and turn to hear him, but Andrew shoos me away and insists I worry myself with my health and not the problems of the planet.

"That's my job," he says, and winks.

Inside the emergency room, the halls are all white, but far from clean. There are queues of what my people would call innocents—children and elderly men and women, some in wheelchairs, others deformed. I cringe as Andrew marches me through the crowds after Kallie, and they part like a sea of followers, allowing their leader to show them the way forward.

The way people once did for me, I think.

"Mutants," Kallie growls, "because of the nuclear pollution. Don't let them touch you; it can be catching."

"It won't always be," I utter, but she doesn't hear.

Despite Kallie's behaviour, they bow their heads as Andrew walks by, and I smile at the effect he has on the people he might rule soon.

"Come in, let's look at you," says Kallie. "He'll be waiting for you here."

Andrew ushers me in and promises he won't leave until I've been given the all-clear. But suddenly, I'm more afraid than I've ever been.

When the door closes, I narrow my gaze. "You're not here to help me, Kallie. Are you?"

TWENTY

Kallie looks a lot like her sister apart from her hair colour. They have the same button noses and thin, angry eyes. I wonder if they are twins, too. In Andrew's car was a photograph pinned beneath the steering wheel, and two of his daughters looked identical.

"Why would you say that?"

"Because you don't seem to like me very much."

"Arriette, I don't know you." She gestures for me to take a seat on a bed covered with a thin piece of paper. "Have you fallen and banged your head?"

"Andrew said I had."

She scribbles something down on a piece of paper attached to a board. "Alright, and could you have taken any medication which may have caused confusion or harm to your memory?"

"I haven't taken anything, not since I woke up."

"And before that?"

I shrug. "I don't remember."

"What do you remember since you woke up, then?"

"There were trees and a large green beast that tried to eat me. I don't think these are my clothes."

"They fit you." Kallie sighs. "If you walk through a swamp, an alligator will certainly try to eat you."

"Alligator?"

"Yes," she grumbles. "The animal you fought off was

a gator. They have sharp teeth and scales; we're seeing them more and more, hunting the homeless mutants."

"That sounds right. Like a dragon," I agree.

"Dragons are mythological."

"They are most certainly not."

Unconsciously, I reach for the fading scars across my face from the dragon's talons, then snatch my hand away before Kallie can ask questions.

She straps a band around my arm and presses a red button. I begin to squirm as it tightens, and my pulse beats beneath the shiny material.

"I'm taking your blood pressure." There's a bleep and Kallie leans forward to read it. "How odd."

"What is it?"

"I'd like to take some blood... for testing. And if you can pee into this little tube, I'll test you for a water infection. That can cause confusion."

I take the tube. Kallie pulls a curtain around a little seat with a hole in it, and instructs me to use it as a toilet. It's uncomfortable and embarrassing, and I ache as I squat, but do as I'm told and produce a sample, then wash my hands in a small white sink.

Kallie unscrews the lid and dips a piece of card into the liquid. "Clear? Hmm."

She then asks if she can take a blood sample, so I hold out my arm for her to do as needed. I'm familiar with this procedure; retainers take blood all the time in the infirmary, and Tabitha took plenty during my pregnancy.

Pregnancy.

Tabitha.

My eyes must widen as Kallie asks, "Are you remembering something?"

I force myself to look away as she jabs me with the

needle. "Nothing."

Kallie jabs me a second time, then a third.

"This isn't possible."

"Is something wrong?"

She examines my skin and tugs it gently to test the elasticity. I frown, confused, and ask if Andrew can come in and sit with me.

"Uh, sure." Kallie presses a buzzer then speaks into a handset to ask a passing nurse to fetch him.

"The needle snapped. Your skin is like leather."

I gulp. "Is that... bad?"

Kallie doesn't answer, but I see the concern in her eyes. She taps her own arm and demonstrates how human skin should flex and fold between the fingers; how when pinched it changes white for a few seconds before the blood returns. I study her lesson and glare at my own body in disgust.

"Yours doesn't do this. Look."

Kallie pinches my skin and releases. It's stiff and thick; the blood doesn't return. Not for a while, anyway. My body reacts slowly and lazily.

"How do you feel in yourself?"

"Tired. Heavy," I tell her, honestly, because it's impossible to hide.

"And where did you say you were from again?"

The door opens and Andrew pulls back the curtain. Kallie jumps. "Oh, it's you."

He sits gently beside me, taking my hand in his. Kallie watches the interaction, but she continues to ask her standard questions.

"Can you raise your arms above your head and hold them there?"

I attempt this task and succeed for a few seconds

before they come crashing down in my lap. I groan and retry, but it's no use.

"Exhaustion?" Andy quizzes.

Kallie shakes her head. "Arriette, I need you to come with me. I have a friend in another department. I'd like to take a look at your bones, and his machine can help."

She helps me off the bed and walks me to a white room. It's a short walk from the examination room we were just in, and though Andrew accompanied us, he's not allowed inside. There's a safety notice on the wall and a red light. I don't particularly want to be alone with Kallie and this other stranger, but Andrew winks.

"You'll be fine. I'll be right here."

I struggle to find the courage to release his hand and allow Kallie to close the door behind us. She hands me a pale blue, unattractive gown. I strip, pulling it over my head, then press my chest against a cool slab on the wall. It's over in seconds, but now she needs to check my limbs and my hips. We're only in the room for a few minutes before I'm given a pair of thick grey jogging pants and a matching t-shirt. It's an ugly combination, but more comfortable than the rags. She also hands me a first aid kit and tells me to clean and cover my open wounds. None of them are deep enough to need stitches, which stuns me, and it turns out my toe is only dislocated. Some of the cuts were certainly gaping when I stumbled out of that water and onto the muddy embankment. Now, not so much, but I can't tell her why.

"You should give Andrew his jacket back," Kallie says. "Christine bought him that for his birthday." Then, she turns her back on me.

I move swiftly through the exit into Andrew's comfortable arms. He hugs me briefly, then shows me the way to the women's locker room where he tells me there are showers and nicer toilets.

Kallie hurries down the corridor in the opposite direction to consult with another doctor, giving him a document filled with paperwork and notes she's presumably made whilst examining my combined results. I glance back, wondering why she's so concerned, then decide a shower might just be what I need to relax my muscles.

"Should I be worried?"

Andrew eyes Kallie over his shoulder, then gives my hand a squeeze. "No, she's just busy. Usually, the doctors and nurses will do all this for you, but there's a fire in the city so lots of patients to see."

"Thank you for getting me seen so soon," I tell him. "I know there are others with more serious injuries. Kallie says mine are not that deep."

Andrew scowls. He feels the back of my head and pulls his hand away, but it's dry. "She's the expert. I can't come in there with you, so I'm trusting you not to run away."

"There's nowhere to run," I say, but I leave the door unlocked, figuring if Andrew's guarding it, there's little need to take any extra security measures.

I take off the hideous gown. There's a plastic stool in the corner which I use to hold my clothing, and turn on a tap. I'm met with a gush of warm water; it's so welcome I close my eyes and imagine a familiar sensation back home. A waterfall and a gorgeous steady river. A petite blonde woman, whose beauty stuns me, and a red-head who flies, twisting and turning in the air like a gracious acrobat. There's laughter all around me, and a husky voice churns my stomach.

I *know* him. I *love* him.

I have plenty of time to wash my hair and scrub the blood from my body, careful not to sting my wounds. When I step out of the shower and turn the tap off, I am careful to dry every inch of my skin before I apply some cream Kallie told me would prevent infection, and enough dressings to cover my injuries.

I wipe the mirror clean of condensation to check out the damage. The ugly pants and shirt fit snugly to my curves.

"You can't go in there! She's dressing. Hey, I said—" Andrew's voice booms through the walls, and I hear him arguing with another male. My heart pounds, and I scurry to apply the lock but halt when I hear the stranger tell Andrew to bring me to them when I'm finished.

"This is a serious matter, Mr Kaines."

"Don't be a fool, she's an innocent woman suffering from amnesia. I can take care of her at my house."

The man disagrees. "She's a security risk, sir."

I place my ear against the door and listen intently to the flicking of pages and the low mumbling of their not-so-private conversation. Andrew huffs and tells the man to get lost; he's going to do what's necessary. The man leaves.

There's a brisk knock at the door and I have to force myself to open it, hoping to see Andrew's face when I do.

"Feeling better?"

I smile.

"Then let's get you out of here."

Andrew grabs my arm and pulls me down the corridor, tugging me left and right and through an emergency exit. His eyes are wide with alarm and he's bouncy. White walls and ceiling tiles pass me by, one boring room and empty corridor at a time, then I'm hit by the musky air of the early evening.

Our car is in the parking lot at the front of the hospital, but Andrew doesn't head straight for it. I'm a rag doll, being thrown in many directions until Andrew decides the coast is clear. Together we jog and he folds me into the passenger seat, slamming the door and running to the driver's side. There are others on the grounds, but nobody seems to bother us.

"Where are we going?" I ask. "Why the hurry?"

"I don't know yet," he replies, checking his mirrors and starting the engine. "Away from here."

"Did I do something wrong?"

"You appear to have done everything right," he says, "and have given the people what they want, actually."

"I am not sure I understand."

Andrew reverses. He slams his foot on another pedal and we speed out of the hospital in the opposite direction of his home. I turn and watch the world fly by through the back window, hugging my body as my many wounds begin to throb again beneath the dressings.

"I had to get you away from there, Arriette."

"They helped me," I told him.

"They want to *use* you."

I sit back. "For what?"

"Those tests are standard health checks for humans, Arriette, and you failed all but one. Your skin is twice as thick as a humans, your bone structure and density is like nothing we've ever seen, and you're completely clueless as to your surroundings."

I nod. "I told you I wasn't from this planet."

"I know, and I believe you."

"You do?"

"But now *they* know and *they* believe you. Humans

on this planet are looking for a way to stay alive, Arriette. If you're really from another world, that means space travel is possible and there's hope. While you were in the shower, Kallie told the consultant about your test results and they want to study you."

"I'd be happy to help."

"They'd lock you up. Treat you like a lab rat!"

"So they think I am an alien?"

Andrew sighs. "You kind of are."

"That *is* what I've been trying to tell you, Andy."

He nods frantically as he swerves through a junction, ignoring a red light.

"If what they say is true, and you are in fact from another world, do you have *any idea* what they'll do to you? What the government have been searching for, for hundreds of years, is proof that humans aren't alone in this universe and that we can escape Earth. If Haeylo exists and you're not crazy, you'll become the most wanted and most valuable thing in this country. On the planet!"

"Haeylo may not exist yet, and I am not crazy."

"What?" Andrew shakes his head. "Humans will kill to find you, Arriette, and then they'll *kill you*. Some will think you're a solution, some will think you're a liar, and others will believe you're a miracle. It's the people who believe you're an investment that we're running from."

"But I—"

"You're innocent, and mankind takes the innocent and ruins it; destroys and *crushes* it. It's what we *do*, Arriette. That's why this planet is dying, because the human race has no compassion, nor do they share anything special or protect it. They just want to make money from it. If I could lead an army to protect you I would, but we're a day early. Right now... it's just me and you."

We drive at twice the speed limit and continue along the highway. Night is upon us like a heavy canvas, and sprayed across that canvas are glorious golden stars. Andrew ignores these, used to their lingering, but to me they are my ticket out of this mess. They can lead me home.

Andrew catches me gazing and pulls into a service station for gas and a toilet break. We sit silently for a few moments before we make a move, savouring the quiet.

"Those people in the waiting area were mutants," I say, breaking it. "Kallie told me to avoid them because it's catching."

Andrew rests his arms on the steering wheel. "About two years ago, there was an explosion at a nuclear plant in the next county. Those who survived were evacuated to our city and became refugees, but slowly we noticed a difference in our people. They were *changing*."

"Ugliness is what terrifies you," I say, startling him.

"No, and it's not the only cause for the mutations I'm sure," he says, offering half a smile.

"I *know* it isn't."

"Ugliness isn't what worries us. It's the costs to our health and the health of our children; these people became deformed and dangerous, because it can mess with a person's mind, Arriette, like a disease, and some of them attacked other citizens. I said there were a few serious cases, well the police attempted to control them, but eventually it was the army who stepped in."

"They stopped them?"

"They massacred thousands. We quarantined the city and those with enough money moved to the outskirts into mutant-free zones, like where my family lives. I'm sure you noticed the difference. Obviously, you saw the posters."

I struggle to grasp this concept. "But *you* are not unwell."

"Well, that's something I'm not proud of. When we realised the effects of the nuclear explosion might reach our county, the government released a type of antidote that speeds up human defences within the body, you know like the natural cold and flu warriors."

"We get sick where I come from. I understand. They created a cure, then?"

"A preventative measure to the fallout, but I'm not sure that has anything to do why some are suffering and others aren't."

"Your family is immune?"

"Sort of, yes," he says, lost in thoughts and guilt. "I often wonder why if they could scientifically manufacture a protective drug, why didn't they attempt to develop one which had the power to reverse the damage, too? Anyway, we were rich enough to pay for it, but others weren't so lucky."

Reverse the damage. Attack the citizens. Having healing qualities within your bloodstream. Having species different from human beings.

This is all sounding so familiar. I shrug, needing air, and open the car door.

I fight with my conscience as to whether Andrew did the right thing by accepting the antidote. Protecting your family is everything, but to leave those who cannot afford this treatment to die or become a mutant seems... inhumane. So I step out of the vehicle and head for the shop to clear my head. Andrew catches up and hands me a twenty dollar note. I'm so hungry and desperate for the toilet that I forget to thank him. There's a man behind the counter reading a newspaper, and another young female in the store buying a glass bottle of something. I ignore them both and head to the toilet, then decide we should buy some food to take with us, too, just in case.

Andrew follows me in to pay for the fuel, then waits whilst I pay for our snacks. I buy two large bags of potato chips, bottled water, chocolate, cereal bars, and toilet roll.

"What medications do you sell?" I ask.

The man grunts, "All I have are pain killers."

"I'll take some."

I cram them in the top of a brown paper bag filled with our supplies and Andrew and I climb back in the car. I open a bottle of water and take two tablets to ease my pain as Kallie didn't offer me anything in the hospital.

It's far too late to drive any further. Andrew's eyelids are narrowing.

"This car will be all over the camera systems, so we can't stay with it too much longer. But, there's nothing else around and we need to get some sleep first," he tells me.

I place the bag in the footwell and climb into the back seat. Andrew locks the doors as I lay on my back and gaze out of the hole in the ceiling.

The night sky here is truly beautiful without the city's light pollution to ruin it.

"Like the human race and the Earth," I whisper, then close my eyes.

***

Morning greets us with whistling birds and bright, warming sunshine. I shuffle upright and rub my eyes, stretching my muscles and circling my shoulders. I'm stiff, but I feel tons better, and despite the way I look, these clothes are certainly more comfortable.

Andrew sits on the bonnet of the car, sipping a take-out coffee and eating a sandwich from the station.

I open the door and step out onto the gravel.

"Andrew *Kaines*, right?"

Andrew's eyes meet mine, and he waits patiently for me to say something. I place a gentle palm against his cheek and smile.

"You *are* Andrew Kaines?"

He nods, puzzled. "Of course, Arriette. Are you alright? Is your memory worsening?"

My friend. It's you.

I wrap my arms around his neck, squeezing gently. His presence is so welcoming and surreal that I squeak with joy.

"Apparently, sleep does wonders for your memory when you travel through time and space." I wink. "I *do* know you, but *not* from your posters."

Andrew sits his coffee on the bonnet beside him.

"You can let me go now."

"I don't want to."

He's nervous and afraid of me for the first time. But he doesn't need to be. My mentor and my best friend—how did I not realise who he was sooner? How could I have forgotten him? I gaze into his eyes and fight the urge to kiss him.

"I've *missed* you," I tell him, tears welling.

"You have me confused."

I shake my head. "If you can believe I'm from another world, Andrew, then you can believe I'm from another time. What I'm about to tell you will sound totally crazy, but you *have* to believe me." I check our surroundings for prying ears, but we're completely alone.

"You *are* going to become the President of the United States today."

Andrew laughs, "You're right, that *is* crazy. Arriette. The vote is tonight, and not only am I missing in action, but I'm also an outlaw. I've kidnapped a being from another world. We're bordering mutant territory here, do you get that? I can't take you further without hitting a quarantine barrier and *hundreds* of soldiers. This is it for us. We stop here and we travel on foot until we can find somewhere safe to hide you."

"I disagree," I say, frustrating him. I can tell. His nostrils flare and his eyes tighten, crinkling the skin at either side. I've seen this reaction before. "You *will* be the president, and you *are* going to fulfil your dream of helping this planet." I smile, and Andrew smiles back, grateful for my attempt to lighten his mood. "By saving my life, you have also saved the future of your people, and a new world."

Andrew hops off the bonnet, tearing his face from my hands in one swift motion. He's prickly and unshaven, and slightly grey around his hairline, but those generous and gentle features are clear to me now; they shine like the night's stars. No amount of masking in the future can hide that kindness.

"How could you possibly know this?" he asks.

"I might be from another world, but I'm from another time as well. For some wacky reason, I've been transported here, most likely due to my power of time-travel, and I'm trapped here to witness the end of the world —your world—with my own eyes." I swallow hard, unable to stop myself from blurting everything out. So I tell him about the Recruit, and about my gifts. I tell him about the HPS and Pandora's box and the war I survived. I tell him I'm a leader—a saviour—and I tell him about Christine. I tell him about Pandora's soul, too.

"P-Pandora? Christine? This is ridiculous, Arriette. You fall asleep and all of a sudden you're able to predict the future?"

"I *am* the future, Casper!"

I reach out and take his hand, forcing him to touch my flesh and bones. I'm real, and I'm here, and he's stuck with me whether he likes it or not.

I need his help to get home.

"Casper?"

"It's not amnesia, Andrew. Time-travel. It's the effects of the wormhole. Travellers are known to suffer memory loss for a short while until time and space catches up with them. My friend lost her father that way; he never regained his memory. I need you to take me to my landing site. The wormhole might still be open. I'll be able to get home."

"I can't take you back there, it's dangerous."

"Not for me. I have gifts, Andrew, if only I can tap into them again."

How do I prove this to him; show him I am a supernatural creature from the planet Haeylo? I hold out my hands and point them at his coffee cup, sat peacefully on the bonnet of his car. Andrew watches me worriedly and waits for me to do something spectacular.

For a while I look a fool, and Andrew's interest begins to slip. Then, like a gust of hot air, the power surges through every cell in my body and shoots through my fingertips. I raise the coffee cup and throw it at the side of the shop. The cup explodes against the brick and the last mouthful of coffee spills across the gravel.

Andrew is still.

I have my powers back.

Did telling him the truth, remembering who I was and where I came from somehow trigger them?

"What *are* you?"

"Not what," I correct him. "*Who.*"

"*Who* are you, then? How can I trust you?"

I back off, sensing he's not quite accepted this yet. Andrew calms as the distance is increased between us.

"It all makes sense now," I say mostly to myself as I pace the length of the vehicle. "When I first met you, you said you needed to be sure I was who you thought I was. You'd been searching for me, and you said you'd met me before, but none of it made sense. I *looked* like the girl you needed, sounded like her, too. You were telling me about a memory, Casper. This memory."

"Why are you calling me Casper?"

"This is too difficult and painful to explain," I begin, "so I'm not going to try. Later today, you will sign a *very* special contract."

"What kind of contract?"

I sigh, unsure how much of this I can give away without risking changing the timeline. "A spiritual contract, in your dreams. Sign it. When you wake, everything you've ever worked towards will be granted, but at a cost. I can't explain any further. Please, trust in me. Hand me over to your government and claim you were on my tail, chasing the runaway alien. Tell them anything! You've *got* to get back for the vote."

"I won't let them take you," he promises. "It's not in my nature to sign the death warrant of a friend."

"I'm touched that you should consider me so already, but this is important."

I can't stop moving, I'm so excited.

"If I had realised who you were sooner, we would be prepared for what happens next."

"And what's that, exactly?"

I huff. "I can't tell you any more."

"Then I can't agree to this idiotic idea."

"If you won't hand me over to someone who can take me there, then I'll find the wormhole alone."

Andrew groans. "And risk them following you to the future?" He opens the passenger door and gestures for me to get in. "All I did was buy a cup of coffee. How was I to predict you'd wake up a witch?"

"I'm not a witch!"

"You can't just spring this on me, Arriette. It's not fair! We barely know one another but this past twenty-four hours, I feel as though you and I are meant to be together; there's a force pulling me to you, and I can't control it or explain it and frankly, it's driving *me* insane!"

I storm around to join him and retrieve Andrew's wallet from the dashboard. I steal fifty dollars and cram them into the pocket of the hideous grey joggers given to me by his sister-in-law, then offer him my hand.

"Please shake it," I beg, "for it has been an honour to meet you in your prime, my mentor."

Andrew hesitates before taking my hand, but then refuses to release me. "I'm sorry, Arriette, sorry for everything. I just can't take you to them. They'll kill you."

I tug my wrist free and turn on my heel, heading down an endless dust road. I'm sad to leave him clueless and angry, especially after my doing, but this is something I have a responsibility for.

"Wait!"

There's distance between us now, so Andrew is running toward me. Sprinting. Filth and dirt flicks behind as his feet leave the roadside, causing a cloud of light dust to gather, protecting us from the view of the people in the car park and the station. He flies into my arms, his lips meeting my cheek, and I give myself to his energy, holding him closer than I have ever held another creature.

We linger in the red dust, forced together by fate. We are intertwined; locked together. I feel his heart flutter and the butterflies in my stomach panic.

"Arriette, I can't let you leave me."

I catch my breath. "We don't have long."

He lifts my chin with the tip of his finger, and I fold into him once more, feeling the roughness of his stubble grate my face. His scent overwhelms me with familiarity and longing for my home.

My mentor. My best friend.

My grandfather.

"I must be a lunatic!" he says.

"Andrew, you need to stay away from me now. Hand me over and return to your family, or let me go my own way. I've done some terrible things—things that if you knew, you could never forgive me. It was once my duty to serve you, to learn from you, and to then replace you. That was before—"

"What? Before what? You can tell me."

"I can't, because it could change history. And we don't have time."

I pull away and drag him back to the car by his arm, just as he dragged me out of the hospital.

"Drive me home. We need to be there for the vote."

"I won't let them hurt you, Arriette."

"They can't," I tell him, feeling my angelic electricity roaring through my veins. "But if they try to hurt *you*, they will certainly fear me."

***

After twenty questions as to why I call him Casper, references to a ghost and plenty of huffs of frustration, Andrew finally agrees to driving in silence.

I gather my thoughts. I can't tell him why I call him Casper; it was a slip of the tongue. I've already said too much. Giving away the future might change it, I tell myself, and that jeopardises *everything* we've built since my reign.

He must sense my dilemma because Andrew places a hand on my knee. He knows I'm stressed; perhaps my memories of Haeylo are better lost than on his shoulders yet again. I smile and link my fingers with his. It's nice to have somebody I love willing to risk everything to help my cause.

"There's a lot you can't tell me."

I turn my face away.

"If you are unable to explain your new name for me, can you at least offer an explanation about Pandora? You mean the Greek goddess, and the box with all the evils in and stuff?"

"You should know about Greek mythology, as it was supposed to have occurred on this planet."

"I want to hear it from *you*," he says and smiles.

"Well her box was said to be the cause of evils released into the world, and Haeylo suffered because of this too. When Haeylo was created, God as you call him used it as a way to re-test us. The same story and the same circumstances. When Haeylo begins, the spirits from this planet are also spirits of ours; we're interlinked and born from one another. You'll live through it all one day, so

you'll figure the rest out for yourself."
    "So... she's *real*?"
    A voice in my head laughs.
    Pandora.
    She's in there... somewhere.
    "Yes," I tell him, laughing too. "Very much so."

TWENTY—ONE

The White House looms on the horizon and I dread having to face those longing for my capture. I fear what they will do to Andrew when he refuses to hand me over.

We pull into an underground parking lot and switch off the engine. Andrew glares at me, almost awaiting orders. I open the door and jump out.

"We should leave the car here. They'll find it soon because it's mine," he says. "We need to move fast. The building is heavily guarded and protected."

"Where do we go?"

"Take a left here," he says, checking if the street is clear of police before we round the corner.

The streets are over-populated and manic. There are traffic jams heading into the city and empty roads out of it. We were lucky, navigating down back streets and avoiding patrol cars. But now we must face the sheer volume of mutants and everyday troubles of city life, and it starts with the smell of the sewers. It's disgusting, and I cover my nose and mouth with the back of my hand to stifle the stench.

A device in Andrew's pocket chirps, but he ignores it.

It chirps again.

"It'll be Christine," he tells me and continues to ignore it.

The fog descends as the day progresses, and the sun warms the city. It distorts our vision, and Andrew points out an accident up ahead. We veer to the right and pick up the pace, jogging rather than walking. My limp has eased, but a twinge of pain plagues me every few steps.

There are armed soldiers on every corner as we near the White House, and Andrew shoves me into a shop entrance as one passes. We wait for a few minutes until the guard disappears around the block, then head out again.

Something isn't right. This is *not* humanity; this cannot be how Earth ended. The living conditions? Cries of desperation? Gunshots?

Andrew drags me to a sprint. We bolt around the corner and face a roadblock with armed soldiers in camouflage combats carrying automatic weapons bigger than my torso. They're pointing them right at us, recognising Andrew from the posters.

"We need to get through without them recognising you. Kallie will have alerted the authorities."

"You! Stay where you are!" they shout.

Andrew nudges me, "Run!"

Two soldiers break away from the patrol and chase after us. We are both on the police's 'wanted' board by now, and they'll capture us in a matter of minutes.

Andrew takes my hand and sighs as the first police officer catches up to us. He grips Andrew by the collar, and I stop alongside him without having to be asked.

"Don't hurt us. I'm the guy running for president."

The second officer approaches and they lower their weapons. "*Why* are you in the centre of this chaos? You're supposed to be at the conference. They've been looking for you, Mr Kaines. You'll get killed out here!"

"We got stuck in the traffic a few blocks back.

There's been a car accident."

The device sounds again.

The first officer shoulders his rifle. "I nearly shot you! Why did you run away?"

"We were running because we're late."

"Come on," he says, "I'll escort you. Quickly!"

The look on Andrew's face is of reprieve, and I let loose the breath I've been holding. As we pass the checkpoint, holding hands, the officer in charge receives a brief message on his radio. Andrew is oblivious, but I shift to my cat-like senses and pick up that law enforcement has tracked the car to a parking lot three blocks from here. The registration matches that of two criminals the police have been tracking, and the officers have been requested to head there now instead of escorting us to check it out. The owner's name isn't mentioned.

"Good luck," says the second officer.

"I hope you get in," says the first. "I voted for you."

"You should answer Christine."

Andrew grunts. "She's been calling since yesterday. I don't have the energy to deal with her yet."

When we arrive late to the conference, men and women with cameras are taking photographs of everyone going into the building. I hide my face in fear that the knowledge of my presence will somehow affect the course of history, and skulk inside when Andrew pries himself free of their lenses.

"Let's go make history," he says.

"You're going to win."

I smile and we shake hands, memorising everything about one another, then he goes one way and I go the other.

"I'll wait back here for you after," he shouts.

Most of the candidate's speeches and campaigns were over weeks ago. Now all that remains is one last word, and a grand total. Andrew told me during our jog here that voting for a president now is much simpler than it once was, but with that comes the risk of appointing the wrong person, and he hopes his voters don't regret theirs.

He takes a firm stance at the podium and awaits his cue to speak, a little out of breath and sweaty, worrying about where I am. We only just made it in time and manning the exits now are armed officers and even soldiers. The other guy speaks first and there are cheers and clapping, enough to make the floor beneath me vibrate with energy. He's likeable and dressed smartly, perfectly groomed, and well-spoken.

"Ladies and gentleman, Andrew Kaines."

Andrew looks like he's been through the swamp with me, but he's confident and honest as he steps forward

"I… I should be dead," Andrew tells his people, and my attention snaps immediately from hiding to his brutal statement. "And death still chases me. I *feel* it."

The audience dies down and glares in horror at Andrew's opening sentence. My mouth is agape, too.

What the hell are you doing?

I push my way through the crowd, trying my best to blend in, and stare up at Andrew, who is nervously twiddling his fingers without notes to read from. The other candidate is already straightening his tie and preparing his gracious winner's smile for the cameras.

But Andrew continues. "It sometimes feels like I'm the only human being on this planet who cares about our future. We are animals... *animals...* who are soon to be extinct." There is a mild chatter echoing around the conference hall and when it hits me, my stomach churns.

"And recently, I've been shown just how terrible we are."

Andrew is driving fear into the hearts of his citizens as a tool. And I know he signs his contract because human nature and greed take over; the very thing he preaches about now. But I force myself to accept he won't sign because of me, and has to become president in his own way for Zïnnyi to offer him the deal. Everything is happening as it's expected to, so I can't be disappointed in him.

"We always ask for the bad news first, right? Here it is. Earth is dying. But the good news is that we're not done for yet. Make me your president and I promise I will do anything within my power to ensure that our future is peaceful, painless, and hopefully the beginning of something incredible." He inhales deeply and closes his eyes. "One world has to collapse for another to flourish. Save the people, save the world."

Surprisingly, there is hardly any panic. His people are cheering, are accepting and excited, like they've been expecting this kind of speech from him.

Those at the front repeat the catchphrase back to him in a chant, waving and taking photographs.

His gaze meets mine and I blow him a kiss, preparing to take off and disappear once and for all into the crowd instead of waiting for him. But Andrew crouches and the rows part for me. I walk to him, and he places his hands on my face. I flinch at how surprisingly cold he feels, and imagine having the time to show him just how warm my heart can truly be.

I hear the click of a camera behind me, but there's nothing I can do about it now.

"I love you, Arriette. I will *always* love you, and I will *always* find you."

Andrew is tapped on the shoulder, so he releases me. A perky blonde woman in heels hands both candidates a sealed envelope, and in unison, they rip them open. We await his news patiently.

Andrew lets out a sigh of relief and holds his envelope high in the air.

***

"Christine?" Andrew gasps.

"Well, you made your intentions clear, Andrew. And to the entire world, too. But you couldn't find it in you to tell me first?"

Andrew doesn't take more than a few steps through the illuminated exit before his wife confronts him, waving a small white photograph in his face.

The click.

Her angry eyes find my sorrowful then, and she narrows them.

"Christine, I can explain."

"Don't bother, tramp," she snaps. "Congratulations, Andrew. I hope you're both happy."

As she turns to walk away, I nudge Andrew and gesture for him to chase after her. At least to retrieve the photographic evidence of my time here.

"We're not having an affair," he tells her.

"Liar!"

"Christine, this *isn't* what it looks like. Arriette and I aren't in love," he explains, "but we do love each other."

She pauses, and Andrew almost runs into her. "Didn't you already ruin our family? Now you're running off with this mental patient?"

He cringes. "Christine, Harriet wanted to tell horrible

242

lies to the press about you. I did what I had to do to protect our twins from that kind of media attention."

Christine makes haste for the exit. "It's not her fault, Andrew. And she's not wrong."

"She's old enough to take care of herself. She called you a *witch*, Christine! People are stringing mutants up in the street and you want to risk someone accusing you of dark magic or demonic worship or whatever the hell Harriet said you were into?"

Christine slows to hear him out. I hang back, standing beside a security guard, who is also trying not to eavesdrop.

"You love Arriette."

"I admire her. I can't yet understand, so it's hard to explain. By tonight, everything will make sense."

"But do you love her?"

Andrew sighs. "Yes. I love Arriette. And I think I have loved her for a very long time. Though I don't know how that's possible."

Christine folds her arms and hangs on her hip. "There are accusations against her."

I interject, "They are true."

Christine gasps and seems to consider the implications. But as Andrew reaches out to embrace her, he is saying goodbye. I try to remember that in a few hours, it will become their reality.

"Christine, you may hate me, but I need to borrow your husband again, and I need you to give me that picture."

"Haven't you done enough?"

"There's nothing romantic between us. I *promise*. Andrew loves you, and he always will."

Andrew nods. "If you don't believe me, then come

with us to the White House. You'll see she's telling the truth."

Christine glances between us with suspicion, then holds out her hand to Andrew, handing him the photo.

"If you're lying, you're both going to regret this."

TWENTY—TWO

We race through four more security roadblocks, two small riots, and patches of denser fog. Christine and I are crammed side-by-side in a black SUV, with Andrew in the front seat and a bodyguard in the passenger side. I have no idea what an SUV is, but it's bigger and fancier than Andrew's car. When we pull into the grounds of Andrew's new home, I'm in total awe. We jump out and are ushered quickly inside. A lady offers to take the children, who are already waiting for their parents, upstairs to their new bedrooms. Christine slips her a few dollars as a thank you.

Tonight is the night Andrew Kaines signs the contract in his sleep and agrees to give up his family for the greater good.

He has no idea.

"Are you ready?" Christine asks him. "A hundred years ago, this would not have been so easy," she tells him. "Your bodyguards would have been far more insistent on your safety, and you would *not* have been given the job via an envelope on a conference room stage!" She frowns and congratulates her husband, nevertheless. "Times have changed."

"We're not living in the past," he tells her. "Though I just announced to millions of viewers that our planet was dying, so I'm hoping Arriette isn't lying to us."

Christine scowls. "You're betting this office on *her*?"

"I can't bet it on myself. I'm clueless. We won, but I've no idea what to do next. She seems to know exactly what's about to happen, though."

I find it difficult to believe Christine Kaines considers his 'end of the world' speech a big lie to get into power. Though her attitude and behaviour towards me is harsh, she's intelligent and strong. She already knows where this planet is heading, and she's been preparing.

"Can't you just go away now? You've made your point, *future girl*."

Andrew growls at his wife, taking my hand and releasing hers. I worry this will give Christine the wrong impression and possibly prompt a further, heated argument, but she inhales deeply to calm her nerves and agrees Andrew needs time to say goodbye to me. So she decides to put the twins to bed; she has a lot to explain to them. She snatches two apples from a bowl on her way.

"This is weird," I tell him as we enter a study filled with books and armchairs. It reminds me of the new library at HQ. "What happens to your home now you're here?"

"It'll be sold."

"Already?"

"We have no control over that," he says, "and if you're telling the truth, none of it matters anyway. The previous president will move in for a while as a temporary settlement. He has nowhere else. He isn't married, nor does he have any children."

"But the sentimental value? All your things?"

"Already here, and we hadn't lived there long enough to make memories. I have a third daughter, but she lives somewhere else."

Harriet. He's talking about the daughter he murders. For me.

He shrugs off my concern for his family, and gestures I sit with him. "Come on, Arriette, we need to figure a way to get you home. This planet is of no matter to you. You did your job, you warned me to accept the contract, and I will."

"*Not* why I'm here," I reply.

He's too busy fumbling in the desk for a pen and paper. He draws a rough perimeter around a scribbled forest and plots my landing site. That's where the wormhole is, although by now, it would be closed and inaccessible. I don't particularly want to trudge back there via the dragon's territory, either, but I take it and thank him anyway.

"I did not time travel *thousands* of years to tell you to accept a contract, because you are smart enough to figure it out for yourself."

"Am I?"

I roll my eyes. "This goes deeper. Like maybe I'm supposed to die when Haeylo is created. I have already tried to re-open a wormhole intentionally and nothing's happening. It is the only one of my powers I cannot access."

Andrew stops scribbling and glares at me. "Haeylo doesn't already exist? And you want to die here?"

"Maybe I have said too much. I don't *want* to, but I'll be re-born in a few thousand years, so it's not the last time you and I are going to meet. Let me go now, Andrew. I can find sanctuary on this chaotic planet and wait for my end."

"But why would I save you only to watch you die?" he says. "I don't know how, but you mean too much to me for that."

I force a smile and tell him, "Everything, that is... *everything supernatural,* happens for a reason. My death here completes some kind of cycle, and in my place, my daughter will take over."

"You have a daughter?"

"The last thing I remember is giving birth to her."

I stare out the window at a riot in the distance, where blazing fires illuminate the sky with an orange and red glow. When Haeylo is created, Zïnnyi chooses those he deems worthy to move on with it, but having met these people and moved among them, none of them deserve to die. Even though they don't care about anybody but themselves, and their society revolves around making money, they are just trying to survive given the circumstances. It's hard being human.

There's a knock on the door.

Kallie is standing next to a man in a white overall who is carrying the notes she passed to him in the hospital. The overall covers most of his body, and a white medical mask covers his face. As does a hood.

"I told him you're not infectious, but he wouldn't listen," Kallie says. "His colleagues are waiting outside."

Andrew barely thinks before diving in front of my body and warning his sister-in-law not to take another step. He's the president now, and he has the authority to remove imbeciles like Kallie from his property, or perhaps even his country. If he ordered her dead, would a soldier enter and end her as easily as Casper ended Harriet? But what would be the point, when soon she and every other selfish human on this planet would be crushed by the force of the sun, or sucked into the pretty circling vortex above this room? I cannot help but beam that we've already won.

"Security!" Kallie shouts over her shoulder. "Remove

this woman immediately."

"No!" I shove aside a burly looking security guard in a black suit, lighting my fingertips and allowing Baby A's angelic inheritance to blaze through them. I catch my reflection in a glass cabinet behind her; my eyes are wild with blue electricity.

Kallie panics and elbows the entering security guard out of the way to make a run for it.

"I told you she's an alien! GET HER!"

I lurch past Andrew and dash into Kallie's scientist companion, head-butting him unintentionally and knocking him down. He sprawls across the expensive carpet, unconscious, and their paperwork scatters. Kallie barely looks back to check if he's following, or if I'm on her tail. She forces open the nearest window with the palms of her hands and bends to escape through.

"We're all doomed," I tell her, allowing my wings to materialise and fill half the hallway, blocking her view of Andrew and his study. My glare returns to normal. "You should be with your family in these last hours, Kallie. Be with Christine and the children."

"You're a maniac!"

Andrew yells after her to come back, and sends the security guard to pull her away from the window. He carefully side-steps around me, and Kallie screams at the guard's touch and thrashes in his hold, biting and clawing for freedom.

"You can't protect her, Andrew. Christine will not allow it! She will come for you both."

The scientist on the floor suddenly wakes and scrambles to pick up his paperwork. I can't let him to keep it—any evidence of my presence here needs to be destroyed. So I leave Kallie and as I kneel to scoop up the remaining sheets, he whacks me with a silver candlestick, which re-opens the earlier wound. I'm bleeding again, but not badly.

"Security, arrest this man too," Andrew demands.

The security guard throws Andrew a pair of handcuffs as he continues to wrestle with Kallie, and Andrew tightens them around the man's wrists.

I rip the paperwork into tiny pieces.

"Are you hurt?"

"I heal quickly. Angelic blood." I smirk and Andrew examines a few feathers in disbelief.

"They're... real," he gasps.

"We should set these notes on fire just to be sure."

He leans angrily toward the man. "Nobody will ever believe your accusations. You can't have her. Our damaged society lives to destroy, and when something beautiful and different comes along, you crush it because you don't understand it!" Andrew asks the guard to get rid of both Kallie and the scientist, but he doesn't specify how. "It's a shame you'll see the end of our world from behind bars."

As the enormous fireplace at the back of the study hasn't been lit in a long time, I throw the scraps in, then pitch a fireball to set it ablaze.

"I've got to go," I tell Andrew, who is shielding his face from the sudden heat.

I place a hand on his arm and squeeze it, then put away all traces of my supernatural gifts, wings first. Before Andrew is given the chance to follow, Christine rounds the corridor and pushes him into the study, locking the door. I hear bangs and shouting, but then all falls quiet.

I know he's OK; he signs the deal.

I wish I could share a kinder goodbye. Haeylo's

future is more important. But I can't leave the grounds before the contract is signed, or be too far away from witnessing his big moment, so I duck out of the open window and skip across the lawns to hide behind a large hedge, separating a garage filled with limousines and SUVs from the public eye. Inside there are three other shiny vehicles, all displaying the American flag, and a motorcycle. There is no dust, and I don't see any scurrying rats or spiders in the windows; the place is immaculately clean for a garage. And it's *huge*. So huge, that in the centre, parked perfectly beneath an automatic roof, is a helicopter.

I sneak inside the garage and climb in. It's quiet here, and perfect for my last moments. I wonder how long I have left and what Andrew and Christine are doing. Part of me cringes at the thought, but love makes you do crazy things.

I should know.

My time on this planet was worth it. I miss my friends on Haeylo now I can remember their names, but a voice deep within tells me I'll see them again.

It's powerful and not entirely my own, but I trust it.

Closing my eyes, I drift into a peaceful slumber. I pray Zïnnyi will allow me to share a small piece of heaven with the Casper I knew.

After all, he owes me.

TWENTY—THREE

I wake with a stiff neck and shoulders, unable to move too far or too fast, and glare out the front window of the helicopter. It's still dark outside and people are crammed tightly on the grounds of the White House, glaring at the sky and pointing. I don't join them because I already know how this ends. I've been asleep for a few hours, I figure, but soon my sleep will be permanent.

No regrets. I am ready to face death head-on.

The kitchen staff, cleaners, secretaries, and other members of staff linger. Some are crying, others awestruck and still. A young woman screams at the sight of a colourful vortex, and runs toward the garage, slamming the door behind her and cowering. I scramble to my feet and move inches at a time, debating whether to alert her to my presence. She must hear me shuffling because she jumps, but once aware I'm hiding too, she heads towards me.

"Sorry I scared you," I tell her.

"You didn't. The president went live on telly and said this planet is dying. And then the sky lit up and everyone started running and I didn't know what to do!"

"Yes, I was at the conference."

She sniffles. "Do you believe him?"

I'm not going to lie to her on her last day on Earth.

"Wait a minute. You're that girl, aren't you? The one

Andrew reached out to during the vote. You've got to be important to get access to those things," she babbles. "Even *I* couldn't gain access, and he's my... never mind. It doesn't matter now anyway. So which is it? Are you famous? Can I get your autograph?"

"No, and no."

"I recognise you from *somewhere*," she says, brushing back her long blonde hair.

I nod. "He and I are old friends."

"Oh, you're *Arriette*. You talk funny. I overheard my mother talking about you."

She accepts a trembling handshake. "Who are you?"

"I'm a *long* story," she says through deep, calming breaths. "I came to patch some things up after hearing his end of the world speech, but I can't bring myself to do it. It's all a bit too... overwhelming."

Now I understand; this poor girl has something to say to Andrew. But it's too late.

"He'll be sleeping now," I tell her.

She hesitates, but climbs into the helicopter with me. "Arriette, can I ask you something?"

"About the conference?"

She nods. "Andrew said he *loved* you. Do you love him, too?"

"Well," I begin, "sort of. But not in the same way he loves his wife. Not in the same way he loves his three daughters."

She sighs, long and hard. "Why aren't you with him for the end of the world, then? I voted for him. He's my favourite of all the candidates, though I'm biased. The people trust him." She sweeps an escaped tear away with a single finger. "Why be stuck in a garage, sleeping in a helicopter, talking to Andrew's... well, to *me*... if the love of your life is in there?"

"Besides Christine?" I smirk.

The girl glares at me. I turn away and slump against the seat, but she follows and perches beside me, waiting for a solid answer.

"Are you afraid of dying?" I ask her instead, and she doesn't deny it. "Don't be. This isn't the end."

She pauses, then says, "To hell with Christine. And you didn't answer my question."

"Yes," I say, grinning, "I did."

Outside, chaos erupts.

There is banging on the garage door, and she's up and away before I can say goodbye. She presses a button, which opens both the external doors and the panels in the ceiling, then disappears into the shadows. A man in his mid-thirties runs in, wide-eyed, dressed in overalls.

Quickly, I stow behind some cargo boxes that are strapped in behind a wall of dark green netting. The man starts up the helicopter and lifts it out of the garage roof, none the wiser, flying only a few metres before setting it down on the lawn and gesturing for Andrew to jump in.

Tears swell as I see him say goodbye to his twins, one of them my mother.

He slides in and leaves the doors open, choosing to sit beside his pilot. Andrew places some headphones over his ears so they can talk and waves at people below.

Andrew calls the pilot Daniel.

I dare not breathe in fear he will re-direct us. By now, Andrew has signed his contract, and I can see it in his eyes. He's exhausted, as though he's taken part in a life-or-death conversation.

We gain height and speed. Still I hide. I nervously peer from the window and witness thousands of inconsolable people congregated in the streets. An awful smog hides half the city, traffic accidents and fires. The rest sits beneath an eerie red dusting. It clogs the propeller.

"You've got to go, Daniel," Andrew tells the pilot.

"But Mr President, I—"

Andrew hands him a parachute pack and yanks him from the seat. The helicopter jolts until Andrew grabs the controls and presses a switch. The helicopter hovers. Then he follows his pilot to the exit and watches him strap on the pack.

"Thank you for what you're doing," says Daniel.

"Tell my children I love them."

Before Daniel answers, Andrew launches him into the air. I scream and hurl my body at Andrew, hitting him several times, but he lies on the floor with his head over the edge and allows me to punish him.

When I've tired, he pulls me to his side.

"You *knew* I was back there," I manage.

He nods. "I saw my other daughter tonight," he admits, nearly shouting.

"She came to visit you, then?"

"Not exactly. I saw her running for her life."

We're being pulled higher. The helicopter's controls have been overridden and Andrew doesn't challenge it, nor my anger at him pushing Daniel out.

He keeps talking.

"We parted on difficult terms, and I haven't seen her in a long time. Her name is Harriet."

Andrew gazes at the people below, now tiny panicking specks, and heaves a sigh of relief.

"I met her. She came to say goodbye, and says she's sorry," I tell him. "But she knew it was too late to disturb you."

Andrew smiles through his tears.

The vortex spins and grows, glowing radiantly; a swirl of fiery shades of orange, red, and yellow. In the centre is a black hole. We're heading straight for it.

I squeeze Andrew's hand. "You regret not speaking to her?"

"There's nothing I can do now, is there?"

"You can be proud of yourself."

Andrew laughs. "Yeah, a career of maybe twelve hours? Perhaps it would have been better for me to allow the Earth to die. We deserve death; we destroyed our world. I'm not perfect, Arriette, but during my campaign I met enough religious groups who *all* wanted the same thing, and they came together. To pray for a second chance."

"If this world was created in seven days, why not another?"

The helicopter spins out of control. It tips, and Andrew and I slide to the opposite door, gripping each other's clothing.

Andrew grabs the edge of the helicopter with one hand and the back of the pilot seat with the other. I wrap my hands around his waist and hold on with all my might. I release my wings and use them as a barricade, but it's so noisy and so hot up here that my feathers smoke, and I can't hear Andrew's straining voice telling me to *let him fall*.

But he deserves a more heroic death, so I extend them as far as they'll reach and grab a hold of him, shouting above the roar that he should brace himself. We jump and watch the helicopter spin away, then disappear through a black cloud. It's up to me now to get Andrew through that vortex. He's heavy but the vortex races to meet us, as if Zïnnyi is giving me a helping hand.

I no longer need to flap my wings. An unknown force takes over, dragging us out of this world's atmosphere.

Into oblivion.

TWENTY—FOUR

"It's been *days*, Tobias," Sebastian urged. "Look at her; she's lost weight. She may not be dead yet, but if we don't figure something out, then she will be soon. From starvation and though I've tried, dehydration!"

Baby A wrapped her arms around Sebastian's neck and they sobbed together. It was the first time she'd seen him cry since Arriette's death. So far, he'd done nothing but try to figure out how to bring her back. But it didn't take long for him to compose himself, especially in front of Tobias and the baby.

"Please, Tobias, we need to hydrate her body," Baby A said. "Tabitha knows what to do."

Tobias placed his free hand on Arriette's coffin and inhaled deeply, missing the scent of her perfume and the sound of her determined, yet always slightly concerned, voice.

"Alright."

"I appreciate this is hard on you," Baby A said.

"It's just a little... difficult to believe," he admitted. "But I'm doing this for Sebastian and Jet—they're adamant; it's not like we can kill her any *more*, is it?"

"Thank you," Sebastian said, relaxing.

Tobias stormed off across the meadow with their new baby in his arms. He didn't look back. When Sebastian tried to follow, Baby A gripped his forearm.

"Let him go," she uttered. "He needs time to think and to mourn."

"He can't mourn someone who isn't dead," Sebastian reminded her, shrugging her away. "Nobody would listen, but I was right."

"Now is not the time to say 'I told you so'!"

"I can't think of a better time."

Sebastian and Jet positioned themselves at the top and bottom of the coffin. Together, they lifted the glass lid gently. It was heavy, but the wind in the meadow was picking up, and they were afraid it might throw off their balance.

"Let's get this over with," said Baby A. "I'll get Tabitha; she'll identify what Arriette's body needs."

"Will she be safe here?"

"She won't be alone," Baby A told Jet, "because you're both going to stay here. Shall we put the glass back?"

Sebastian nodded. He'd feel better if she was still protected until Tabitha and Baby A returned. Carefully and respectfully, Sebastian lifted Arriette's head onto a larger silk cushion first. He fought back tears at how soft and healthy her hair was, and at how he could still smell her favourite fruity shampoo.

Baby A didn't see any of this because she was already sprinting back to the square, so Jet helped him to replace the glass. Baby A *had* to find Tabitha Hope or one of the Four Saviours—any of them would know how to rehydrate Arriette's body without the use of alchemy. But as the lair's beautiful scenery rushed by, she couldn't help but also think about the Enzoian women. Despite the coincidence and their connection between their terrible change and Arriette's demise, her gut instinct told her to let it go. And to let them all go. Her gut hadn't let her down before, but her heart was overruling it, anyway. She *had* to confirm if the happenings were connected, or if their mutation caused everything that had happened since.

Baby A needed closure, and Tobias needed his fiancée back.

And as the sun rose in the Recruit's underground lair, Susan and Dion made their way to take over from Sebastian and Jet temporarily, allowing them an emotional break they denied needing.

Dion had towel-dried her spiky red hair, and it stuck out in fuzzy little ringlets at all angles. Compared to Susan's glorious blonde shimmer and her naturally glowing eyes, Dion appeared to be the darker soul, but as they approached the coffin, Jet couldn't help but notice that both women were equally stunning, and if they weren't both extremely out of his league, colleagues, friends and well... *dead*, he might have been tempted to ask one of them out on a date. The idea of befriending Susan was less terrifying since Reiko's synthetic blood had them in great shape. Both were luminous and eager and supportive. Neither had experienced a blood-lust for their preferred meal in over twenty-four hours, either, and so Reiko had deemed the trial period a complete success.

Whether they stuck with the manufactured substitute, however, was an entirely new conversation.

Dion was the first to greet them. "How ya holdin' up?" she asked Sebastian, who was now sitting with his back against the coffin and his head on his knees.

"I'll live, which is more than can be said for Arriette if Tabitha doesn't hurry."

"Baby A's on it," Susan said, examining every inch of Arriette's body for movement. Since Arriette had ceased to dream, the blinking lids had also stopped completely, and she was now beginning to adopt a drawn, vampyric complexion. Alive, but not quite. She lacked the fangs, but Susan had often thought Arriette's attitude would suit being a part of her species well.

"What's the matter?" asked Dion.

"Nothing," Susan muttered, tilting her head. "I was just... *considering* something."

"A way to save her?"

"It is not preferable."

Susan leered over the coffin to better examine Arriette's body. Despite the removal of her hunger, she still remembered how easily sinking fangs into the flesh of a victim could be, and how pleasurable.

How *appealing* taking a life was for her kind.

And easy.

"I have an idea."

Dion's ears pricked, perhaps sensing Susan's intentions or reading the vampyr's body language in the way only another could. She pulled her in one swift, vicious motion, and flung her aside.

"Absolutely not!" she ordered.

Susan's fangs protruded from her gums in anger, glistening in the early sunlight. Sebastian jumped to his feet, shuddering, rousing Jet from a half-slumber by his side.

What were they considering? It only occurred to him when Dion's face turned a sickly green.

"It could save her life," Susan hissed.

Jet's hands trembled, and his invisibility flickered.

"You're not suggesting—"

"Wait!" Baby A interrupted, re-appearing with Tabitha at her heels. Both were out of breath. "Let Susan talk. Tabitha says it may be too late for us to intervene without the use of magic."

"You're not considering this, are you?" Sebastian asked, disgusted by the suggestion.

Baby A blushed. "It's mad, but if it saves Arriette and gives her the chance to live happily ever after with her family, then is it worth an attempt?"

"But she won't *live* happily," Tabitha uttered, "because she'll live thirstily, and dangerously, and put that baby girl at risk."

"Maybe," Susan replied. "*I'm* different. Dion is different. Arriette will be as well. We have the synthetic blood."

"Arriette *did* say she was drawn to it earlier."

"Enough!" The harsh boom of Sebastian's voice abruptly halted the girls. A voice he rarely expressed in such a way.

Baby A lowered her head in shame but held on for a glimmer of hope in that Recruit sunrise. If reasoned with, the others might allow Susan to give this insane plan a shot.

"I'm going to pretend I didn't just hear all of this," he said, "because if Tobias finds out, you're all dead! I mean that literally. The man is not in a forgiving mood. He's already beaten a security guard half to death because he forgot to lock the loading bay door."

Baby A gasped. "What? Nobody told me about this! Is he alright?"

"*Tobias* is fine. A little guilty maybe. The security guard has been granted three months of leave and has agreed after that to remain as a member of our staff, but it took a lot of convincing. Can you blame him? Between the death of our leader, *zombies,* and now this?"

"We're losin' Tobias, ya know," Dion groaned, rubbing her head. "And this idea is so far-fetched an' may go *completely* wrong. Ya need total strength not to keep suckin'."

"Strength you both possess," Baby A said, "for a reason."

"We *were* designed differently, Dion," Susan reminded her, taking a step closer to Arriette once more to assert herself.

But Baby A seemed puzzled by her statement.

"Arriette once told me I was special, and Zinnyi chose us both to become what we are for a purpose. He gave Dion immunity to our evil nature, and he gave me the gift of astro-projection, to be in two places at one time. I believe that's so I can help Angelica. How many other vampyrs like us have you met?"

Dion shook her head. "If there were any, they'd be in hidin'."

"We are stronger, Dion. Physically, mentally, emotionally. Think about this. Arriette *knew* something about why we are the way we are; she never tried to change us because she loved us. When she found out about my plan to undo all this with Reiko, she was angry, but she let us do what we had to, what was in our nature and our morals. I've killed people in this form, but in all my existence, I have chosen those who deserved it. Murderers, rapists, thieves, other demonic beasts. I can project, just like Angelica. Sure, it's only when one part of me sleeps, but I'm sure it's because it's my *destiny* to protect Angelica. She's talented and she can do things I can't. And it was my *destiny* to hunt evil even as a vampyr. Arriette saved me for a reason. Dion, you have immunity to the bloodlust and held onto your human soul because Arriette needed a friend she trusted, and someone to teach her to trust even the most unlikely of creatures. Someone to help her through *this*... when she herself owns fangs."

"I wish we could ask her first," Baby A said.

"You convinced the leader of the Recruit to see vampyrs in an entirely different light, Dion; you saved her from herself and that awful plan to live alone. In return, she helped you. Now you're the best of friends. And thanks to my ability, I could find Arriette again and help her locate Pandora's box. Our gifts were assigned purposefully to serve this woman." She patted the glass above Arriette's head gently with her long fingers.

Dion shrugged. "So what are ya sayin'? Where are ya goin' with this speech?"

Susan lifted the glass without aid and placed it gently on the ground. Jet stammered, remembering how heavy that lid was and how he and Sebastian struggled to move it together.

"How d-did you—"

"Vampyr," Sebastian whispered from the corner of his mouth.

Susan glanced at them both as she took Arriette's limp white wrist and held it by her fangs, hovering nervously. Baby A and Sebastian both gasped, but nobody attempted to intercept her.

"Tobias will k-kill you," Jet told her. "We w-won't be able to s-stop him."

Susan thought for a moment, then said, "If that's my purpose, then so be it."

"What, to let Tobias *stake* you?" Tabitha said.

"If it saves Arriette's life."

"Please, Susan," Baby A begged her. "I agree it's worth a shot, but let the others have their input first, and let Tobias hear everything you just said."

"I don't think we have enough time," Jet told them, cringing as Baby A's glare suddenly found him. "Arriette's paler and weaker, even more so than when we started this debate."

"I'm warning you *both*," Sebastian said, raising his voice again. "Nobody else will want this. She will wake up and she will kill us all. *Dead dead.* And then if he's not already dead too, Tobias will kill Susan!"

"*You,* of all people, Sebastian, should agree with me," Susan said. "You were the one who said she—"

"It's not right," he stated.

Susan growled in return. "I won't allow Arriette to suffer anymore. I can *end* this, for better or worse. Her pain will be over."

Sebastian dived forward to catch Susan as her fangs punctured Arriette's wrist. Blood oozed from the wound, caressed by her long tongue. Susan's pupils widened at a flavour she'd missed and tried so hard to forget, but as Arriette's unique supernatural blood gushed down her throat and into her bloodstream, Susan's eyes illuminated and her energy increased.

Sebastian was no match for her vampyric strength.

Baby A forced him away. "You'll get yourself killed," she told him, but he roared with anger and thrashed forward, calling for Susan to stop and let Arriette go.

The blood drained quickly.

Each limb twitched in response to Susan's venom and the torturous pain it was inflicting on Arriette. Susan hoped she wasn't conscious enough to feel anything. But Arriette's body was responding as they'd expected, and her limbs were contracting.

"Dion," Baby A gestured, "can you help her? Speed

this process up? I bet if both our unique vampyrs worked together, Arriette will have a better chance."

Jet stammered. "What a-are you d-doing, Baby A?"

Sebastian pushed Baby A aside to witness the effects of the venom himself. Arriette's lips had pursed, and her lungs filled with air, causing her chest to rise and fall gently as the venom kick-started her.

Dion stared at the wrist she held so dearly and closed her eyes. She *hated* the tang of human blood; it made her sick. But if this would help her friend, and if it was indeed her purpose, like Susan claimed, then she'd do it.

So Dion bit down and pierced Arriette's skin, feasting in rhythm with the other vampyr to speed up the process. For the first time, the flavour was pleasant. But Arriette's blood wasn't ordinary, because she had an intense supernatural potion of power circulating her body.

What the concoction would do to Susan and Dion, there was no way of knowing. But she wasn't conscious enough for them to worry about power-saving; neither Dion nor Susan wanted to inherit any of her powers.

They injected more of their venom, and Arriette's steady breathing ceased once again. Vampyrs were technically dead, and so her body's response shouldn't have come as a shock, but they were all beginning to worry their plan had backfired.

On the count of three, they bit into their own wrists and squeezed several drops of their blood into her mouth, then closed her lips and waited.

Baby A realised she'd been holding her breath in anticipation and dread.

"I can't... this is... I don't..."

The vampyrs released Arriette's hands, deflated. For a transformation to be truly complete, the process often took a few hours to a few days, but with Arriette's position on the HPS and their circumstances, everyone had expected an instant fix.

Sebastian swore. "We had a chance to do this properly and you didn't listen to me! AGAIN!"

"I really thought we'd be able to change her," said Dion, solemnly.

"Yeah, me too," said Susan.

TWENTY—FIVE

Sebastian had been watching over Arriette's body for several hours, protecting it from any further attempts to re-animate her. She had twitched and groaned a few times, but there were no other signs that the vampyrs attempt to turn her had worked. If anything, he now worried about their leader being in writhing pain, but being unable to show it or ask for their help. His only comfort was knowing those vampyrs would face Tobias's wrath once he found out.

And soon.

He looked over the meadow, waiting to see the top of Tobias's head appear, but so far there had been no sign of him. So Sebastian picked a few rocks and plants to cast spells on, keeping his mind busy until Tobias gathered the guts to say goodbye properly. That's if he wasn't off on a vampyr staking spree.

Until then, Sebastian would stand in his friend's place and guard her until the inevitable happened.

In the early hours, he drifted off to sleep. It was impossible to find a comfortable position, so he gathered some long grass and wild flowers and settled upon them, gazing up at the lair's false sky and imagining Arriette's body changing. Maybe there would be progress by the time he woke; progress unseen by his unworthy eyes until the venom had done its job internally.

He hoped. He prayed. But he didn't believe.

Within Arriette, the vampyrs' venom ran. It had plotted a direct route from the bite marks on both wrists to her heart. From there, it would be pumped furiously into every other part of her body and then eventually her brain would respond, bringing her physical form back to life. But it wasn't as easy as her friends had first expected. They had assumed, given her rank on the HPS that she'd transform faster. But living within Arriette's temporarily frozen form was another being; one dormant until the piercing fangs woke it, but still immensely powerful. Enough to resist the venom's pull until she had intercepted Arriette's returning consciousness first.

Living within Arriette was the goddess, Pandora.

And there were things her host needed to know.

The dark tunnel of Arriette's consciousness opened. Before her, blocking a brilliantly lit exit, was a woman in soot-grey rags. The same silhouette she'd seen standing amongst the mutants. She was a gorgeous tanned doll, standing in bare feet with matted hair that hung loose and eyes a painted pool of golden sunlight. They had met before. Arriette recognised the stranger as Pandora.

She was suddenly optimistic about seeing her again. But Arriette didn't understand where she was, or what was happening to her.

"You're s-still here?" Arriette asked as soon as her ability to form words returned. Her voice was hoarse, and she was stammering, stunned by Pandora's presence.

"I thought f-for so long I had imagined our u-union in that cave, but here you are."

"I'm real. A part of me lives inside you."

Without warning, her image flashed and reappeared closer, sending Arriette staggering. Pandora reached to take Arriette's chin in her right hand and guided her; the glance was soothing. And then she was beside her, holding her hand instead, and leading her carefully toward the light at a slow, steady pace, leaving neon footprints on the sand.

"All this time we have been protecting your box from unknown, potential threats," Arriette said. "And we weren't sure if you had perished or become trapped within it."

"We bonded, and so it's only fair of me to step in now when our life hangs in the balance. Is *this* what you want?" she asked Arriette.

Arriette sighed. "You mean... to die?"

Pandora paused and shook her head. "This isn't death, Arriette. Not yet. This is just a temporary pause I've created so we can converse."

"The long dark tunnel leading to a single bright light," Arriette replied matter-of-factly, "gave me the wrong impression."

"You're not dying. I mean, you *are*, but there are things we can do to prevent it. Do you want to live in this newer form?"

"*Their* form," Arriette whispered; the tingle of the venom nudged Pandora's barricade aside. "A vampyr is... trying to *save* me?"

"*Vampyrs*. Your friends."

She nodded. "Susan and Dion bit me."

"You weren't dead, Arriette, you were travelling," Pandora told her, "and so your friends were misguided, but they were trying to save your life. To turn you into a vampyr before your time would be up. Their intent is pure, if a little... rushed."

She tugged Arriette gently forward again. The intense light ahead scolded her eyes, and she held up her free arm to block the glare. If this wasn't heaven she was headed towards, then what?

Beautiful and warm, like a long hug.

"They are changing you," Pandora said, "and, if you think about it, they are killing you. Or should I say, they are killing *us*."

"Your soul is still hiding here. What do *you* want?"

She squeezed Arriette's hand. "You're my host, and this decision can only be yours. If I allow the venom to take you, it will also take me and will create something unique and dangerous, yet capable of miracles."

"Why haven't we talked sooner? It's a bit late!"

"It was not my time."

"Could it be your time *now*?"

Pandora replied, "If *you* want it to be."

"I'm not sure I understand what that would mean for Haeylo," Arriette admitted. "How it might change *me*."

When she looked down at her form, Arriette mirrored this beautiful woman in every way. They were like twins locked in a strange but noble place; a place of bravery and truth. They stopped and stared at one another. Arriette didn't really want her appearance to change. Her face, body, and her personality had attracted Tobias, and she loved him; she wanted him to recognise her heart. A change from human to vampyr wasn't as simple as a change of clothes, which she now assumed was Pandora's doing.

"It's too late to turn back now," Arriette said.

"Not quite."

"The venom is pumping. Who knows what I might turn into? But they did this to save my life and so I should be grateful. It's a gift, right?"

"You were not dead, though," Pandora reminded

Arriette, "only travelling through time and space."

She scoffed. "Impossible."

"Not for me," Pandora assured her. "An infinite thought is all I am. It is all I have ever been since arriving here, because my original form is still in that cave, rotting. Only my soul exists, and now within *you*. I have been travelling through space from host to host, waiting to find *you*, Arriette."

"So you're a traveller of what, then?"

"Of spirit," Pandora replied. "Or of consciousness, but I don't know what I am, exactly. A memory? A story. A myth! A lesson, mostly. But it was through me that your mind travelled, though your body remained behind. Once your daughter was born, you tapped into *my* power."

"My... daughter..."

Arriette's stomach was flat in this place. Her human pregnancy was over, and somewhere, her daughter was waiting for her.

Pandora tugged at the chain around Arriette's neck, releasing her everlast pendant and, behind it, a key to the vault in the basement of HQ where Pandora's box was hidden. It hung on a silver necklace between her breasts.

"You have done well to keep my box safe."

"You could return there and live. Why suffer in here with me if you don't have to?"

She smiled, and Arriette smiled back. "Separating my soul is the best way to remain connected to the box whilst still having some control of it from the outside. Once I fully return, I am relying on the Recruit alone to ensure nobody ever opens it again."

"I didn't know I could activate your power," Arriette admitted. "I would have sooner. I didn't know you were here, not for certain."

She was warmer at the thought of her daughter, and her skin was glowing against the light of the tunnel's exit. But the vibrancy was buried somewhere deep, and hesitant to give itself to this goddess. Whether it was life returning, hope, or the venom slowly killing her cells, she had no way of knowing for sure. Not until Pandora released them from limbo.

"I can stop the venom," Pandora said. "I can hold it back long enough for you to wake up and warn your friends of their mistake. They could reverse it with fluids or suck the venom back out. I could leave you completely to their will and return, as you say, to my box."

Arriette pondered the implications. If she allowed the venom to weave her into a new existence, what might it look like and how would it affect her temperament? Could she still nurse and love her daughter, or would it harden her heart and drive her to long for her family's blood?

Without Pandora's soul, Arriette could never call on her for help or knowledge around the box's protection.

Then she thought of Dion and Susan, whose special natures meant they walked Haeylo in unique ways, allowing them to rouse her now. Perhaps that was, after all, *their* purpose. Their paths had led them to this moment to turn Arriette and Pandora into something... new.

Arriette stopped walking and released Pandora's hand. "Why did they think I was dead? Did the travel," she swallowed hard as she formed the end of her difficult sentence, "*harm* me?"

"It weakened us," Pandora finally admitted.

When Arriette said nothing further, Pandora exhaled deeply and gestured for them to sit. There was a large smooth rock by the tunnel's exit, and Arriette sat upon it to hear Pandora's explanation before she could make an informed decision. They had a little time to decide whether to let Pandora protect them from the venom, or allow it to take her body and change her, potentially for the better.

"The travel lasted longer than expected, and I miscalculated how much physically your body could withstand after giving birth," she admitted. "Your friends were running out of time; you have eaten nothing in days. Despite the warnings of the red-headed sorcerer, your friends did not realise soon enough that you were alive."

"They thought I died when the travel began."

"Yes, but when you did not decompose, the sorcerer realised something was amiss. Though your body is now struggling, and malnourishment is becoming apparent."

Arriette's fingertips were tingling, so she wound her palms together to distract herself from what the venom was doing as they lingered here in Pandora's dream world.

"If we can wake and warn them, what are our chances?"

Pandora hummed. "Your body is... hungry."

"You didn't answer my question."

Arriette stood and narrowed her eyes through the glare. On the other side, she saw the wild flowers in the meadow and the clear blue sky waiting for them. Upon its horizon were the castle's towers, the Recruit lair's buildings and trees. It beckoned to her, but in the distance the skyline was darkened with storm clouds and a blood-red hue.

"Were you with me when I began my journey?"

Pandora nodded, confirming it was not Casper who had accompanied her.

"I can't do this to Tobias again," she told Pandora. "I mean, he's had to mourn me once and plan a life without me; a way to raise our daughter, to protect your box without really knowing how or why, to lead the Recruit in my place and who knows what else? I cannot... I *will* not... put him through losing me again. To wake and warn them, only to be too late and to die for real this time?"

She sighed as she accepted the lesser of the evils, praying silently to Zïnnyi that he might make her worthy of a kinder vampyric existence.

"You can release the venom, Pandora. I know what it's doing to us, and how much pain we're about to be in. But it's necessary. I won't leave them again."

Pandora offered Arriette a hand, and she took it.

"Are you sure?"

But could Arriette manage such an important responsibility? To lead such a huge organisation, raise her daughter, venture on to discover her accurate family history and now manage the raging hunger of a vampyr?

Pandora's ghost morphed into Arriette's soul and their bodies became one before Arriette complained about her ever-growing responsibilities. There was no use fighting either side, and so Arriette gave in to Pandora and allowed her to seek sanctuary once again within her body; they would endure the transformation together. Pandora owed her that much, and there had to be a reason for their connection. She wished to live on within Arriette, and Arriette simply wished to live.

She had to trust that Zïnnyi had a plan and would guide her from this point forth.

The light rushed toward her, like a fast-forward of thousands of Haeyloian years, and a beautiful silver whirlpool sucked them in. Arriette thought of Andrew Kaines's last moments on Earth, and how a similar vortex had swallowed that helicopter. She remembered what he'd done for his people, and how she must now do whatever it took to be there for hers.

We save the people, we save the world.

No sooner than the light had swallowed Arriette did it spit her out, and she felt her lungs fill. A sweet sensation, but immediately Arriette experienced the pangs of hunger in the pit of her stomach and the lasting aches and pains of the venom down her back and her legs. Her eyes flicked open to a confined space where she lay inside a glass box no longer than her body or wider than her shoulders, and she was trapped and stiff. Her muscles throbbed, but coursing through her veins moved something newer, powerful, and it healed and strengthening her with every passing second. It wouldn't be long before she'd be running and fighting again.

"I... I can breathe?" she uttered, stunned.

Arriette shoved upwards to try to lift the glass. It wouldn't budge, but she turned her head enough to see a red-headed man sprawled on the floor beside her. Her arms were still like jelly. The man's head sagged and his awkward posture told Arriette he was probably asleep. With no need to shift to her cat-like senses, she suddenly heard him snoring. She tried again to lift it, but it had been locked at the base, so she shuffled lower and kicked the bottom with her bare feet, noticing someone had dressed her in a white gown and surrounded her with colourful wild flowers. In the glass's reflection, she could see they'd brushed her hair and her cheeks were flushed, though she appeared thinner in the face.

Arriette hammered on the glass with her fists, trying to get somebody's attention.

"Sebastian!" she called to the man, recognising his auburn hair and the way he was dressed in sorcerer robes.

Sebastian's ears pricked; he stretched and yawned but he didn't turn. Instead, he rummaged in a satchel for a canteen. When he turned to check on Arriette's body, he dropped his water and froze. He took a few steps back, and without trying to free her or talk to her, he set off running across the meadow. He bolted faster than Arriette had ever seen him run and disappeared with a tip of his hat in a puff of smoke a quarter of the way towards the town hall.

"Hey! Come back!"

Arriette rolled her eyes. When the shock wore off, somebody would be along to let her out.

But time ticked by slowly, and all she could do was fidget, growing more and more claustrophobic. Arriette had given Sebastian a jolt. He needed to find somebody else—Tobias or Baby A, maybe—to double-check he wasn't seeing things or going crazy. But she realised the glass case she now called home was, in fact, a coffin.

She'd been dead.

And the dead aren't supposed to call your name.

The strength in her muscles gradually returned, and her determination to escape this chamber grew. Arriette let out a sharp cry as she punched upward with both hands. She brought her knees to her chest and aimed them high, winding herself briefly and gasping, then bolted them upright at the glass ceiling at the same time. It cracked down the centre enough for her to push it apart, and as she did so, it crashed to the ground into a thousand pieces.

Getting up would need to be a slower process than she'd expected, because she was light-headed now, and her vision seemed brighter and sharper than before, throwing her balance. She could see right across the meadow to examine the brickwork of the town hall, and hear each snapping twig, ruffled leaf and approaching voices in the surrounding trees.

Panic overwhelmed her. Arriette jumped up, landing on her toes. She grabbed the coffin base to steady herself, then prepared to fight or flee. Across the field, Arriette saw a group of people. But she recognised them, and exhaled with relief when she saw Reiko was at the head of the group, closely followed by Susan and Dion. Pouki stood at the back, accompanied by Tabitha Hope and, finally, Sebastian Sky.

"I'm telling you, she was staring at me!"

Reiko was about to tell Sebastian he needed to get some more sleep when the group was met by Arriette's awe-inspired expression.

The vampyrs halted and circled her, examining her body and her eyes without a greeting as if to test how dangerous this newly created creature was. Arriette followed every inch of movement, wondering why they didn't welcome her home with enthusiasm, but allowed them to check her over until they were satisfied.

"Arriette?"

"Yes, it's me, Dion."

"Oh, blessings!" Dion gasped and ran to her.

Her vampyric instincts relaxed, and she embraced her friend with no need for any further evidence. Arriette squeezed her back, lifting her off the ground and swinging the red-headed vampyr around with excitement.

"Put me down, ya hurtin' me!"

"Whoops, sorry." Arriette let Dion drop to her knees. "I don't know my strength yet. I'm... woozy."

"Do you know what happened?" asked Susan, her eyes still narrow, inspecting her.

Reiko interrupted before Arriette told them about her

conversation with Pandora. "*You* have the explaining to do! What the hell happened, Arriette? We assumed you'd died and then Sebastian said you'd look... well... and then you didn't, so he wanted to monitor you and we didn't believe him."

Arriette took a single step toward Reiko to offer Pandora's explanation, but Reiko didn't seem eager to be any closer to her than he had to be.

Her approach halted his rambling, though, and he held up his palms. "Not until I confirm you're the same Arriette you've always been."

"As opposed to...?"

"A monster."

Dion said, "Aren't ya hungry, Arriette?"

"I could eat." She shrugged.

Susan added, "You should be starving."

"I'm thirsty."

She reached down for Sebastian's discarded canteen and took a swig, then placed it on the top of her coffin, inhaling deeply as she did so.

"You're breathing, too?"

Susan's fangs protruded from her upper gums, prompting Arriette's to involuntarily do the same.

"Thirsty for *water*, and yes, I can still breathe," Arriette insisted, feeling the tips of her fangs with her tongue as she investigated this new, natural reaction to being around another vampyr.

"Odd."

"You don't want blood?"

"I'll have some synthetic stuff, if Reiko's up for it? I'd like to see what it does to me."

Arriette scanned her friends until her eyes met Pouki's. He half-smiled, moving towards her with his arm outstretched, wanting to touch her beautiful, pale skin. He wanted to see for himself how real this all was.

"You're a vampyr," he said. "And you... know everything already? How?"

"I figured it out but I had help. I almost died, and you did as necessary." Arriette retracted her fangs with minimal effort, then grinned. "Nice coffin, by the way. Did everyone cry at the funeral?"

Pouki sighed with relief, tears streaming down his cheeks. "You're still *you*."

"And ya don't hate us," Dion said.

"No!" Arriette beamed. "I'm fine, look."

"But, we killed you and turned you into a vampyr. Don't you feel an overwhelming connection to us? Haven't you inherited any memories or urges or instincts?" When Arriette didn't reply, Susan grabbed her wrists. "We bit you!"

Puncture marks on both her wrists seemed to be healing, but visible. They'd be a pleasant addition to the others she sported on her neck; further scars to prove her resistance to the species. Other than appearing slimmer, Arriette hadn't changed at all. The dirty green eyes of the human woman she'd once been were now golden, and her brunette hair shone brighter. If anything, she looked healthier.

"Explains why vampyrs could never kill me," she said. "I don't feel any different. So, does somebody want to fill me in? What happened with the mutant women?"

Pouki shook his head. "Tobias doesn't know about this yet. He's going to need time to... adjust. And you have a daughter we need to consider before any of the Enzoian women."

Arriette's eyes filled with tears. "Is she... healthy?"

Tabitha nodded, finally gathering the courage to speak to this new creature they had all helped to create.

"I've been helping Tobias take care of her and monitoring things. She's absolutely gorgeous. She looks just like you. At least she did, before..." Tabitha gestured at Arriette's golden eyes, which she examined in the reflection of a large shard of glass.

"I hadn't noticed, but the colour of my eyes and fangs is a small price to pay. I have a lot I need to tell you, but first, I want to see my daughter."

"Wait," said Reiko, "because we should get some synthetic blood in you. It's remarkable you remember us, Arriette. That you remember... anything, and that you look *better off*. Most vampyrs look the way they died and have to spend years learning from their vampyr parent."

"I'm not the only unique vamp on this planet," Arriette reminded them, folding her arms and resting back against the coffin. "You all took a tremendous risk doing what you did. I'm sure Zïnnyi has rewarded it by allowing me to keep my humanity. I prayed for it."

"Certainly looks that way to me," Pouki said, a little hesitantly. He grasped her hand and led her across the meadow. "We should also check that your original powers are still functioning."

Arriette scanned the field until she found a rock. She quickly flicked it away with the use of telekinesis, then checked behind her before releasing her wings.

"Being vampyric, my shifting will be intact, as will my everlasting life, and I just got back from travelling, *so*..."

Pouki halted the group. "You... *what*?"

Arriette laughed and tucked her wings away. "Like I said, I have lots to tell you."

"You travelled where, exactly?"

"To Earth. Andrew and I witnessed the end of the planet together. But before we get into any of that, how are you going to break the news that I'm not dead to Tobias, and *when* can I hold my daughter?"

TWENTY—SIX

How beautiful is the Haeyloian language? Arriette contemplated, as Pouki surrounded her with incense.

"Zohla mightie Zïnnyi, illumina et ze dezra. Et'ternan ira ze marê." He and the Four Saviours muttered powerful protection chants to free Arriette's inner vampyr, and Arriette watched as he re-formed their individual triangular symptoms in salt at her feet, as he had once done in the dirt in Manaia Forest. Nothing else had worked, and it seemed neither would this.

Pouki was sure now that there wasn't anything to free. And Arriette trusted his judgement; fluent in the language after years of practice and study, mostly thanks to him, she too could understand the outcome of each of these little tests.

On the surface and to those less experienced, his words meant, 'Oh, mighty creator, shine your light upon the dead, watch over the fearless for eternity.' Or, Arriette knew it also roughly translated, to those willing to read between the lines, to a prayer, and as he drew magic up through the symbols and through the Four Saviours, using their individual gifts to boost his final test, Arriette re-created his past chant: *Urt, Ayre, Fori, Walta.*

Pouki was asking Zïnnyi to show him, or *illuminate* to

him, what Arriette's death meant for the Recruit. To take away his fear of her; a fear that knows no bounds, and one that he would hold infinitely. And he was using the Four Saviours' magic to support his enquiry.

But Pouki's underlying fear of Arriette's intense power was not what her friends needed to see or hear. And it was not something Arriette wanted to concern herself with, either. He had no reason to fear her, because she would do nothing to harm any of them. If her vampyric instincts did ever attempt to rule her, she had already promised she'd leave them and venture off into the forest alone for as long as it took.

Forever, if necessary.

And with the goddess' influence now active within her, she could call for Pandora's help, too.

But for now, she had to see her fangs and increased stamina as only a benefit to their organisation, and to protecting Pandora's box from others like Falkon Lou, who would wish to use it against them. To her friends, Pouki's chanting was the deliverance of a Haeyloian blessing and nothing more. He and the Four Saviours had worked with the language long enough to respect the power it held; in every word and phrase, and in not only how it was used, but who by. If their results proved Arriette wasn't an imminent threat, she'd be contempt.

"You've inherited a vampyr's physical appearance without their thirst," Pouki told her, "but your control of what should be natural instincts is only usually seen in weres."

"How do you mean?"

"Some werewolves cannot distinguish between friend and foe when shifting, but some can. And it's a skill not to give in to their urges."

Then Ruby and Pouki conversed in the language, deeper than Arriette ever thought she could grasp. But with Pandora's ancient soul active within her and the vampyr's venom seeming to only boost her other gifts, the translation was smoother and came to her like another sense.

"Zo verefrows forendo litte?" Ruby asked.

So, were the werewolves involved too?

"Nol, verefrows elitia Arriette Monroe."

No, the werewolves respect Arriette Monroe.

"Arriette Monroe ze lanya et Earth?"

Arriette did not really travel to Earth?

Pouki said, "Yei, de'va demetran, Arriette proniba."

Well, she is a spirited lover of the planet.

Arriette grunted and interrupted them. "You don't need to be *rude*."

"We don't mean to be," Ruby said and gnawed on her lip. "I didn't want to worry anyone."

"They do respect me, by the way. They would never step out of line—Susan and Dion did this to me alone, and they were *trying* to save my life. He's right, too. Earth has fascinated me my whole life, and it turns out we do not know as much about their last few years as our books indicate."

At the back of the lab, the corner of Reiko's mouth upturned as he mixed Arriette a batch of his synthetic blood.

"I didn't realise you had studied the language to such a degree," Ruby admitted.

"Well, it's not only me in this body."

Reiko dropped his beaker. "Excuse me?"

"I'm not the only one translating. I meant what I said. Pandora helped me to break free of that travel to Earth, and she also tried to prevent me from becoming a vampyr."

"Why didn't you let her?"

"Because her plan wouldn't have worked. I trust her, Reiko, and she trusted me enough to allow this to happen. She and I are a part of each other now, and it has only confirmed a question we've all been asking since we defeated that dragon."

"Pandora isn't dead," Reiko said, matter-of-factly.

"It's because of her presence that Susan and Dion could do what they did. That it worked. And that I'm different as they are. We're unique for a reason."

Pouki seemed lost. "Pandora is inside of you?"

"Well, her spirit is, and I sense her power now. A little. I couldn't sense her at all before. The vampyrs activated her. I believe I am what I am now for a reason."

"Where has she been, and why not show herself until now?" he argued.

"She said it 'wasn't her time'."

Jade asked, "And it is now?"

Arriette wasn't sure. "She's leaving that decision up to me. Perhaps to call upon her when I feel she is most needed. When you eventually tell me what happened with the mutant women, perhaps we can put her to use."

"There's another threat to face?" Di interjected.

"I think somebody will try to steal Pandora's box again; someone who can do terrible things with it."

Pouki took a beaker of red fluid from Reiko and insisted Arriette drink it, then he gestured for Reiko to clean up the one he'd dropped.

"We may already have identified who that is," he said.

The blood substitute tasted bitter and salty; she didn't

care for it, so she also drank half a canteen of water to wash it down.

"Ah! Much better."

"Do you have any desire for blood yet?"

"No, Reiko."

"Are you... sure?"

Arriette growled. "Just *yours*." She laughed and waved a dismissive hand. "Kidding. Honestly, it tasted like feet. I don't know how Susan and Dion drink that stuff."

"You said it called to you," Dion argued.

"It did, maybe for a reason. A hint I was about to become one of you." She rolled her eyes and said, "Reiko, I'm not going to bite anyone. I'd *die* first."

Pouki mumbled, "Yes, well, let's not think about that right now."

"How can we not," Reiko said, "when she has bigger fangs than Susan? If she's a vampyr, she's technically dead anyway, right? But she's not because she's breathing, but her heart isn't beating... much. And she doesn't look the way most vampyrs do when they turn."

"That's because I didn't die. I travelled. Like Susan and Dion, I didn't have a gnarly, gruesome end. I might have fangs, but there's nothing so far to suggest I'm venomous... or dead."

"All vampyrs are," Ruby said, shrugging.

"Shall I bite you and double-check?"

Pouki swatted her. "That's enough!"

Ruby and Arriette chortled, much to Reiko's disgust. At least *someone* understood her dark sense of humour.

"Venom is something we can check," said Saph.

Pouki walked to a small refrigerator and pulled out a chilled slab of meat. Arriette was already sick at the thought, and she could detect it had been there several days; perhaps it had been the victim of other laboratory tests. It was gross.

"What *is* that?"

"Doesn't matter." Saph shoved it at her. "Bite it."

"*No way.*" She cringed.

Pouki raised a brow. "She wasn't asking."

Before agreeing to try it, Arriette gave it one final sniff. She regretted it. She bit down hurriedly, hating the texture, then quickly retracted her fangs. The skin turned black and hardened as Arriette's venom soaked through it —venom she hadn't activated.

Pouki dropped it on a tray before the venom reached his hands.

"That answers that."

"Wait, vampyr venom doesn't do that," said Reiko, pointing at the meat. "It's transparent. Never have I seen it internally *solidify* another creature, or turn that colour."

"Is that bad?" Arriette asked, worried. "I didn't even feel it come out. Should I?"

"Perhaps Pandora has something to do with it. It's got to be a little crowded in there, and you said she's got powers. Maybe the two of you combined are something unique, like a brand new species of vampyr?"

"Watch your mouth, Jade," warned Pouki. "If others hear you speak of new vampyrs, we can kiss goodbye to hosting HQ here, especially after the zombie outbreak."

"*Zombie* outbreak? That's what you're calling it?"

"Whatever you want to call it, Arriette has some kind of venom capable of changing the form of its victims. I suggest, for *now*, we keep that nugget to ourselves."

Reiko rolled his eyes and continued cleaning his laboratory. Arriette downed the rest of the blood in the beaker and handed it back to him.

"Given your other powers are still fully functional, I presume your everlast pendant will still offer you some help during battle, though you no longer need to rely on it to extend your life. Vampyrs are... undead."

"I told you, I'm not dead! I didn't die! And my heart is beating, just faintly. I'm some kind of hybrid, and I fully intend on marrying out of the everlasting life if Tobias will still have me. If you're sure I'm safe, *now* can I see my baby girl?"

Pouki nodded. "I suppose so. With an escort."

"Tobias will be there, right?"

Pouki nodded again. "There's something you should know, though, before you go running off."

Arriette hastened to the door, only to pause at the knob. Heavy footsteps approached the lab, and Arriette braced herself to face Tobias. Pouki noticed she'd frozen as she listened intently to the quick breaths and weeps of heartache that followed. Then through the door, sending Arriette jumping back to avoid being knocked in the head, burst Tabitha.

Her cheeks were red, and her eyes panicked.

"Arriette, it's Susan and Dion. They've collapsed!"

"What? Vampyrs don't get sick," said Reiko, quickly grabbing two viles of the synthetic blood and heading to the door. "Is Dion awake? Is she alive?"

Arriette and Pouki exchanged knowing glances, then dove after him through the exit, navigating through the endless span of corridors within HQ.

Susan and Dion were sprawled out in a corridor, exactly where they had fallen on their way to see her, to offer her comfort and advice.

"Susan was complaining of a stomach ache," Tabitha

explained to Pouki, "and Dion said her head felt heavy." She cried. "They went down without warning. Like they'd been shot! BAM! I didn't think vampyrs could get sick."

"They can't," said Pouki.

Arriette knelt beside Dion first to examine her body, sensing Reiko's concern as he crumpled, panting, beside her. The vampyr's glowing skin was fading and her protruding fangs were sinking slowly back into her gums. Arriette lifted her upper lip, startled.

"They're... vanishing!"

Her luminous red hair was turning dull, and her open eyes were darkening.

"A-Arriette," she managed. Her lids narrowed, and she writhed in pain, but Arriette couldn't tell where the pain was coming from.

"What's happening to them?" she asked Pouki, who rubbed his face with his hands and exhaled sharply.

He pointed to Dion's wrist. "I think you should bite her back. Let's test that venom."

"*What?*" she startled. "Are you insane? You saw what it did to that meat! You want me to turn Dion into a crusty black steak? You *just* said we should keep it a secret!"

"I think doing what they did for you, Arriette, is changing them. When they bit you, they ingested something they shouldn't have. Something acting as a defence mechanism."

"You mean, *Pandora*?" Arriette felt faint, if being light-headed was possible for a newly turned vampyr.

"But Susan drank from me before," she told him, "on the way to the temple. She was fine then. Why not now?"

Pouki shook his head. "Because you offered yourself to her the last time. You volunteered. This time, Pandora's spirit must have initiated some kind of kill code. When they bit you, it changed them."

"Into what?"

"*Prey…* for you, potentially."

"WHAT? NO!"

"It's only a guess," he said.

"What's going to happen if I *don't* bite them back?"

Reiko slumped, head in his hands. "Dion will be human?"

Pouki whispered, "I-I don't know."

Without a word or a motion more, he left them—Susan and Dion were now struggling to keep their eyes open, but Susan was crying, and Arriette took her temperature with the back of her hand. She was burning up, and Dion would soon join her. Vampyrs, normally freezing to the touch, were causing Arriette to hiss from the heat.

Dion swallowed hard, as if fighting for a breath she had never needed to take.

"Arriette, what did he say to you?"

"What's going on?" Susan strained.

"You're turning human again," she said, watching as Dion's chest began to rise and fall. "Because of me."

"Arry! Don't let this happen, bite me now," Susan urged, but Arriette couldn't bring herself to do it, even at the sound of her nickname. "Please!"

Reiko placed his hand on Arriette's shoulder. "You *can* do this," he urged.

"Are you sure, Susan? You were the one fighting to find a way back to humanity."

"Never mind that. BITE ME!"

As she wept, distraught at what she'd have to do to please Susan, she sank her giant fangs into the flesh of her wrist and pulled away quickly, terrified it would start a longing she didn't want or need. Especially since she was about to meet her newborn daughter.

Susan's body vibrated and thrashed as Arriette's hardened venom coursed its way to her heart.

Dion squeezed her hand. "It's OK," she said, then glanced at Reiko, who clutched her hand. "It h-hurts."

"I don't know what to do for the best, but it's going to be fine. Hang on, alright? I'm right here. You can change your mind."

"No. This... is... right."

From within Dion's chest came a light thump. Arriette tucked her hair behind her ear and leaned down to listen. There it was again. *Thump! Thump!* The faster heartbeat of a human had replaced her lazy, unused vampyric organ. And blood—Arriette's blood, the blood she had sucked from her leader's body when saving her life—had saved Dion's.

Life ran through her, and her body wriggled.

The vampyrs, in unison, ceased to writhe in pain. It happened suddenly, like candles being extinguished in a breeze, or a switch had been flicked.

Arriette glared down at their bodies. Susan's fangs were visible again, and her glorious electric blue eyes returned. Her skin lit up the room in a blaze of power. She rolled to her side to inspect her companion, lifting her hands and arms, thrilled to see they were milky again. But Dion's body had been totally transformed from the muscular and intense red-headed hunter she once was, to a stunning pale-skinned human with lake-green eyes and auburn locks. She lay still for a moment to catch her breath, then wrapped her arms around Arriette's neck.

"Thank you, Zïnnyi," she hummed. "Thank you, Arriette. *Thank you... Pandora.*"

TWENTY—SEVEN

Arriette broke from the havoc in the room to give Dion and Susan time to compose themselves, and to talk through Dion's transformation with Pouki. She scowled at him, but ultimately knew he'd left her there for a reason. Choosing to use her venom for good was a pivotal moment; it identified Arriette's intentions as a vampyr, and solidified his predictions that she was the same messed-up supe, who would do *anything* to save her friends.

Susan hadn't changed at all. She'd avoided most of the pain Dion was forced to endure, but it was obvious to Arriette why Dion wanted to transform back to her human self when she saw the way Reiko looked at her.

They were in love.

The intense strain of being made 'normal' again had exhausted her, though. She longed to sleep; something Dion hadn't done properly since being made vampyr the year before she met Arriette. A beating heart, breathing lungs, pulse points, and the human sensation of lust had already caused her first migraine. One she was proud of.

Human suited Dion. And Arriette told her so before leaving her to come to terms with her new body.

But Susan couldn't have been less jealous. It had taken almost being made human again for the vicious astro-projecting vampyr to realise she could think of nothing worse, and the concoctions she'd asked Reiko to work on were now in the past, never to be explored or tasted. Reiko promised he would cease work on such a potion because Arriette reminded him they still had Casper's recipe for the one he'd made for Baby A—she'd given it to Arriette in the first days of her Recruit adventure, who had then given it to Dean, stripping his memory.

Susan had made her choice.

To be fragile and vulnerable again, enough for another Falkon Lou to take advantage of her? Enough to *kill* her and for real, this time?

No.

She thanked Arriette for acting quickly and under the pressure they both placed on her simultaneously. To save a life and to re-take a life.

"It was brave of you," Susan told Dion, "but I just couldn't go through with it."

Arriette was fine with leaving them alone for a while. She had a baby girl and a fiancée to catch up with, and neither was expecting to be face-to-face with a vampyric version of the woman they loved.

Arriette was halfway down the corridor to her room when Pouki followed her out and called her name.

"Are you visiting Tobias?"

Arriette smiled. "That's the plan."

"You should... brace yourself," he warned her.

"What for? She's OK, isn't she?"

Pouki ushered her aside to allow a group of Recruit followers to pass them, allowing Arriette extra space.

"Your angelic blood was passed to her during the pregnancy," he explained, "and it has helped to speed up her growth a little."

"So she's... what?" Arriette asked, scowling. "Is she

like a *giant* or something?"

"No!" Pouki stifled a laugh. "She's healthy, and she's beautiful, and she looks just like you, but she's already around three human years old. You weren't on Earth long, but it was long enough to miss quite a chunk of her infancy."

Arriette gasped. "I missed *three years* of her life?"

"No, only three days," he assured.

"Will she stop ageing at this speed?"

"Oh, I am confident she will! Once she comes into her powers properly, the process will slow. I believe, like an Everlast, she will become of age. Like a defence mechanism; she's the product of two extremely powerful supernatural beings and on the HPS, she likely doesn't exist. Born at a dangerous time, too, so it's an instinct. She wants to be ready to fight with you."

Pouki walked Arriette to her bedroom where a rocking bassinet would sit unused and outgrown, and in its place, a wooden cot suitable for a toddler would be nestled beneath the window.

"She's giving up her entire childhood to protect us?"

Pouki shrugged. "Give it a few more days, then ask her yourself. By the end of the week, I predict she will be walking and talking properly, though she's already half-way there."

He rapped on the bedroom door for her, gave her arm a gentle squeeze, and walked away.

Tobias was reading through a storybook when she poked her head around the door. He almost jumped out of his skin and grabbed his daughter, moving her behind his leg. She grasped his trouser leg with both fists.

He held up his palms, ready to dream and defend her.

Arriette raised hers. "Please don't be afraid of me."

"You're not real. You can't be. Who *are* you, some shape-shifting monstrosity?"

He pitched a fireball in warning and Arriette ducked, but she didn't retaliate. It singed the door frame, but caused no other damage.

"I'm real. It's me. I won't hurt you. *It's me!*" Arriette inched closer and held out a hand. "Sebastian was right; I didn't die, I travelled."

She reached over the bed. Tobias's muscles relaxed.

Keeping their child behind him, he edged forward and accepted her touch, enjoying the softness of her pale skin and pulling her in to examine the golden eyes she now possessed.

They were hers.

Despite the odds, this *was* Arriette.

He suddenly yanked her across the room, cradling her against him and caressing her face. Their lips met in a sentimental, wanting kiss, and his fingers smoothed her hair.

"I... thought you... were dead," he sobbed, rocking them both left and right, then turning to bring their daughter into the family reunion.

"Your daughter... *our* daughter..." He quickly lifted her onto the bed and said, "This is your mama."

Arriette inhaled Tobias's familiar scent and smiled. She was home, but she didn't know what to say to the daughter she'd effectively abandoned. A daughter she expected to hold and love as a baby, but who was now a three-year-old toddler.

Arriette smiled widely and bent to offer her a hug.

"I missed you both," she said.

But Tobias pulled back.

His eyes narrowed as he studied her features, then

cautiously lifted her upper lip to check out the two huge, sharp fangs beneath.

"*That's* why your eyes are different." He gasped.

"I'm not dangerous, Tobias. Pouki and the Four Saviours have tested me. I drink water. I can eat solid food, and I'm alive." Arriette took a deep breath. "I just look a bit... off."

He shuddered and stammered. "I'll say! Are those... *real*?"

Arriette peered over his shoulder at their little girl; her beauty was unmistakable, and they recognised one another instantly. She outstretched her arms and cooed, and Arriette lifted her gently to hold her close to her heart —a heart that because of venom could no longer beat fully, though her child's pumped furiously. Arriette could feel it through the hole in her chest, excited and longing. Everything about her daughter oozed innocence, from her vibrant green eyes to her fluffy, mousy hair. Her long, strong nose was definitely Arriette's, but she had her father's hair.

Tobias watched Arriette like a hawk, but their daughter seemed to already understand this creature's nature.

"I won't hurt her."

Arriette sighed, placing her daughter gently in her cot, adoring the sound of her laughter.

"*How* did this happen?"

"It wasn't planned. I travelled through time to Earth. Pandora helped me, actually. You all thought I was dead, and you were right to."

Then she explained everything, sitting beside him on the bed, and told him where she'd been and how she'd met Casper in his youth. He folded his arms angrily when he heard that Susan and Dion had played a part in her physical change, but softened once he learned their fates for trying, and their motivations.

"If they hadn't, I might have starved to death. They saved my life, Tobias, and they were reluctant. Baby A agreed it was the safest option and gave us the best chance to be together."

He rubbed his eyes. "I'm... *relieved*, but they should have told me something."

"They kept you in the dark because you had a baby to care for. And my mother, so I hear. Where is Ma?"

"She went for a walk. She will be back soon, and we'll have to go through this reveal and ordeal again."

"It'll be worth it," Arriette replied, beaming whenever her daughter giggled or reached for her. "And I have a plan now. A purpose."

"You didn't before?"

"I thought I did, but now I *know* I have to leave you all. I can't risk your lives, not this time. This family is my entire world, and if Christine Kaines, my grandmother, finds out I'm still walking around, she's going to come for you both."

"You know about the mutants?"

"Pouki filled me in," Arriette groaned. "I'll lose you forever. So I'm going to travel across the Barren Fishtail to the Edge and deal with her on my own. When she's dead, I'll return."

Tobias gripped her arm and dragged her toward him. She didn't fight it. She allowed him to cuddle her and nuzzle her and kiss every part of her body. Arriette's vampyric senses were tingling with delight at how masculine his scent was, and how sticky his human skin was against her porcelain.

He caught his breath, then said, "I *know* you don't want to leave your family."

"You're right, but I don't have a choice! I think my soul went to Earth so I might witness the fall of the planet. I saw the vortex, and I met Andrew Kaines. I have to prevent Christine from using Pandora's box to destroy this planet, too. If she can't rule it, I think that's her plan."

Tobias didn't interrupt. She splurged on the details, leaving a messy trail of destruction and guilt behind her.

"A version of me died on that planet. I waited, Tobias. I waited for so long before I woke up on Earth for Zïnnyi's presence, but he never came to guide or reassure me. And I waited for Casper. I thought he'd be there, but all I heard were those screaming women. But on the way back, there was Pandora. From a beacon of light, she beckoned me and pulled me home. I knew, then, I had to do this part on my own."

Tobias shuffled closer. "You have me, the Recruit. You have Pandora."

"I always did. She and I became moulded to one another, but before she allowed Dion and Susan's venom to change me, she prepared me to call on her. It hadn't been the right time until now, and she offered to return completely to the box and stay there, but she made a valid argument to continue inside me."

Arriette tugged the key to Pandora's box hanging from the same chain as her Everlast pendant.

"In the box she cannot help us. Out here, we have access to her powers. This key is in danger. Somebody wants the box, and Pandora has tasked me with its protection, although now I know she's not willing to stand by and watch me do all the work. I feel her strength and her personality within me. I'm not the same person,

Tobias. I've *changed*."

"Yeah, into a vampyr!" He lowered his head, saddened, but willing to take her in any form.

For that, she loved him.

"And are Susan and Dion alright?" he asked. "Did biting you and Pandora harm them?"

"That depends on your point of view. They bit me, and I had to bite Susan back to make sure she stayed a vampyr."

"And Dion?"

Arriette couldn't help but grin. The thought of two of her best friends beginning an exciting romance filled her with hope.

"Dion opted to be with Reiko. She's human now. I think my venom—Pandora's venom—is extremely powerful."

Tobias bit his lower lip. "Must be."

"Perhaps it's the way to get rid of Ze Entit Sehde Eyeh once and for all?"

"You want to *bite* The All Seeing Eye?" Tobias shook his head and sighed. "This is all my fault."

"I don't see how you're at fault here," Arriette said.

Her lips pressed to a thin line and her eyes fell suddenly solemn, their golden shine now a deeper bronze.

"Everything I did was to protect you, but as usual, you were more than capable of protecting yourself. I pushed for the supernatural pregnancy. I encouraged you to hibernate in our room in fear you'd be assassinated. I insisted we involve Pouki and the Four Saviours when those women arrived... and I just assumed you were dead! But I wasn't there for any of what's happened since you travelled, Arriette. I wanted to keep this little girl—who still needs a name, by the way—from the pain and the grief. I'm so sorry."

Arriette lifted his chin. "You did a *great* job. Look at her! She's amazing! We made all those decisions together, Tobias. Neither of us had any idea I'd go into early labour, or that I'd time-travel to Earth and leave my body to waste away here on Haeylo. And how could any of us have predicted the heinous crimes Christine committed against those poor women?"

Arriette gestured at their daughter, who had already learned who her mama was and how to call out for her.

It was the most incredible sound.

"She needs a strong Haeyloian name," Tobias said, "but I couldn't without you. I told the others I had decided so they'd stop asking."

From her cot, she gazed at Arriette with undying love. There was nothing for her to forgive, because in her heart, her mother had done no wrong. And as soon as she could form the words to reassure Arriette of such, she would.

Despite being only three days old, and appearing three human years old, Zïnnyi was already feeding her amazing memories and visions, Haeyloian words and, through them, encouraging her to develop her powers.

As Arriette gazed at her in awe, in the child's eyes, their creator had written her name.

In Haeyloian, a name that meant *honour.*

Anora.

"Arriette and Pandora: Anora. *That's* what we should call her, Tobias. She's a miracle; birthed from the source of both good and evil."

"Then let's honour our history, her bloodline, and the

goddess that helped to save her mother's life."
Tobias took Arriette's hand in hers.
"*Anora*. I like it."

TWENTY—EIGHT

Hiding Anora from the planet Haeylo was a decision made to protect her, but already the infant perceived hiding as dishonourable. Despite being only days old and several years in appearance, Anora's mind and powers were developing at an incredible speed. She had decided merely minutes after meeting her mother for the first time that being named after honour itself in the Haeyloian language was a symbolic thing, and would force the whole family into the open when it came to locating and defeating Ze Entit Sehde Eyeh.

Anora meant *honour*, and eventually when Arriette and Tobias left the planet to rejoin Casper and Zïnnyi, Arriette wanted Anora to lead the Recruit in her place, guiding Haeylo to a prosperous future. Travelling to the Edge where Christine Kaines supposedly still ruled without her organisation or capable family behind her would not set the best example.

She needed air.

Just thinking about all they'd have to go through and risk caused her silent chest to tighten, stinging more than the venom. So with their heads held high, they decided to involve the Recruit in Arriette's fight to avenge the Haeyloian women's suffering, and to prevent anyone else from having to bow to this so-called *queen*.

"We should call a meeting," Tobias said, "and bring

everyone up to speed on our..." He coughed. "...our situation."

"You mean these," Arriette said, grinning and running her tongue playfully over one of her fangs.

"And this," he said, nodding his head at Anora, who chose not to respond.

"And to our new threat," Arriette finished.

She reached into the cot for Anora, then took Tobias by the hand. As a family, they walked the corridor to accept the sceptical glances, baffled expressions, and gasps of shock at Arriette's new form.

It didn't take long to spread the word from follower to follower within HQ. Arriette also thought it best to invite the werewolf masters who could attend; those not currently guarding the Enzoian women, along with Pouki and the Four Saviours. They held the conference in one of the larger empty office spaces to accommodate the extra bodies, leaving the wolves and the saviours standing towards the back.

By now, they had all heard of Arriette's 'death' and her reincarnation as a fanged fiend, and it was clear not everyone was accustomed to the idea. Arriette wasn't sure she liked it either, but after deciding with Pandora to allow the venom to do its job, they were all stuck with the consequences.

Though she could eat, drink and breathe like a human, she hadn't yet tried to sleep like one. It comforted her that she was tired—mentally and physically—but there was no time for rest. Her vampyric body had already been out in the lair's fabricated daylight, but they had yet to discover if she could travel on Haeylo's surface during the day.

"I'm sorry to have to call you all here on such short

notice, but as you can see, circumstances have changed dramatically." She took a deep breath to stabilise her anxiety. "The rumours are true."

Mild chatter filled the room, and the werewolf masters' posture changed from relaxed and interested to defensive.

"I *am* a vampyr, but only physically. From what Pouki, Tabitha and the Four Saviours can determine so far, only my venom is dangerous. I do not thirst for human or supe blood and have had a satisfactory, ordinary meal already. I can only occasionally feel my heart beating, but I can still love. As for other bodily functions?" Arriette cleared her throat and grinned. "Sleep is yet to be determined, but it will thrill you all that I have used the bathroom successfully."

This earned a chortle from a few of her friends and a wry smile from the wolf masters who were now softening.

"Also, my powers are fully functioning. I can only assume I am now technically immortal, although nothing there has changed, as I did already inherit my everlast pendant from the Indalo store last year. Tobias is still willing to marry me, so my everlasting life is hopefully temporary."

She lifted a dusty desk with her telekinesis just to prove her point, then checked she wouldn't knock anyone off their feet behind her before releasing her wings.

Baby A exhaled. "That's a relief. And sunlight?"

"In here? Fine. Out there? I guess we'll find out."

Tobias wrung his hands together and sat Anora at his feet to play quietly and happily with a stuffed tiger. Then he explained what happened to Arriette and what she'd discovered whilst on Earth.

Arriette interrupted only to clarify that Casper had

been young, and she'd met him as Andrew Kaines the day before he was sworn in as the president of the United States of America.

"Our books are all wrong. The planet was a mess. There were mutations and segregation, cannibalism and rioting. Humanity was *not* thriving, nor were they united when Andrew Kaines decided; he simply wanted it the most. Whilst none of those living conditions can help us now, they give us an insight into where Christine's cruelty was born, potentially where she drew her inspiration for the Enzoian curse we experienced. Cannibalism, missing limbs and violence? It all seems so familiar, leaving me with no doubt that Rain Irontome's account is accurate. Christine is after me because of what I did on Earth. She remembers what feels like such a brief encounter, from thousands of years ago. She thought Casper and I were in love."

"So that all really happened, too?" Sebastian asked her quietly from the front.

She nodded, but said nothing.

"And she hates you *why*, exactly?" Reiko asked from behind him. "Surely you and Casper didn't—"

"Oh, no!" she said, firmly cutting him off. "But Christine isn't convinced because she wasn't there for the entirety. She was fearful of me because I was a stranger. But Andrew insisted on helping me and once they began to listen, Christine's sister was involved in the attempt to capture and experiment with me. He never found out that he's really my grandfather. I thought it was too risky. He saved my life, and he listened to me when I told him what he had to do. Clearly, or none of us would be here. That's why Christine hates me and wants me dead; not only is she after Pandora's box and the key so she can possess the ability to control the world's evils and rule as she once did, but now she knows I'm real, and Pandora's soul lives within me. If she got hold of both of us and ended my life, there's a chance she could replace me."

"She believes so anyway," Pouki said, rolling his eyes, "because I'm not convinced Pandora would be willing to jump to her body. When Susan was killed, Pandora's spirit was surrounded by viable bodies and instead returned to the cave to await *your* arrival, Arriette."

Arriette snapped her fingers. "However, if Christine controls the box and Pandora's spirit returns there?"

"You make a valid point," he agreed.

Joy leaned forward in her seat. "So, what do we do about it? Are you willing to go now, Arriette, given you're now a mother?"

At that, Anora's head lifted. She met Joy's gaze and beamed, and Joy had to double-take.

"Did she just understand me?"

Anora got to her feet and took an unsteady step to take her mother's hand.

Tobias laughed. "About that. Uhm... Pouki?"

"She may not speak much at the moment," Pouki began, "but here's the thing about our little Anora..."

Pouki explained his theory that because of Arriette and Tobias's combined power and Pandora's presence in her mother's body at the time of conception, that Anora was an extremely unique child. Though she may only be days old, she looked almost three years, and it was possible that Anora's mental development already far exceeded that. Given Arriette's family history of slow-ageing curses, it was possible magic was simply reclaiming those years.

"Maybe whatever Christine's curse did to my mother's development," Arriette told them, "has simply skipped a generation and, in the opposite way, affected Anora. Like those years are being *reclaimed*. Ma doesn't know any of this yet; we're going to ease her into this."

"Will Anora stop growing when she comes of age?" Baby A asked her.

Pouki shrugged but confidently replied her development may mimic that of an everlast. Anora's body would reach eighteen years old, but she'd cease to age after that, at least for a while. His theory was that after reading Arriette's thoughts and listening to the messages received from Zïnnyi, Anora's premature delivery and speedy development since then may have been intentional.

"She may have sensed her power will be needed sooner rather than later, and so she's done this to herself to protect her parents and our organisation."

"With Zïnnyi's blessing?" Baby A asked.

"Until she decides to speak to us in full sentences, we can't be sure, but by all means ask him if you're able."

As if prompted or perfectly timed, Anora released her mother's hand, then tugged at the material of her pretty pink dress at the base of her spine.

"Wings? Surely not!" Baby A jumped to her feet, but Pouki waved her back.

"I don't think it's wings," he said.

Anora dragged her dress up and tucked her body into a ball at her parents' feet. Pouki, Tobias and Arriette knelt beside her and examined her skin, where what appeared to be a tattoo was forming, similar to how Arriette had received her runic identifiers.

"I don't recognise this symbol," Arriette admitted.

"Me neither," said Tobias.

But Pouki did.

He waved at the Four Saviours to look as Arriette ran her fingers through Anora's mousy brown hair and hushed her.

"It's a unicursal hexagram," he confirmed.

The symbol looked similar to a hexagram, but with an unusual twist. The six-pointed star had been created initially over a diamond-shape, but also included two interlinking opposing triangles to create a confusing design that few in the Recruit had ever seen.

"It's a protection hex."

Arriette scowled then. "A *hex*?"

"I've seen these before, too." Jade added, "I once met a coven of wiccans who stood in the centre of this symbol to perform their spells. It is supposed to prevent access to what lies within, like a forcefield."

Di seemed to remember the coven, too. "They believed the elements held greater significance than the spirit, and that if they protected themselves within this unicursal hexagram, they could look darkness in the face to better understand and therefore defeat it."

"Like a shield," Jade said.

When Arriette's scowl didn't fade, Jade continued. "Think about how we might study Falkon Lou, Arriette? If we wanted to see how he moves, we might observe him from a place of safety, keeping him behind bars. Within their symbol, those wiccans can observe and learn about their enemies to tailor their spells and potions safely, then defeat them."

"I understand," Tobias said, "but it's technically a hex? So where does *that* come from?"

Anora was no longer squirming in pain, but she sat still and allowed them to continue their examination and conversation. It didn't look red or sore, or infected, or as if it had been branded or forced upon her either, merely a tattoo or a birthmark like their own runes.

Pouki gestured they should allow Anora to sit up, and he offered her a hand. She stayed close to her mother but continued playing with her tiger as if nothing had happened.

Ruby interjected, "I hate to be the one to say this, but you can place a hex upon yourself... if you have enough power."

The room's gaze shifted from Ruby to Anora again. The child didn't react and didn't seem to care about the additional attention.

"This is far too intricate to be anything but creator or goddess-inspired, Arriette," Ruby insisted. "Hex symbols are used for many reasons, and be assured *most* of these are for good rather than evil. It seems this one averts dark forces and is in place for Anora's protection."

"If she can force her growth and development, I'm sure she can hex herself to prepare for what you're about to face."

"She senses a threat from her great-grandmother," Pouki advised. "And I'm sure the ladies will agree that such symbols can also be specific to a family line. Like stories, they can change a little as they are passed down, but Christine was a practising wiccan, which means it is likely her mother was and even her grandmother. They may have used this symbol, like a crest."

"Harriet was a wiccan too," Arriette confirmed. "And I met her on Earth but she obviously looked different. Explains why *she* hated me. I was the reason her father abandoned them all, but she expressed how sorry she was that they'd lost touch right before I returned to Haeylo.

She may have been embarrassed."

"Did anyone ever see this symbol or anything similar on Harriet?" Pouki turned to Jet. "You were close, weren't you?"

Jet held up his hands. "Not *that* close! She and I were friends, but if she knew how to hex herself, whose to say it wasn't part of her live-forever-unless-kissed curse? And Casper broke that!"

"So does that mean a blood relative can break *Anora's* hex?" Tobias asked nobody in particular.

"Harriet did not know she would be that close to her father again when she cast hers; Anora knows *exactly* what she's doing. This is to protect her against Christine Kaines specifically," Baby A said. "Do you want my honest opinion as a traveller?"

"Very much so," Arriette said.

Baby A bit her thumbnail, then cleared her throat. "Well, I think Anora sent Arriette to Earth so she could identify Christine and study her. She wanted to view her like those wiccans from a safe distance, then gave herself that tattoo to deal with her personally when the time came back here on Haeylo."

"But Arriette gave birth *before* she travelled," Tobias argued.

"Not immediately. I'm an experienced time-traveller, Tobias, and I know from past ventures that I can be gone what feels like days and return just seconds after I disappeared in our time." She paused in thought, then said to Arriette, "You met Christine early, right?"

It dawned on Arriette that she had encountered Christine only a few hours after meeting Andrew Kaines; he took her back to his home for safety before Christine cast them out. Then Andrew drove her to the hospital.

"Anora knew exactly what she was doing. Arriette passed out and her heart stopped. *Then* Anora was born. We delivered her once she'd seen what Christine looked like. Then, you continued alone."

Baby A sat back and folded her arms as if to rest her case.

Tobias stifled a laugh as he said, "Hang on, are we really talking about a *baby* hunting and killing her relative to do her parents a favour?"

"The *planet* a favour," Reiko grumbled from somewhere at the back of the room. "Christine be crazy."

"Rubbish, she's *days* old!" said Jet.

Arriette pinched the bridge of her nose and exhaled.

If *she* could demolish the HPS, then what must her daughter be capable of?

"She may be now," Arriette said, "...but not for long."

It was then that Anora pulled herself up and took a few tentative steps toward the group. She gazed at their awe-struck expressions, smiled, and turned to face her mother.

Determined, she uttered, "Save... the... people."

Arriette fell to her knees and wept. "*Save the world.*"

The HPS

THE HAEYLOIAN POWER SCALE

1: Everlast - There are three classes of everlast, all with the power of everlasting life and the ability to communicate with other everlasts through an assigned pendant (*Mirror of the Soul*).

2: Dreamer - Power of telekinesis and power to turn imagination into reality. When in large groups, dreamers can mirror another's reality for observation purposes. This is referred to as Mirroring, Jumping or Spying.

3: Sorcerer/Rulecast - Power of wizardry through the use of magical items, potions and spells. Rulecasts specifically work with/for an everlast and have a higher level of experience.

4: Time-Traveller - The power of travel in time and space by opening and using wormholes.

5: Invisibility - The power to turn themselves and their sensory footprint invisible.

6: Angel - Possesses wings and has the power to communicate with the creator.

7: Shape-Shifter - The power to change physical shape. They can temporarily inherit the power/s of their chosen form.

8: Demon/ Werewolf/Vampyr -
- *Vampyr* – power to change physical shape. Power of eternal life. Weakened by silver, sunlight and sharp wooden objects. Drinks human blood — their bite is fatal.
- *Werewolf* – there are blood born, bite born and shifter born breeds of werewolf. They form packs or clans. They can change their physical shape to that of a wolf. The three most powerful clans are the Shoku, Tri and Shou, named after the moon/s they worship.
- *Demon* – there are two species of demon, the spirit and the horned. A spirit or shade demon's claws are poisonous. Horned demons have increased strength and armour.

9: Telepathy - The power to read minds and emotions. They can read human minds clearly and most supernatural minds. From the demonic family they can only read orc minds. Vampyric minds can be accessed but only until the end of their human memories.

10: Retainer - The power to control their eidetic memory.

11: Astro-Projection - The power to separate their spiritual and physical forms. Most are able to control both forms and duplicate their existence—one as a spirit, the other as a shell. Due to experimentation, some are forced to use only their spiritual forms whilst their physical shells sleep.

12: Wiccan - The power of witchcraft using basic spells and potions. The power can be taught.

13: Orc - A demonic slave with no supernatural power.

14: Human - No supernatural power, however, most potion masters are human, which is a skill that can be studied.

ABOUT THE AUTHOR

I'm an Amazon international #1 bestselling author from the UK, and I write (mostly) fantasy and adventure books for young adults and teens.

I believe in entertaining readers by offering them a temporary escape from reality. My stories are fun, fast-paced and addictive—the ideal vacation companion, and I aim for relatable characters who embark on meaningful journeys, get into tons of trouble, but overall discover the depths of what it is to be human. Through my emotive *Noah Finn* novellas, I also hope to encourage you to look within; to find *your* story.

Through books, I believe we can face our darkest fears, explore infinite new worlds, and realise our true purpose. Creative writing helps me to understand what that purpose is.

Since starting my self-publishing experience in 2010, I have worked with many individuals to help make their dreams of publishing a book reality, including school children! My imprint, *Curious Cat Books (CCB)*, has been responsible for producing gorgeous children's books, memoirs and more since 2017.

***

Scan to visit Rachael's website or visit www.rachaelhardcastle.com for more information.

If you enjoyed reading this title, please consider leaving a short review and/or star rating on your favourite retailer website, as book reviews will help Rachael to reach more readers.

Thank you.

PRAISE FOR THE PREVIOUS EDITION OF
THE CHRONICLES OF PANDORA
WRITTEN AS *FINDING PANDORA*
BY READERS FAVORITE

"The world of Finding Pandora is interesting on its own, comprising a mirroring history and an assortment of creatures that will make for consuming contemplation sessions.... This is testament to E. Rachael Hardcastle's ability to choose carefully what to show and what to suggest... It is with this skill that E. Rachael Hardcastle delivers a light-pierced sombre story with a compact, multifaceted plot." - **Book One**

"There is a spiritual, moral and instructive quality to this book, asking us to look at ourselves as a civilization, our values and our actions. That is where its strength lies and that is something very commendable." **- Book Two**

"Finding Pandora beats at a pace that keeps the reader's attention and interest. The story flows remarkably. The imagination, planning and execution of E. Rachael Hardcastle's work is the strongest I have ever seen it... Finding Pandora is rich with societies, environments and cultures that are bustling with life, history and tradition... But perhaps the strongest feature of the book is found in its insightful themes and discussions on evil, morality, purpose and humanity." - **Book Three**

"It is all action, anguish, emotion, twists, blood, and light. It is laced with feelings of triumph and defeat, anguish and happiness, closure and continuance. The lean economical style of E. Rachael Hardcastle accelerates the tense, quick pace... However, this isn't at the expense of depth... One thing is clear at the end, the Finding Pandora series is about sacrifice, the demands of living a purposeful life, and hope in the face of calamity. It is these poignant themes that make the series the moral force it is. As we close this chapter, we are reminded that this may not be the last time we see Arriette and the Recruit, and that should bring some excitement to fans because this story has more to offer." - **Book Four**

A NOTE FROM THE AUTHOR

Dear Reader,

If you've made it this far, thank you wholeheartedly. I wanted to give you a brief overview of the story's origins, as the path I took to share it with you is deeply important to me.

I started writing Arriette's adventures in 2010, when the series was titled *The Recruit Adventure* and was self-published in four parts: *World, Heaven, Infinity* and *Eternity* to reflect the poem it was inspired by: William Blake's *Auguries of Innocence*. A short snippet of the poem briefly features in the series in its honour—it brought me here, and continues to inspire me almost 14 years later. If you haven't read the full poem, I highly recommend the experience.

As with most indie titles, I've re-written and re-released the book a few times, most recently as *Finding Pandora* in 2018, which existed as a paperback collection of all four novels, or individual e-books. Whilst the production of that book was successful and beautiful, with *World* reaching #1 on Amazon's bestseller list, I always felt something was missing. I so desperately wanted to return to the adventure's origins to re-capture the magic I experienced all those years ago.

Writing a book is a thrilling, fun experience, but it's also hard work and takes dedication and time. Since 2010, many have supported my efforts in too many ways to fit on this page. I can't thank them all individually, but they know who they are and they know why they deserve a mention—that's what matters. Please know I am blessed and so grateful, whether we simply crossed paths or we are still in each other's lives today.

Finally, a note on my change of name. In 2010, I wanted to separate two sides of myself, so people I knew wouldn't necessarily associate me with my work, and I could write without fear of embarrassment. Since, I have accepted and embraced that being a writer is *awesome*; I'm ever so proud of it. I think about being E. R. Hardcastle fondly, as I will someday think about E. Rachael Hardcastle in the same way. But for now, I'm happy just to be Rachael. I've earned it.

And I'm so very pleased to meet you.